THE FIFTH JUROR

LORI LACEFIELD

Covers designed by Nick Zelinger at NZGraphics
Editor The Fifth Juror: Michelle Hope
Editor The Advocate: Ellen Larson

This book is a work of fiction. Names, characters, places, and incidents either are products of the author's imagination or are used fictitiously. Any resemblance to actual persons, living or dead, events, or locales is entirely coincidental.

Lori Lacefield
Visit my website at www.LoriLacefield.com

Printed in the United States of America

First Printing: May 2018
Open Book Media, LLC

EBOOK ISBN-978-1-7322890-4-8

READER'S NOTE

Like FREE Books? Sign up to receive news, grab a free copy of my novella, THE RUMOR, and enter to win my latest giveaway at
https://www.lorilacefield.com

CHAPTER 1

The icy full moon hung over the Denver skyline like a spotlight, casting a shimmering blanket of crystals on the snow below. Dimitry Romanov's steps crunched across the ice-crusted top, the clear sky and single-digit temperatures having turned the multilayers of snowmelt into some odd winter desert. Somewhere down the street, a neighbor scraped their windshield, and a trail of gray exhaust smoke from the person's warming car clouded the air. His own breaths did the same, adding brief but heavy wafts of vapor. Others disliked the cold, but not he. He thought when he'd arrived here some weeks ago, in a city so famous for its snow, he would find like-minded people, appreciative of the frigid blast that stunned your lungs and made them expand, like an electric shock on a dying heart. Yet, even here, he found the inhabitants whiny about the temperature and days without sun. They thought a few days in single digits was cold, a lone day without blue sky dismal. They did not know cold. Back in his home country, in Saint Petersburg, where the subzero temperatures helped dig you a frozen grave, that was cold. To breathe air as frigid as the arctic wind and exist under a blanket of dark gray for months on end. That was dismal.

Tonight, all Dimitry wore was a thick sweater overlaid by a brown wool coat and gloves. No scarf. No hat. The Americans he passed along the city streets were bundled in parkas, with scarves around their necks and mouths and hats pulled so low that you could only see their eyes. But, he knew, most of the time that was all a person needed to judge a man, his eyes. Be they cold or indifferent, frightened or wounded, the vessels into the soul told of a man's history and future intent like no words could easily convey. He often wondered what his own eyes spoke to others, if the practiced intimidation and murder he performed for a living was displayed there in his pupils, a dark and distant spiral. That others cast such a wide berth for him as he passed them on the streets indicated it to be so.

Dimitry chuckled under his breath. He bet the man he was soon to visit would know his intent immediately. He wanted the man to see his face and hear his words, understand why he was about to die.

At the next corner, he turned south off Colfax, a street that ran for miles across the city, and walked a few more blocks. When he grew close to the Park Hill neighborhood where his target lived, he left the streets and maneuvered through the alleys instead. A couple of dogs barked behind the tall fences he passed. One menacing, a deep pull at the throat and a growl, the other smaller, a high-pitched yap. At the corner of the next block, he saw a cat chewing on what remained of dinner pulled from a trash can, its eyes luminescent in the night. The thing looked like it'd been involved in more than a dozen fights—half an ear missing, a crooked tail. It seemed to give little thought to the human who could do him harm though, far more interested in fulfilling its basic needs. He had seen much of the same behavior in the men in his home country. After a time, it didn't matter what else they did to you, as long as they threw you some scraps.

At the home he knew belonged to his target, he checked the high windows on the two-story Tudor structure for lights or movement, any signs that one of the family was awake. When he was satisfied they appeared to be asleep, he checked his pockets, ensuring he had everything he needed. Syringes, drugs, duct tape, knife.

From the side alley, he scaled the fence with ease and crossed the backyard. He looked for any new signs of trouble—a dog bowl or chain, a security camera—but none of those things existed. Instead, the entire lawn was filled with items that spoke of family. A toboggan for sledding, a basketball hoop, a trampoline, a skateboard. He stared for a moment at a small bicycle and felt a gnawing in his chest. Dimitry's daughter had once owned a similar bike, pink, with trails of ribbons on the handlebars that rippled as she rode. Another world, another time.

He strode to the back door, opened the screen. Tested the knob. The door was locked but the lock was loose. It proved ridiculously easy to pick, the door not even secured with a deadbolt. That would play in his favor in the investigation that was sure to follow, making the suspicion of a break-in less likely.

Inside, he stood a moment to listen. Hearing no signs of stirring, he checked out the house. Hardwood floors with Victorian rugs. Matching dining table and hutch containing lots of antique glassware, plates, cups, vases, bowls. There were also signs of the modern era, a laptop on the kitchen table, an Xbox next to the television, a tablet on the sofa. Americans loved their technology. Down the hallway were two bedrooms and two baths, one an empty suite for guests, one the master. He let that one alone for now. He had business to attend to first.

He crept up the stairs, trying to step lightly, but the house was old and the stairs creaked in places. After crossing a small loft, he saw the doors to the kids' rooms, one open, one closed. He grabbed the knob of the closed door, the one he assumed belonged to the older son, and slowly pushed it open. Inside was a typical teenager's room—posters of rock bands and superhero movies, a mound of clothes that appeared to have gone through combat. Dimitry removed one of the syringes from his pocket and quickly injected the drugs in the son's vein, a special concoction prepared just for him. It was most important the son be nearly unconscious the entire time, so he remembered nothing when he woke the next morning. The son barely moved before rolling onto his back and flopping his arms to his sides. "Sorry, kid."

Next, he checked on the daughter, who was twelve years younger than her sibling. He looked upon her as she slept quietly, curled among a mound of stuffed animals on her bed. For her, he applied a light sedative, enough that she would sleep soundly and not awaken during the ordeal that was about to unfold. Back in the son's room, he scooped him up in his arms along with his baseball bat and carried him downstairs where he propped him up on the couch.

The next part would be ugly, but in his experience, he knew to do it swiftly, with no hesitation. He took the baseball bat and hid in the family room, just behind the corner. With a remote, he turned on the television and upped the volume, added the stereo for good measure. In less than five minutes, the dad was out of bed, cursing under his breath.

"Justin? What the hell?" *Whump.*

Dad was down. Dimitry moved quickly, taping his mouth, hands, and legs, then dragging him to a far wall. The father wasn't a light man, maybe six-two, two-forty, but Dimitry had handled much bigger men in his home country. He returned to his former position and waited for the mom. Heard her sleepy voice call from the bedroom.

"John? What's going on? You'll wake the kids."

He heard a distant stirring and a light came on. More rustling, then a shuffling of feet. Maybe grabbing a bathrobe and slippers. He waited until she was fully clear of the hallway and could see her husband slumped against the far wall before he struck her from behind. She cried out as she went down, reaching for the back of her head. He turned to the loft above, making sure the drugs were doing their job on the daughter and the cry hadn't awakened her. The last thing he wanted was for her to see what was about to occur. If she did, he'd have no choice but to kill her too.

He moved the wife next to her husband, taped her mouth, hands, and legs as well. By then, the husband had begun to stir, trying to figure out what had happened. A trail of blood oozed from the top of his head, down his temple and left cheekbone. His eyes widened at the sight of his wife, stretched even further as he noticed his dazed son on the couch. When he turned his attention to the man standing over him, Dimitry could see the plea in the man's gaze, practically hear the words out of his sealed lips.

Don't hurt my kids. Don't hurt my wife. What is it you want?

And soon enough, he would know. With one name, he would know.

Mikael Kriskan.

Dimitry went to the son, untied his hands. They were limp, like the rest of him, but he was still breathing. He dragged the kid in front of his mother, collapsed him to his knees, then positioned himself behind the son with his own arms wrapped around his. The mother trembled, appearing as fearful for her son as for herself. She looked to her husband, back to the stranger kneeling in front of her. Made an icy, guttural noise, one he'd heard many times before.

Pleeeeeaaaaase.

Dimitry watched her reaction as he opened his coat to reveal the knife. This was the part that always gave him a thrill, that moment when a person realized they were about to die. He smiled as he slid the eight-inch blade from its sheaf and positioned it squarely between the son's hands with the blade pointing toward the mother. He delighted in the cold electricity that zapped his heart as he watched the father's eyes nearly explode from their sockets.

"Ah, I see you have some memory," he whispered.

The father began to scream and writhe beneath the duct tape, red-faced, straining to make use of worthless hands and feet. The mother's head whipped toward her husband, the desperate look in her eyes begging for help, but her husband, her protector, could do nothing, say nothing, to change the events at hand. When she started to sob, Dimitry leaned toward the husband.

"This one is for Mikael Kriskan."

Dimitry thrust the knife into the man's wife using the son's hands, seven times, until it was finished. Blood spatter covered the kid, who remained completely unaware. The husband banged his head against the wall, then slumped in a heap, sounds of grainy agony escaping his throat beneath the duct tape. Snot poured from his nose and tears streamed from his eyes, mixing with the blood from his head wound into a slimy mess. His fingers clawed at the tape to no avail.

Dimitry let the father writhe in his harrowing pain for a few minutes before repositioning the son to kneel before him, the kid now covered in his mother's blood. To Dimitry's surprise, the father tried to reach out and stroke his son's face with his taped hands, looking upon him longingly as if to say he was sorry. The father glanced up one last time, then simply closed his eyes and waited for what came next.

When the job was complete, Dimitry let the knife drop from the son's hands and raised him from the floor, careful not to make a mess of the spatter, and lay him on the couch. The drugs would keep him passed out well into morning and begin their chemical breakdown within hours, making them harder to trace. And even if the police drew his blood and it tested positive for various chemical substances during the investigation, it wouldn't matter. The analysis would show traces of ecstasy and everyone knew kids his age liked to take ecstasy.

Later, he'd wake, unknowing of what fresh hell had been unleashed upon him. The police would tell him what he'd done, and it would destroy him, as much as it had Mikael Kriskan. He was sorry he had to ruin the kid's life in such a manner, but his father had brought such carnage upon his own family by first condemning Mikael Kriskan to death.

He stood looking at the scene, admiring his work. He exchanged the bloody gloves on his hands for a clean pair in his pocket, shoved the old ones in his pants to be disposed of later.

The only thing left to do now was to get the daughter.

CHAPTER 2

Jess held the fork with the bite of cut pancake in front of his mouth as syrup dripped on the tablecloth. "Please, Ricky, just one bite," she begged. The six-year-old launched himself backward and screamed. She put the piece aside, cut a new slice, dipped it in syrup, showed him it was free of butter. Tried again. He swung his arm and knocked the fork from her hand, sending it to the floor with a clang and a splat of syrupy mess.

"You know he doesn't like his food to touch," her husband, Tom, said. He stood before the hallway mirror, tying his tie. "I have depositions this morning. Do you think this suit works?"

"Nothing touched. I swear. Ricky, look, the pancakes are not touching." She showed him the plate and grabbed a new fork, one of six set on the table in advance because he wouldn't eat from the same utensil more than once.

Another scream. Ricky slouched down and wriggled beneath the wooden arm of his chair, away from Jess. Now, he was on the floor, writhing. Jess sighed, watching him roll around and kick his bare feet. Just once she'd like a morning without this battle.

She pulled at the waistband of his green pajamas, trying to get him to stand up, but the more she pulled, the more he resisted. The pajamas had been a Christmas gift, the only pair she could find with a hood but without feet. He insisted his head be covered but not his feet. The previous winter, she'd had to cut the feet off a pair of new pajamas just so he'd have something to wear to bed. Even though his feet grew as cold as the snow and ice outside their Colorado home, he always had to have an out. An escape. And this, she understood. It was difficult to be cornered into a situation you didn't ask for and couldn't control. In many ways, it resembled her life with him.

"Here, let me," Tom said. He took the fork from Jess's hand and coaxed Ricky back into the chair. Ricky brushed his bangs from his eyes and stopped fidgeting. Jess bit her bottom lip. Ricky always calmed down in Tom's presence, and Ricky wasn't even his child.

She stood. "Fine. I have to get ready for my interview anyway."

She poured herself a cup of freshly brewed coffee, tasted its bite. Behind her, in the adjoining room, the gas fireplace fought to cast a warm glow against the harsh light from the television, but the blue light was winning. Post-holiday blues. Someone on *The Today Show* was talking about New Year's resolutions and finding the resolve to stick to them. Jess wondered why people tried to make changes at the most depressing time of year, a month that followed five weeks of holiday gatherings and pummeled you back into reality: winter, work, bills, sick kids.

She burst up the stairs, anxious to leave the house. She loved Tom and Ricky. She did. But sometimes she needed her space too. Her out. Away from the tantrums and the destruction and the constant disagreements that came with having an autistic child. It was one of the many reasons she wanted a job—adult time and conversation.

She took a quick shower, scanned the closet for what to wear. Slid into navy leggings, calf-high brown boots, and a cream-colored sweater. Topped it off with a scarf and gold earrings. She kept the makeup light, just a touch of foundation, liner, and mascara. She never needed much anyway, blessed with fair skin and bright-green eyes.

She stopped in front of the full-length mirror, gave herself a once-over. It was good. Just the right outfit for an on-the-go journalist. She'd been trying to get a job with a local newspaper or radio station for months now with no luck, and she was growing tired of a process that, so far, had ended in the same result. The old "you have no experience" dilemma. All the positions wanted previous experience but no one cared to grant you any experience, especially to a woman in her mid-thirties who'd graduated from college a decade ago. She'd explained countless times that she'd needed to stay home with her son until he was old enough to go to school but that didn't seem to matter. It only made matters worse that her journalism degree was as stale as she was, granted in the final age of paper and dust, not smartphones and social media.

She hoped this one would be different. They, she, needed the money.

She bounded down the stairs where Ricky, now dressed, sat quietly on the couch with his tablet, playing games his school recommended. They were supposed to help with the way his mind sorted facts and figures but Jess loved them most for the moments of peace it gave her. Tom was in the kitchen, rinsing the dishes and loading the dishwasher. Above the sink, frost blanketed the window. The thermometer outside rested just above zero.

"Supposed to snow again this afternoon, another two to three inches," Tom said.

"Great. Like adding bricks to the wall. By February we'll be fully surrounded."

"It'll break soon."

Jess sighed. "Feels like I haven't seen the sun in days." She sorted through her purse on the kitchen island, unable to find her favorite lipstick. Tom wiped his hands on the kitchen towel, looked past her to the television, the local news. An avalanche in the high country. Heavy traffic on I-25. And a tragedy, a family brutally murdered in their own home.

"Jesus," he said. "Hope that's not my jurisdiction."

"What's that?" she asked.

Tom shook his head, smirked. She knew he thought her filter was limited to fashion and celebrity news, and in truth, he was right, most of the time. "Family murdered. Husband and wife stabbed to death. They suspect the son."

Jess stilled, tried to shake the icy cold that seized her. She glanced over her shoulder at the photos of the scene flashing on the screen. A Tudor-style house surrounded by yellow crime-scene tape. Police cars blocking entry to the street. A reporter outside in a parka providing details. For a moment, she was transfixed to another time of her life.

It had been nearly fourteen years, during a summer off from college, since she'd served on the jury that had convicted a then twenty-year-old Mikael Kriskan to death for the murder of his family, a case that had both shocked and riveted the tiny northeast Denver community of Montclair. Now, as his execution neared, her memories were resurfacing. It seemed every week now the media gave an update on the case, planting itself deeper into her psyche. She longed to talk to Tom about it, but she'd resolved long ago to never tell him about her time on the jury. As a public defense attorney, he was adamantly against the death penalty and believed the Kriskan jurors heartless and cruel. To tell him now that his wife had been one of those heartless jurors—a participant on the only case in recent Colorado history to be successful in getting a jury to grant the death penalty—was something better left a secret.

She wished the execution would happen and it would all go away.

But the news apparently had other ideas, and just like that, the anchors turned the conversation from the current murder to the former trial. In the top right corner, Mikael Kriskan's face appeared as a small photo, a boy-man with full, round cheeks and unevenly cut bangs, as the newscaster announced that Kriskan's writ of certiorari petitioned to the U.S. Supreme Court had been denied, paving the way for the execution date to be set. Then, with a solemn face, he emphasized that four men in Colorado would then be waiting on death row, and the state could soon see not one, but all four men put to death—the first executions in Colorado in more than forty years.

Jess turned away as a mix of emotions equivalent to leftover stew stirred within: guilt, anxiety, depression, fear. Just looking at Kriskan's face made her stomach twist into an unescapable knot. His photo looked like that of a child, not a monster who killed his family. And soon, she would be partly responsible for his death.

Ignoring the sudden sting in her eyes, she grabbed a long wool coat from the closet and slid on leather driving gloves. She picked up Ricky's jacket from the floor near the back door, where he'd left it crumpled in a heap upon last entry. "C'mon, buddy, let's get ready to go," she called.

On the kitchen island, her phone lit up and danced in a strange vibration against the granite. She glanced over her shoulder, rolled her eyes, grunted.

Tom was drying Ricky's plate, cup, and fork and placing them back in their proper place on the counter. They had to be hand-washed and not placed in the dishwasher and visible on the counter where he could check on them at any time. "Who's that?"

"Who do you think?"

Tom stiffened his jaw. "What's he want now?"

"What he always wants—money." She turned again to Ricky, shook the coat like a matador waves a red flag at a bull. "Dude, coat." Ricky made no move to acknowledge her.

"The well has run dry," Tom said. "We're done."

She stared at her husband. "I've told him that a thousand times. He thinks I owe him due to his fabulous sperm donation or something."

"Well, this time we mean it. I don't have to tell you..."

"No, you don't," she interrupted. "I know, Tom. Believe me, I know. The money's gone." She choked down the lump that had gathered in her throat, the one that rose every time she thought of her father, gone four years now. He'd barely made it to the wedding, just long enough to walk her down the aisle and have their father-daughter dance. One month later, he succumbed to a massive heart attack.

Before his death, he would've helped out, always helped out. Now his money—what was left of it—was in control of her stepmother and a dwindling trust fund.

He raised his hands. Tom didn't want to argue. Tom never liked to argue with her.

She turned back around, waved the coat at Ricky again. Nothing.

Tom took the coat from her hands, walked over to Ricky and slid the coat over his arms one at a time, then zipped the front. Ricky automatically stuck out a foot for one snow boot, then another. Still staring at his tablet, his thumbs pressing furiously, he stood and clomped across the rug into the hall, following Tom. At the door, he paused again so Tom could put his knit hat on. Jess simply stood and watched as she did every morning.

Tom grabbed his briefcase and sunglasses, and kissed Jess on the cheek. "Good luck on the interview. See you tonight." He opened the front door. "Come on, buddy, let's go."

Ricky ran after Tom without giving his mom a second thought. "See you tonight, kiddo, I love you," she yelled after him. No response. Just the sound of the door slamming.

She stood in the silent kitchen and felt the walls closing in.

CHAPTER 3

Jess checked in with the receptionist at the front office of the small suburban weekly newspaper and took a seat in one of the four chairs in the lobby. The walls were starkly absent of anything newsworthy, displaying old photographs of the city's main street throughout the years. She'd thought they'd at least have a few awards or breaking headlines, but then again, this wasn't exactly the *New York Times*.

Odd to think now that, at one time in her life, a big-city newspaper like the *Times* was exactly what she'd envisioned for herself, a career as a hard-hitting newsy asking all the tough questions. She remembered telling her father as much, thinking he'd be excited she'd finally chosen a profession, but he'd responded much in the same way he always did, simply patting her on the head with a "That's nice, Jessie".

She'd felt so deflated in that moment, realizing how his patronizing attitude resembled what he and everyone else thought of her. No one took her seriously. Not her teachers, not her boyfriends, certainly not her family. The world simply didn't believe she was capable of anything except looking pretty and party-planning.

She'd even overheard her father once tell a friend that the best he could hope for her was that she run off to college and get her 'MRS' degree—in other words, to meet a husband. From that point forward, every time she'd see the two of them together, they'd elbow her and ask her how the degree was coming.

No wonder her father had paraded around so proudly when she'd married Tom. She was marrying an attorney and getting her degree. He thought his daughter had hit the jackpot.

Alas, little did he know that the attorney she'd married wanted to free the world of injustice more than he wanted to line his pockets—practicing law to make a statement, not money. She'd secretly cried when out of all the positions offered to him out of law school, he'd accepted the one with the lowest pay, that of public defender. But she'd kept her disappointment to herself. Maybe he wouldn't be the wealthiest of husbands and maybe he wasn't the most exciting of men, but Tom was a good man and great with Ricky. She knew she was fortunate to have him.

Most of his clients were guilty and not very sympathetic, yet some were guilty only by association or not guilty at all, and those were the cases he got most fired up about. Like his current case, where he felt a lazy prosecutor was opting for the easy suspect because he didn't want to take the time to investigate a complicated case.

Jess often wondered if the same thing hadn't happened with Mikael Kriskan, that the prosecutor and the jurors had just accepted the simplest solution. Initially, it had seemed like an open-and-shut case. Kriskan had been found in the house covered in his parents' blood, along with traces of his younger sister's, and no evidence existed of a break-in. Toxicology showed no traces of illegal substances in his blood, yet Kriskan had refused to testify on his behalf, citing a night he couldn't remember, insisting he was drugged. At the time, the jurors had paid little attention to the defense's arguments—the inconsistent angles of the stab wounds for a left-handed individual, the evidence of other people in the house, the missing body of the younger sister.

On the drive over, Jess had heard an Amber Alert go out for the daughter of the family murdered the prior night. The authorities were speculating that she may have fled her Park Hill home during the murder and could be in danger. It seemed crazy a case so similar to Kriskan's was happening now when he was approaching execution.

She snapped from her thoughts as a man with thinning hair and horn-rimmed glasses approached and extended his hand. "Jessie Dawson? Jim Wilson, nice to meet you."

"Jess," she said. "Please, call me Jess." She had resolved to introduce herself as Jess to anyone she now met, desperate to gain distance from the younger version of herself.

They quickly dispensed with the formalities and she followed him to his office. As they passed through the workplace, she glanced at the people in their cubicles to get a sense of their mood. They seemed relaxed and focused, a few chatting over a computer. She thought how nice it would be to be part of such a group.

"Have a seat."

He took a moment to read through the resume she'd given him. It didn't take long.

He cleared his throat, glanced above the rim of his glasses. "I have to be honest. This isn't much of a resume. Just a few odd jobs here and there. You've never had steady employment?"

Here we go again. "In college, my summers were spent helping my father with his real-estate business. He was a developer, owned a number of commercial buildings and strip malls. The tasks I did for him aren't relevant to journalism. After graduation, I worked for a temp agency. Magazines and newspapers were dying by the day, so nobody was looking for a new journalism major. Six years ago, I had a son. As I stated in the cover letter, I had to stay home with him until he was ready for school. He's autistic. Now I'm ready to get a career started."

She took a deep breath. All of what she'd said was true enough, although maybe the career part was a stretch. What she really wanted was the money, and more specifically, money to spend on a full-time nanny. Someone knowledgeable and experienced with autistic kids who would know what to do with Ricky. Because if she was being honest, even after six years, she didn't know how to handle him. Every day he made her feel like a bad parent, and she was tired of feeling inept. So, she wanted a nanny. No, more than wanted—she needed a nanny. The career, and the adult time, that was just a bonus.

"I see." He put the sheet of paper down. "Then tell me about yourself. What made you get a degree in journalism?"

"I like to conduct research and write. I think it's important to get information out to the masses, to educate and inform. Uncover the truth."

Oh, and it was the only degree I had enough credits to get after six years. Did I mention that? My real degree was in partying.

"What kind of time management skills do you have? Deadlines are key here. I see it took you two extra years to get a degree. That makes me question your ability to set personal goals, deadlines. You don't finish on time here, we've got a blank page."

Jess felt her cheeks flush. "I understand your concern, but the extra time was actually due to me changing majors midstream. I could've graduated with dual degrees, journalism and international business, but I was short a few classes."

That was true enough as well. She had changed majors—three times to be exact—and she was a few classes short of the international business degree, if you considered ten to be a few, but she needn't elaborate.

Oh, and I also had to retake several failed classes after getting involved with an addict who got me hooked on heroin for a time. I did three separate stints in rehab over a decade. The addict, he's the father of my kid.

"Can you give me examples of things you set deadlines for in your personal life and what steps you take to ensure you make them?"

She thought for a moment, felt a rising panic.

I get my kid to school on time? No, not true, my husband does that. In fact, I can't even get my son to put his coat and shoes on and get in the car.

What else?

I put my hair and fingernail appointments in my phone to make sure I don't forget? I attend yoga twice a week to watch my weight?

Jesus, this was ridiculous. How was she going to convince him she could manage deadlines when she couldn't even convince herself? She decided to not offer details.

"Sir, have you ever had to deal with a child with autism or special needs? They need a great deal of attention. Constant attention. And you have to set deadlines for the smallest things that need to get done that may not seem important to anyone else but are critical for your family."

He looked over the top of his glasses and nodded. "What time to cook dinner, laundry to wash that sort of thing? I get it. I hear that from moms all the time. How hard it is to keep track of everything. Keep the kids' schedules in line." He lowered his eyes back toward the paper. Jess could tell he didn't believe a word of it.

"Did you bring samples of your writing?"

She removed two stories from the folder she carried and handed them to him.

He read. "What are these? Personal essays? Don't you have any pieces that have actually been published? Op-eds? Freelance stuff? Blog posts?"

"No, but I've never tried."

His pursed lips indicated that might've been the wrong thing to say. What kind of writer, researcher, journalist, doesn't try to get his stuff published? Or at a minimum, blog his ideas and musings? She attempted to save herself.

"What I meant is, I've never been afforded the time to pursue it. Of course, I've wanted to publish. I have opinions, several ideas for stories I'd like to pursue."

She felt a flutter in her chest, a little prewarning of getting heated. Defensive. She could hear Tom's voice in her head, telling her how she took things too personally. She tried to push it away.

"Tell me about those, your opinions and ideas. Give me an example." Jim leaned back in his chair and crossed his arms, as if he couldn't wait to hear the musings of a suburban housewife.

She sat up straight, thought for a moment. "Okay, opinions? Let's talk gun control. I believe in the Second Amendment, but I challenge you to identify any other industry where a product can accidently kill hundreds of people a year and isn't immediately recalled. A simple safety switch could reduce accidental firings, especially among kids, and help reduce these deaths and yet, our lawmakers won't give an inch. That's crazy.

"And speaking of crazy, let's talk mental illness in this country. People don't want or like to talk about it, but the lack of available mental health care is ridiculous. I know a woman whose son has episodes of paranoia and frequently talks of mass killings. She's tried every means possible to get him evaluated and treated before he hurts himself or several others and at every option she's turned away. No beds. Not enough counselors. Or they say they can't help until he comes forward on his own because he's eighteen. Given the mass shootings in this country, and the role mental illness has played with many of the perpetrators, you'd think the lawmakers would do something, but again, they just look the other way. Mothers need to demand change."

"You think one mom can make a difference against all those odds?" He smirked.

She felt affronted by that sneer. She wanted to slap it off his face. "Maybe not one, but thousands banded together? Yes. You ever heard of Mothers Against Drunk Driving?"

He raised an eyebrow. A single strand of his thinning hair blew in the heat blasting from the duct above his head. He put his hands back on the desk, studied more of her writing samples, rubbed his pointed chin.

"Not to sound unconvinced, but don't you think you might be more suited for...well, the social page or something? Report on charitable events and who attended? Test and do reviews of new beauty or household products, items of interest to women? Maybe an advice column? I think that's more your lane."

The former affront turned into total disrespect. She'd just presented this man with two relevant, current issues to discuss, and he'd come back with suggestions fit for a women's weekly or Dear Abby.

She started to give him a piece of her mind when she thought of Ricky and her daily battles with him. *Suck it up, buttercup. You need this job.*

Forcing down the shards of lashing insults and stinging comebacks she'd gathered on her tongue, she uttered words she'd never thought she'd say. "If you think that's where I'd be valuable, I'd welcome the opportunity. I just want to get my foot in the door. I can prove myself once I'm here. You'll see."

He smiled, exposing a wayward bicuspid that hung at an unusual angle. "Well, the issue is, I don't currently have an opening for such a reporter, but I think I could make a good argument for one if you're willing and work hard. You're a mom, attractive, stylish. I think women will respond well to you. And men, of course, for other reasons," he said with an underlying chortle. "Maybe we can work something out."

Work something out? Other reasons? What exactly does that mean?

She could feel the heat glowing on her face, her breaths weighted on her chest. She couldn't say anything that wouldn't come out wrong. He might as well have slapped her on the ass and sent her into the kitchen to fetch him a cup of coffee.

When she didn't respond, he glanced up. Her eyes must have bled fire, because he sensed her offense and attempted an explanation.

"You lack experience, Ms. Dawson, and I'm willing to help you, but you will have to start as my assistant and work your way up. You know," he said and winked, "I pat your back, you pat mine."

The firestorm erupted. "It's *Mrs.*, not *Ms.*, and I'm not patting anything." She rose from the chair. "I've changed my mind. I may need experience, but not that kind of experience."

He removed his glasses, laughed. "Oh no, don't tell me you're one of those feminist types who always misinterprets the words of a man to make it insulting to women. You'll never last a day in this business if you twist the words of every person you meet to match your need for drama."

She felt her jaw drop. "Drama? Is that what you think this is? You think it's okay to patronize and harass me just because I'm a mother and have only worked temp jobs? Let me tell you something: motherhood may make me inexperienced, but it doesn't make me stupid."

Jess slammed the door and walked out. Maybe she'd overreacted, but she didn't think so. She wouldn't last a day working for him anyway. She stormed through the reception area and out the glass doors.

Sexual harassment. Just one of many things they didn't prepare you for in college.

CHAPTER 4

Mikael Kriskan paced in his eight-by-ten cell, awaiting the knock on the door that would inform him that his attorney had arrived. Nick Whelan wasn't the attorney who'd represented him during the trial but the appeal attorney who'd stepped in when his original attorney had moved on to greener pastures. Nick was part of the Colorado Innocence Project, a nonprofit that represented clients they felt didn't receive a fair trial, and he'd become one of Mikael's best friends. Nick had represented him for roughly a decade now, through the entire storm of his post-conviction appeals. Now, they were riding their last wave together, waiting to see if they would make it to shore or drown.

Two raps on the door and Mikael stepped up and shoved his hands through the slot. When he felt the cuffs clamp each wrist, he stepped back, awaited the door to open. Two of his favorite guards stood in the corridor. While one attached the leg irons, the other spoke. "How are you today?"

"Living the dream," Mikael said.

The guard chuckled and leaned in. "I got a little something for you. I'll leave them in here for later." The guard entered his cell and slipped a package of Twinkies under his bedcover.

Mikael smiled. He loved Twinkies. "Thanks, man."

"You bet."

He shuffled between the two guards down the hall, pausing as they unlocked each section door before stepping through, then halting again for them to lock it behind him. They had to pass through three sections before they entered the area where visitation occurred, one large room with a number of round tables and plastic chairs for family visitation, the other smaller, private rooms reserved for attorney-client privilege. Nick was already waiting for him in such a room, chewing a nail and poring over the documents in front of him. Mikael took note of the smell of bleach and piney cleanser, as if they'd just disinfected the place. He hoped that wasn't because the last client had crapped his pants after getting bad news.

As procedure dictated, they cuffed him to the table, but not until he'd shaken Nick's hand. Nick knew most of the guards had become Mikael's friends, especially the ones who'd been raised in the same Sterling, Colorado, community where Mikael's parents had grown up, part of a German Russian population whose relatives had settled in the area over the last century. They, like much of the old community, had grown to believe Mikael was innocent.

Usually, Nick was dressed in a navy suit and a colorful tie, with not a mottled brown hair out of place, but today, he didn't much look like himself. His clothes hung loosely over his body, his skin was gray, and his eyelids appeared heavy, as if someone had stretched and folded them in places. Mikael didn't think he'd ever looked so tired and beat. He felt a buzzing in his chest, like an alarm going off.

This can't be good.

When the guards closed the door, Nick sighed. "I don't have the best of news."

Mikael took a deep breath and studied his hands. He often wondered if the lines in his palms told of his fate and was glad he couldn't read their message. He should've known better than to hold out any hope. For the past ten years, on multiple occasions, Nick had come to the prison to bring the joyous announcement that he'd filed a new appeal, only to return later with the news that it had been denied. Why should this one, the last one to the U.S. Supreme Court, be any different?

Nick hung his head, like a dog that had chewed Mikael's favorite shoes. "You know I've tried. Over the years I've tried to show inadequate prior counsel, begged to admit new evidence, filed a writ of habeas corpus to raise issues outside the trial record. Nothing has worked. The judges always take a hard look but come back with the same conclusion—that none of the issues I've presented would change the outcome of the original verdict. The last step was the petition to the U.S. Supreme Court and I'm sorry to tell you it too was denied. I'm sorry Mikael, but other than the governor granting you clemency, we've run out of options."

He sighed. "I don't have to tell you how difficult that is going to be. As you know, the political climate has changed in the past few months. Ever since the new governor was elected, he's made it clear the former flag of liberalism had waved its last stripe under his administration. Just days ago, he lifted the indefinite stay the former governor placed on your three fellow inmates who had long-ago completed their appeals, and now he wants to throw a big death-row party. He wants all four executions completed within the next six months."

Mikael slumped in his chair, all the remaining breath leaving his lungs. Of all the times for political change to take effect. Even though he knew this day would surely come, its finality landed like a hammer to the chest. "Lucky me," he said.

He turned away and stared at the gray concrete wall. The sounds outside the room pained his head, the constant rattle of chains and stomp of boots, the biting commands of the guards. How he longed to hear anything besides the reminders of confinement—a dog barking, a bird singing, the whispers of the Colorado pine in the high country.

Before his arrest, his days had been anything but confining. Filled with hikes at nearby Red Rocks and bike rides through Waterton Canyon. Weekends home from school to see his parents, filling himself with piroshki and honey cake until he was sick. He'd long since stopped trying to recall the taste of his mother's cooking, the memories too painful.

And college, how he missed his days on campus at the Colorado School of Mines. Since he'd been a boy, he'd wanted nothing else other than to build rockets and shuttles, dreamed of working for NASA someday. And at nineteen, when his parents were murdered, he'd been well on his way, attending on a full ride and already earning enough credits to be a junior when it had all come crashing down.

For nearly fifteen long years, a third of his life, he'd stared at these blank walls imagining what it would be like to fill them with photographs from a new life. Friends, family, and a future.

Now, there would be no chance of that. His appeals had run out and he would die. Without an ounce of ever understanding who, or why, someone had killed his parents and chosen him to take the fall. Without knowing what had really happened to Anya, the little sister he loved and would never harm. It seemed so unfair, so wrong.

He tasted the bile rise in his throat. "How soon will it come?" he asked.

Nick sighed. "The governor will set all four execution dates in the next two weeks. If you go last, maybe this summer. If you go first, early March." He wiped his eyes. "I'm sorry."

Mikael waited for his own emotion to surface but he'd long ago emptied the wells and the bucket was dry. Only anger remained, rusting the rest of the bucket away with its acidic nature. "You have nothing to be sorry for, my friend," he said. "You believed in me when no one else would. More than even God."

Nick reached over and took his hand. "Please don't lose faith."

Mikael blinked. He looked sorrowfully at his attorney. He knew Nick was a religious man, just as Mikael's parents had been, but Mikael wasn't sure he had any such belief left in him. I mean, what good had it done him to be faithful thus far? What good had it done his parents? They'd believed in a mighty power, prayed at meal and bedtime, displayed Orthodox crosses on the walls for protection, and they'd been murdered in cold blood. Struck down in the prime of their life.

What kind of God allows such a calamity of justice without intervention? What kind of God allows evil to win?

No, he had long given up on faith.

"Will I see you again?" he asked Nick.

"Yes, of course. I'll keep trying Mikael, you know I will."

Nick buzzed for the guards and they entered. He turned to Mikael, gave him a hug. Mikael would've liked to hug him back but the restraints didn't allow for it. "I'll see you soon. Very soon," Nick said.

Mikael nodded but didn't respond. A lump had gathered in his throat, blocking any vocal ability, like a cancerous tumor that spread nothing but death. The walk back to the cellblock felt suffocating, as if he were heading into the death chamber itself.

What did they say? *Dead man walking.*

When he arrived back at his cell, the guard who'd given him the Twinkies sensed his troubled mood. "I take it the news wasn't good?"

Mikael shook his head.

The guard examined his shoes. "What can I do?"

"Nothing. There is nothing anyone can do now. I'm a dead man."

CHAPTER 5

E than Stantz returned from his evening bike ride to a flurry of beeps, buzzes, and other noises signaling e-mails, messages, and replies to his latest blog post. He'd written it two nights ago, before the U.S. Supreme Court had made their latest ruling, and he thought it was one of his better posts the past month. In it, he debated whether Mikael Kriskan, Russian immigrant and death-row inmate, should be granted an appeal on his fourteen-year-old conviction for killing his family. The Russian had been found guilty of two capital offenses for the murder of his parents, plus a second-degree murder charge for the death of his younger sister, Anya, although her body had never been recovered. Getting a murder conviction without a body was a tough charge, but traces of her blood had been discovered at the scene, including on Mikael's hands, so the jurors had deemed her death the logical conclusion. That included Ethan, who'd served as juror number four.

Over the years he'd kept track of them all: John Berman, the foreman; Hazel Winwood, the retiree; Libby Allen, the feminist; Saku Priyanka, the restaurant owner; Gerald Fowler, the libertarian; Emmanuel "Manny" Perez, the gay Mexican; Kevin Ryland, the advocate; Linda Lopez, the young mother; Myrtle Hays, the gospel singer; Fred Patterson, the accountant; and, of course, Jessie Gaylord, the University of Colorado Boulder student he'd developed a crush on during the trial.

Jessie and Ethan had been closest in age and naturally bonded during the three-month ordeal. It had been one of Colorado's most notorious cases of the past decade.

It was the jury service and the case that had prompted Ethan to start the *CrimeSpree* blog and forum two years later, to discuss all things of a crime-related nature. Forensics, evidence, investigators, conspiracy theories—few topics were off limits except the occasional whacko who wanted advice on plotting a new murder. Unsolved cases were his specialty, everything from Jack the Ripper to Tupac to JonBenét, but he also kept current with features on highly publicized cases across the world. He'd started with just a hundred subscribers and now had over ten-thousand. Crime, it seemed, never stopped fascinating.

In his posts, Ethan never took sides, instead choosing to present both the pro and con arguments and opinions from every rank and file in life. He was well respected for eliminating the trolls that came with an online forum, those who spewed their variety of hate and wrath upon the world like a plague of insects. He had no use for trolls, for those who didn't listen and engage and debate properly. He kept a few of the subscribers that often skated the edges but issued stern warnings and posted his rules and bylaws regularly, trying to keep the peace.

Sometimes subscribers left, offended, and sometimes he had to notify a subscriber they were no longer welcome to comment, but that was part of the job as forum administrator. It was his site, his rules. He was proud of what he'd created.

Today there were three especially combative arguments going on. One, the debate surrounding the original question he'd presented, whether the Colorado death-penalty system was fair, a structure that left the fate of a suspect to the selection of random jurors and a lone holdout, a method both the prosecutors and defense attorneys often referred to as craps, a roll of the dice.

This he'd demonstrated by a number of trial outcomes, including Aurora theater shooter James Holmes, who'd executed twelve people, including children, and injured seventy others. Though his guilt was unquestionable, he'd received life in prison and not the death sentence because two jurors held out, citing Holmes's mental illness as the reason for their decision.

That compared to Mikael Kriskan, who'd allegedly murdered his parents, his guilt questionable, yet got twelve jurors who chose death over life. Ethan had openly admitted to his audience in his initial posts on the trial that he'd been a juror, and in his defense, noted the lack of Kriskan's counsel to prove any abuse that Kriskan had received at the hands of his parents prior to their deaths—such as in the Eric and Lyle Menendez case—nor offered any hint of mental illness, as in the James Holmes' case.

To make matters worse, the prosecution made mention of Kriskan's genius-level IQ numerous times, but the defense never objected, making Kriskan appear even more menacing and calculating. Kriskan had also refused to testify on his own behalf, to offer a shred of defense, saying he couldn't because he didn't remember anything about that night. When the tox report had come back clean, that left jurors feeling suspicious.

The second argument being debated was specific to the Kriskan case, the discussion of any role that anti-immigration sentiment played in the trial, along with a side theory that Russians had only allowed adoption to Americans in the past because they were planning to develop the kids into future spies. Ethan wasn't sure about this theory but it appeared to be gaining momentum.

The third trending thread on the blog was about the death penalty itself, which, as usual, appeared to be teetering dangerously and crossing over into the pro-life and abortion debate. For Ethan, this was an argument that never had a winner. And how could it, because for most people, you could never have empathy for both the victims and the perpetrator. Pro-lifers advocated for the innocent unborn but were quick to call for an individual's death when that person took another's life.

Pro-choicers believed that guaranteeing health care, food, and education should be akin to being pro-life, otherwise, supporters were simply pro-birth. Pro-lifers came back at pro-choicers, pointing fingers at those who would march in defense of a man who killed and maimed others but would so easily kill a fetus without a thought.

Ethan wanted no part of this discussion so he'd let them debate this one out. He'd watch out for the fringe trolls, both pro-life and pro-choice and the death-penalty advocates and foes, but he wouldn't interject an ounce into the discussion. The key to being a successful moderator was to never offer up extreme opinions of your own.

He spent the next twenty minutes answering questions and thanking a number of responders for their input. Grabbed a second beer from the refrigerator. When he returned, a number of instant messages had popped up on his screen. They were from one of his regular contributors, online name of NSearchofTruth.

"Have you heard the news? John Berman?"

Ethan frowned.

Berman? Their foreman?

The message included a link to an article on a local news station's website. Ethan clicked on it and read. *Parents killed in deadly knife attack. Young daughter missing. Teen son suspected.*

He set down the beer, felt his brow furrow.

Reluctantly, he played the video. The reporter stood in front of house in Park Hill, a two-story brown-and-white Tudor with a well-manicured lawn.

"The couple killed late last night have now been identified as John Berman, age fifty-two, and his wife, Alison, forty-nine. Their young daughter, Bryn, who's just five years old, is still missing, and police hope somebody out there has information about her whereabouts. Police believe she may have fled from the house while the crime against her parents was being committed and are anxious to locate her. The Denver Police Department, along with scores of volunteers, continue to search the area in and around Park Hill, looking for any signs of her. So far, authorities say the seventeen-year-old son, who is still in custody and can't be named because he's a juvenile, is offering no information on the whereabouts of his sister and is claiming innocence in the murder of his parents. Police say this one will take some time to figure out."

Ethan sat back, feeling like someone had zapped him with a stun gun.

Holy crap. John Berman, their jury foreman was dead? In a knife attack? With his daughter missing and his son a suspect?

Just like Mikael Kriskan's family.

The fine hairs on the back of his neck raised.

He didn't like this. Didn't like this at all.

He texted a couple of his sources in law enforcement, asking them for information. While he waited for a response, he paced the room and slapped at his arms, trying to shake the abrupt chill that had gripped his body. Suddenly, he heard a new ping. He raced over. It was one of his sources, an officer with the Denver Police Department, or DPD.

"Got your message. You're not going to believe it. Detectives said the Bermans were stabbed the exact number of times and places as Kriskan's parents. They think the son was infatuated with case. Creepy."

Ethan gasped. Stabbed the same number of times and places? That was more than creepy. That was suspect. Wait until they learned that Berman was a juror on the case.

He stepped back, wondering what to do. He pondered what the killing meant. Was it the son as police suspected? Or something bigger? Did someone else know that Berman was a juror on the Kriskan case? Were they trying to send a message?

He had to blog about it. How could he not? He returned to the keyboard and began to type when another instant message popped up. The username gave him pause— The Reaper.

He didn't know who it was.

"Your friend has a message for you."

"Who is this?" Ethan typed.

"You and your fellow jurors."

Ethan stopped breathing. Again, he typed. "Who is this?"

"The Reaper."

Maybe the guy thought he was being funny, but Ethan wasn't laughing. He took a long swill of beer. Typed, "We don't do pranks here. If you have something to say, leave a comment on the blog."

"No prank."

Ethan waited. He wasn't sure he wanted to engage with this contact. He didn't know the name or the man behind the message and his gut was telling him he didn't want to. The cursor blinked. One minute, two, three.

"Kevin Ryland says hello."

Ethan stilled, his heart abruptly racing. Kevin was another juror, and Ethan didn't like the coincidence. A picture suddenly appeared on his screen. At first it was small, but when he clicked on it, it began to grow, until the image filled his screen.

When he realized what it showed, Ethan Stantz ran from the room.

In the photo, Kevin Ryland was dead, hanging from a rope.

CHAPTER 6

Jess navigated the Denver streets until she reached her designated stop, the Oxford Hotel. It was downtown Denver's oldest, first opened in 1891. The hotel still boasted of its original wood-burning fireplace and elevators, known as vertical railways, and its display of several antiques and fine art. Once a month for the past two years, Jess had become a regular here, although none of the staff knew her real name. Instead, they knew she and the man she was about to meet as the Thompsons, a married couple who liked an afternoon of privacy every so often. Personally, Jess referred to Mr. Thompson as her therapist, as he helped her forget her daily troubles. They'd started their affair two years ago after meeting for the second time at an event for a local charity she'd attended with Tom. The man, David Foster, had remembered her from their time together long ago, when they'd crossed paths during the Mikael Kriskan case. Then, she'd only known him as the prosecuting attorney. Now, he was her lover.

She parked nearby in a local lot, took the stairs up to room 212, and knocked twice. On the other side was a semi-naked David, wearing only boxer shorts and a smile. He wrapped a hand around her waist and pulled her in, kissing her as he shut the door.

Jess pulled back and slid by him, running her hands along his abs as she passed. David was six feet of pure muscle with full dark hair and brown eyes, a martial arts master and part-time ultimate fighter. She could see he was already hard, awaiting her arrival.

The room smelled of a fresh shower and aftershave, the mirrors still fogged. The covers lay in disarray at the foot of the bed, the television on but muted. Outside, the day was a dull gray, the city expecting flurries later that afternoon. As she hung her coat and placed her personal items on the dresser, she felt him press behind her and run a hand up the inside of her thigh up to her crotch. His mouth grazed her neck.

She tilted her head back to rest against his shoulder and reached up with both arms. His hands slipped beneath the oversized sweater she wore and slid it up and off. He unhooked the lacy black bra in the back without a hitch. It fell to the floor.

She turned her head to the side so he could kiss her. His tongue, his lips, tasted like coffee and chocolate. His hands were on her breasts, massaging. He abruptly spun her to face him and stood back to examine her body, ready to devour. Like he was thinking about every single thing he wanted to do to her. She let his eyes take her in as she wriggled from the remainder of her clothes, except the matching lace underwear, careful never to shift her gaze. She slid two fingers beneath the lace and between her legs to tease him. He liked to watch.

He knelt in front of her, took the edge of the panties in his mouth and pulled them down, just far enough to expose her, then slid them off. He shoved his mouth there, tasting her, his tongue slipping in and out, circling. She arched, grabbing the back of his hair and pushing him farther into her. In minutes, she felt the first warm rush of pleasure erupt between her legs and down her thighs.

A sardonic smile graced his lips as he stood and removed his boxers. He gripped each of her hips, slipped his hands down beneath her ass, and lifted her to meet him. She wrapped her legs around him and he shoved her against the wall. As he entered her, she thought about Tom, how this was what he never understood—the forcefulness, the animal instinct, it was such a turn-on for her. Tom was always so careful, so loving, asking what she liked and disliked. Stroking her tenderly.

Like the rest of him, sometimes Tom was just too nice.

She knew how horrible that would sound to the outside world, to anyone who knew Tom and the empathetic, caring individual that he was. He was a good man, a great catch. She'd been reminded of that time and time again. But, oh Lord, sometimes she just wanted to scream at him to raise his voice and argue with her, to man up. Tell her to cook dinner, make the damn bed, be his wife.

And sometimes, yes, she just wanted him to stop with all the niceties and fuck her.

With David that wasn't the case. Fucking was all that David wanted to do.

As he thrust up and in, kissing her chest and neck, she turned her head up and closed her eyes. Lost. She just wanted to get lost. Escape into this momentary lapse of time and responsibility. No troubled kid. No weak husband. No lack of a job, or money, or a nanny to help. No spit to wipe, spilled juice to mop, or thrown food to clean. No husband telling her another six months to a raise or promotion. No stepmother chiding her for her immaturity and lack of financial management.

Just feel, just lust. Get lost.

She had told no one of the affair, of course. They would be horrified. Even her best friends, the bridesmaids at her wedding, all also married now, thought she had the best husband. Not the richest but the best. Nice, kind Tom.

Why did it annoy her so?

All her friends had kids now too, toddlers up to age twelve. The oldest belonged to Catelyn, who'd accidently gotten pregnant while she was still in college. But all their kids were healthy. Cavities and knee scrapes and boo-boos, those were their biggest complaints. They didn't have a clue. Oh sure, they pretended to be sympathetic, give her the *poor Jess, how do you manage and it must be so tough,* but silently, she knew they thanked God every night it wasn't them, that the trade-off for having a more demanding husband might be healthy kids.

He cupped his arms beneath her ass and pulled her from the wall. She hugged her legs tighter around him as he carried her to the bed and they fell in together. He paused and lifted, still inside her, now teasing, pulling out slowly then thrusting back in. He reached up and fanned her hair out behind her. He often spoke of his love for her long hair. They spent the next ten minutes kissing with their eyes open, recognizing the common lust between them.

His phone rang from the dresser. He didn't stop.

Jess's phone soon followed. She didn't recognize the ringtone which meant it wasn't anyone she knew. Not an emergency. No need to interrupt.

David turned her over, entered her from behind. His thrusting grew more intense.

Again, his phone rang, but he was too close to orgasm. They were both panting now, grunting like animals. When they were done, they fell onto their backs, sweaty, staring at the ceiling. Both of their phones rang again.

"Shit, who keeps calling?" he asked.

David hopped from the bed, glanced at the call log, then at Jess. "It's my office." He hit the call-back button. Soon, Jess could hear a voice on the line, rambling off a string of words she couldn't understand. She watched as David's face darkened.

"Are you certain? The family from the other night?"

Jess felt a pit in her stomach. She didn't know why. Something in David's voice and the way he looked at her. She stared at her phone as it also began to ring again. She picked it up. Three calls, all from the same local number. *Maybe it's Ricky's school?* She hit accept.

"Jess? Oh, thank God, you answered. This is Ethan Stantz. We have to talk. You have to meet me right away."

CHAPTER 7

After David left in a rush, no explanation provided, she took a quick shower and arranged to meet Ethan at a nearby café. Coincidentally, he lived in the same LoDo neighborhood as the Oxford Hotel, so she left her car parked in the lot and walked the three blocks to the café. She still wasn't sure whether the frigid feeling gripping her was due to the weather or Ethan's call, but once inside the café she began to warm.

She stripped off her coat and glanced over the tables. The place was crowded for a Wednesday afternoon, college students and telecommuters with their faces shoved in laptops, working on various projects. She was wondering if, after so many years, she and Ethan would recognize each other when she saw a man wave from the back corner. He looked right at home among the crowd of young urbanites, his face unshaven and his shaggy hair pulled up into a little man bun at the top of his head. Only the wire-rimmed glasses served as a reminder of the Harry Potter–like kid she remembered from the jury. Ethan Stantz had grown up.

She wound her way through the café until she reached his table, next to a brick wall covered with photos of various musicians who'd stopped by for coffee or lunch before performing at the venue next door. Ethan stood to hug her. "Long time no see."

She took off her hat and gloves, shoved them in her pockets. Removed her puffer jacket and draped it around the back of the chair. Left the scarf on for warmth. "Yeah, well, no offense, but I was kind of hoping never to see anyone from the trial ever again. I haven't stepped inside a courtroom since the day we were dismissed."

"None taken." He tipped his cup to her. "It is good to see you, though. You look great."

"Thank you. You..." she said, pulling out a chair and taking a seat, "look all grown up."

He laughed. "Thank heavens. I'll never forget when the judge asked me if I was old enough to tie my shoes during the pretrial questioning. The whole courtroom laughed."

"I remember. I felt so bad for you."

He shrugged. "I was used to it. Hell, I got carded at the movie theater until I turned twenty-one." He took a long sip of his latte. Jess did the same with her mocha.

"I had a hard time finding your phone number," Ethan said. "No longer Jessie Gaylord. You got married. Now Jessie Dawson. Congratulations."

"Yes, I did. Four years ago. And please, call me Jess."

"Kids?"

"Yes. Ricky. He's a handful. He's six." She waved her hand. "I had him before. He's not my husband's. From another relationship." She sighed, gave a nervous laugh. "A bad relationship." *Ugh, I'm blathering.* "Enough about me. What about you?"

He pushed his glasses up on his nose. "Finished grad school, started doing some freelance work, ended up writing for *Westword* for three years before I started my own gig, a blog."

She smiled. "A blog? So, you're a writer?"

"Yes, if you remember that was the thing we had in common, besides our ages."

"I remember." It was a wistful memory, back in a time when she still believed the journalism career could happen. Back before her ex and Ricky and her father's death. Life got in the way.

She thought of the prior day's job interview and felt sick.

He spun his cup between his hands. "So, my blog, it's called *CrimeSpree*. We discuss crimes—the evidence, the suspects, conspiracies. It's kind of a whodunit online. I got the idea after the trial. I try to keep the crazy out, but it's like herding cats. Anyhow, it's one of the reasons I called you. To discuss what happened two nights ago."

She tipped her head. "Two nights ago? What are you talking about?"

"You haven't heard? They released the names today. Don't you watch the news?"

"I've been...busy. Whose names?"

He let out a breath of air like he'd been holding it in all day. "John Berman, our jury foreman? He and his family were murdered. Stabbed in their home, just like our case. The daughter's missing and the son is the main suspect, just like our case."

"Wait," Jess said, feeling the fingers of dismay gripping her chest. "That was John Berman and his family?"

She recalled the bits and pieces of the news broadcast she'd listened to the prior morning, Tom's comment about how he hoped the murder wasn't in his jurisdiction. Then later, as she drove to the job interview, the Amber Alert for a Bryn Berman. She'd had no reason to associate the name with their juror foreman—he hadn't had a daughter then that she recalled and Berman wasn't an uncommon name.

Ethan nodded. "Even worse..." He leaned in. "It's not been released to the media, but I have it on good authority that John and his wife were stabbed the exact same number of times and locations as Mikael Kriskan's parents."

It was Jess's turn to lose her breath. She fell back against the chair, feeling as if she'd been hit with one of the bricks from the wall. She knew immediately that also had to be the news David had received an hour earlier and wondered why David had told her the call was nothing. That their jury foreman had been murdered in the same manner as the case he'd served on as a juror wasn't nothing.

David and his team were probably going over all the details at this moment, the similarities and differences between the cases. Though that would take time. If Jess had learned anything during the trial, it was that autopsies and toxicology and blood spatter analysis were slow.

"What do you think it means? A copycat?"

"So far, the police only suspect the son. They think maybe he had an infatuation with the case, so if that's true, then yes, he's a copycat killer. A stranger would be as well."

"Are the police aware that Berman was a juror?"

"I don't know, but if not, they soon will be. I plan to blog about it tonight."

Jess stared at him. An uncomfortableness stirred inside. "Do you think that's a good idea? To reveal his identity?" She wasn't sure who she was more afraid of exposing, John Berman or the rest of the jurors, including herself.

"I think I have to, especially given..." He removed his glasses and rubbed his eyes. Cleaned the lenses with the edge of his shirt then slid them back on. Put his hands in a steeple and blew out another breath.

Jess braced herself. He seemed to be preparing to drop yet another bomb on her.

"There's something else I've learned that the authorities don't yet know."

"What?"

"John Berman wasn't the only juror to die this week."

Sharp stabs like barbwire pricked at Jess's skin. She wasn't sure she wanted to hear anymore. If she listened, it made it real.

Ethan twisted the corners of his mouth, chewed both sides of his lip. "Kevin Ryland was found dead yesterday. He hung himself from his loft. And Jess, he left a note attached to his body."

"Saying what?"

"KJ—do the right thing."

Jess felt the blood flee from her extremities. She swooned.

Ethan grabbed a napkin, dipped it in her water glass, and handed it to her. Immediately, he apologized for being so abrupt.

A wave of nausea ran over her as she dabbed the napkin over her forehead where sweat covered her brow. "Jesus, Ethan. This can't be happening."

"But it is, it is happening."

"Are you saying Kevin Ryland killed himself over our verdict?"

"Yes, maybe. Or maybe..." He leaned across the table, the nervous energy gathered around him almost like a visible mass. "Jess, what if he didn't kill himself? What if someone killed Kevin too and staged it to look like a suicide?"

"What? Ethan, no." She scrambled to think, to make sense of the matter. "No, he must've seen what happened to John and his wife and in his guilt, killed himself. Remember, he was the one who was most opposed to a guilty verdict and the death sentence."

"You were too, at one time. And me, I was on the fence, but you convinced me to change my mind."

Jess erupted. "Don't lay that on me. Don't you dare. Any one of us could've decided upon life in prison instead of death, any one of us. We had a choice."

She hated that she sounded so defensive, as if she didn't believe her own words. Because, well, she didn't.

Ethan gazed at her through hazel eyes, a glance that said he didn't believe it either.

Jess turned away, fighting her anger and fear and grief. She felt her eyes grow moist and hated herself, hated those feelings. She quickly wiped her tears, glad her back was to the crowd.

"Look, I'm sorry to dump this on you like this," he said, "but I thought everyone on the jury should know. Just in case, you know, their deaths are not a coincidence. You need to watch your back."

Jess sat up, alarmed. "What are you saying? You think we're in danger? No, this is just a coincidence." She could not, would not, think otherwise.

"Well, I mean, we don't know that yet."

"You don't understand. I have a son, a very vulnerable son. I have a husband who knows nothing about my time on the Kriskan jury. Honestly, I just want this to be over with."

Ethan appeared like a man who had taken a punch to the gut. "What? You never told your husband about your jury service?"

"No, Ethan, no. He's an attorney himself—a public defender. He's adamantly against the death penalty. It would kill him if he knew I'd sentenced Mikael Kriskan to death. I cannot confide in him about this."

Ethan blinked his eyes. "Wow. Jess, I'm sorry." He seemed to be at a loss for words.

Jess sighed. She rubbed her tired face and groaned. "Look, I'm not angry at you. I'm just...scared. This is such a shock. I mean, that note. What does he mean, do the right thing? We can't change the verdict now. It's done."

She sat back, shook her head. "Ethan, what are we going to do?"

"I don't know, Jess. I honestly don't know."

CHAPTER 8

Jess bundled herself back in her hat, gloves, and coat and headed into the cold. Snow fell from the sky, a light dusting that covered the sidewalks and city streets. Beneath her jacket, she trembled from the anxiety that had taken up residence in her heart. Thoughts and images of a previous time battered her emotions, memories of John Berman and Kevin Ryland. She'd spent fourteen long years trying to push away all recollections of that time, and now, current events had summoned them, like a witch raising the dead from their graves.

John Berman had never been particularly pleasant to Jess, although he'd treated her no worse than the other young jurors, Ethan Stantz and Kevin Ryland. It seemed at the time, he equated young with stupid and expressed a counter-argument to every opinion they made about the case. John, as a father and high-ranking manager at a software firm, had seen himself as the man best suited to assume the role of jury foreman, and no one had objected. Truth was, no one else wanted the position. Most of the jurors had kicked, screamed, and pounded their fists once selected, realizing their entire summer would be spent sitting in a courtroom listening to tales of stab wounds and viewing autopsy photos with a judge who demanded the air-conditioning be set just north of freezing. All except John Berman, who wanted the job.

And Kevin, poor Kevin. Jess and Kevin had grown close during the trial, so close that others had teased them about their budding romance. They'd often hung out after the daily court drama had ended at a nearby bar and talked for hours. She remembered him as a lover of mountain biking, craft beers, and classic rock. He kicked ass at trivia and video poker. And it was possible, if the trial and the deliberations hadn't turned as ugly as they had in the end, maybe they would've dated afterward.

At one time, Jess had been looking forward to it.

As it turned out, Kevin Ryland wanted nothing to do with her by the end of trial and told her as much the day they were finally released. Not that she blamed him.

It was the deliberations that had sent them all over the edge. When they'd started, Kevin had firmly planted himself in the not-guilty camp, stating that the existence of unidentified DNA discovered at the scene was cause enough for reasonable doubt. John Berman was in opposition, arguing, like the prosecution, that Kriskan's family regularly invited church members over to their house and hosted community potlucks, and the unidentified DNA likely belonged to any one of them. Kevin countered that the police had collected DNA from all known parties who'd been in the house the past three months and still a match hadn't occurred. Not so, said Berman.

And so, it had gone on like that for days on end.

What made it worse was that, unlike the time of the actual trial, when they'd been free to return home each night and live a fairly regular life, they'd been sequestered for deliberations. Stuck in a downtown hotel with a court attendant. No phones. No television. No internet. Every day lined up in the morning like school kids so their teacher could take attendance then driven to the court and locked in a ten-by-twenty-foot room to battle it out. Back again at night. Monitored during breaks, accompanied to lunch, even to the bathroom. An endless, relentless hell.

By day five, Jess was perched on the edge of insanity.

Maybe changing her vote hadn't been right, but she still believed that if David Foster, prosecuting attorney, hadn't come to her rescue during that time, she would've died in that hotel room.

She rushed across a street of stalled traffic, desperate to get away from the café and the news that Ethan had heaped upon her. She was so distressed by the memories that flooded her consciousness like tidal waves, she didn't even realize when the traffic began to move once again. One driver honked his horn at her as she stepped in front of his grill and another followed suit when she bumped into his car. On the next curb, she slipped on black ice, her legs as shaky as her nerves. She just wanted to get back to her car so she could gather herself together and warm up a little.

It wasn't meant to be.

At the next block, she felt a presence behind her, a man speeding up and growing closer by the second. With her hood up and around her face, she couldn't see him until he was fully beside her.

He reached out and grabbed her arm, bringing her to a halt. "Hey."

She wheeled to see her ex-boyfriend, Ricky's father. Tyler Cooper.

She felt a thud in her chest, tasted bitterness, as if she'd bit into a rotten apple. He wore the same clothes as always—plaid shirt, jeans, hiking boots, beanie—but the beard was longer and he was at least ten pounds thinner, causing the jeans to hang on nonexistent hips.

Great. This is all I need right now. "I'm in a hurry, Tyler."

"I can see that. What's the big rush?"

She jolted from his grip, kept pushing on. "None of your business. Go away."

He kept step beside her. "I left you, like, three voice mails. I don't like to be ignored."

"I don't care what you like. I know all you want is money and I'm telling you for the last time, I don't have any. I'm no longer funding your habit. Go get clean and get a job. Get a life."

"Well, aren't you all uppity now. What makes you think you're so much better than me? You're no more perfect than me. You don't have a job. You're an addict. You and me, we're just alike."

She stopped in her tracks. "No, we aren't. I'm sober. I went through hell and worked my ass off to get clean. Look at you. Eyes as hollowed as caves. Clothes barely clinging to your frame. And you have the audacity to tell me that my money has been going to rehab? That you're not using?"

He slouched, kicked a foot. The emotions played out on his face—shame, anger, desperation. It's what she'd hated most as a user, that constant clawing of need. His dark brown eyes twitched at the corners, lips trembled in the cold. Underneath the shaggy beard, traces of his former good looks remained, but he appeared at least a decade older now than when they were together. She couldn't imagine how she'd ever found him attractive in the first place.

"I swear to you, I'm going to get clean. And when I do, I want to see my son."

"When you're ready to pay up six years of child support and prove you've been clean for a year, let me know. I'm not trying to keep you from Ricky, but I will as long as you're using. I don't want him to know you as an addict. I have a difficult enough time explaining things to him as it is."

"My mom wants to see her grandson. Don't be surprised if she files for visitation."

He always did this to her, threatened her with his mighty mother. She worked in child services for the city of Denver, and both he and Jess knew his mother could do much to make her life hell. Jess didn't put it past Tyler's mother to create any such lie she wished to get Ricky in her custody, should she ever pursue it.

She'd never approved of Jess, never thought she'd make a good mother. Before Jess had married Tom, Tyler's mother had been relentless in her surprise visits and verbal assaults on Jess, casting suspicion on every cut and bruise Ricky received and examining Jess's arms for needle marks.

It had taken Tom's own threats of legal action to finally make her back off. But Jess knew she was always in the shadows, awaiting an opportunity.

Jess stood her ground, moved an inch within Tyler's face. "I'm done with your threats, Tyler. I'm done with your mother's threats. You tell your mother to get her deadbeat son to rehab and pay up his child support in addition to all the money I've loaned him for the past six years, then we can talk. Until then, I've got nothing to say to you or her."

CHAPTER 9

Jess paced the living room, awaiting Tom's arrival. In the background, the local evening news issued an update on John Berman's murder. The district attorney was planning to charge the son as an adult, paving the way to seek the death penalty. However, a leading criminal defense attorney had come forward to represent the son, pro-bono, stating he adamantly believed the boy was innocent. Unlike the prosecutor, he believed the Bermans were murdered so the killer could abduct their young daughter, Bryn, who remained missing. There was still no word of John Berman's participation on the Mikael Kriskan case, but that would likely change by morning once Ethan published a new blog post.

Jess chewed a nail, gnawing on the idea of telling Tom her predicament. Yet, she really wasn't certain if there was a predicament to discuss. Yes, the jury foreman had been murdered, and Kevin Ryland was also dead, but she didn't yet know whether he'd committed suicide or if someone had made it appear as such. And if she went ahead and told Tom about her jury service now, and then it all ended up being nothing, well, what would he think of her? Was it worth risking her marriage just to be able to talk to him about it, especially at a time their relationship was already experiencing duress?

Ricky, curled up on a rug playing a game, pulled on her pant leg. "What's wrong, Mom?"

Jess noticed his crinkled face, realized her anxiety was bleeding over to him. She knelt down, kissed the top of his head. "Nothing, kiddo. Everything is fine." To her surprise, he stood and gave her a warm hug. She inhaled the smell of his hair, strawberry and oatmeal, felt his breath on her cheek. It was the best thing to happen all day.

It ended when Tom appeared in the door and Ricky bounded from her arms. "Daddy!"

Jess sighed. At least Ricky had paid her attention, if only for a moment.

Tom scooped Ricky into his arms, held on to him for what seemed an eternity. She noticed Tom's expression, dark and distant. His face was weary, his skin sallow, black bags underlining his eyes. "You okay?" she asked.

Tom closed his eyes, nodded. He kissed Ricky on the forehead, then let him slide to the floor. Walked over and gave Jess a peck too. Heaved a sigh as he put his keys and phone on the kitchen island, loosened his tie. "Bad day," he said.

Jess grunted. *You have no idea.*

"Seems to be going around," she said. She poured two glasses of wine, handed one to him. He drank half. She refilled it. In rehab, the counselors emphasized to Jess that she should refrain from using drugs or alcohol of any kind again, as it would always pose a risk, but she'd never experienced an issue with alcohol. After two glasses of anything, she always fell asleep. "I made chicken for dinner."

"I don't have much of an appetite. Maybe after a shower."

While Tom cleaned up, she went ahead and fed Ricky. A piece of chicken deboned, no skin, mashed potatoes, no butter. She tried to slip in a couple of green beans, but he wasn't having it, and they quickly ended up on the floor. He ate nothing green.

Tom came down twenty minutes later, smelling of soap and deodorant. He grabbed the bottle of wine and set it on the table. She dished up two plates, all the while wondering how she could approach the subject of Ethan's news without implicating herself. She waited until Ricky had finished his dinner and went back to playing his games before she brought it up.

"I saw an old friend today," she said.

"Oh, who's that?" Tom asked, moving the potatoes absently around his plate.

"Ethan Stantz. He writes this blog, *CrimeSpree*. Ever heard of it?"

Tom frowned. "Yes, I know of it. Stantz was a juror on the Kriskan case. He writes some good pieces but also plays host to lots of conspiracy theories. Some of those people are two colors short of a rainbow, know what I mean? How do you know him?"

"He went to CU." True enough, he had. Not that they'd known each other during their time on the University of Colorado campus.

"You never mentioned him before."

"I didn't really know him that well, but he was at the coffee shop today, and we got to talking. He remembered I wanted to be a writer so he was telling me about his blog. He was really hyper because—you know that family that was killed the other night? The husband, John Berman, was the foreman of the jury in the Mikael Kriskan case. Ethan said the media doesn't know yet."

Tom looked up from his chicken. "Wow, seriously?"

"Yes, and worse, he said a source on the inside told him that Berman and his wife were stabbed the same number of times and locations as Kriskan's parents. Ethan was really scared. He thinks someone might be targeting the jurors to make a statement, get an appeal for Mikael Kriskan."

Tom wrinkled his brow. "That's crazy," he said. "I heard that the police think the son might've been influenced by the Kriskan case. If his dad was a juror, that would make more sense now. He probably knew all about the case and became obsessed by it."

"You think so?" She really wanted to believe it.

"Yes."

She chewed on a spoonful of mashed potatoes, considered it. "Maybe, but Ethan was also spooked because a second juror died the day after Berman, and the police haven't made that connection either."

Now Tom looked concerned. "Stabbed?"

"Well, no. Suicide, they think, but Ethan thinks maybe not."

The corner of his mouth twisted. "See? The conspiracy theorist."

"Ethan said the juror left a note taped to his chest. It said, *KJ—do the right thing.*"

"KJ?"

"Kriskan jury."

Tom raised an eyebrow. "Compelling. Sounds like juror remorse. With the execution approaching and Berman's murder, maybe it sent the guy over the edge. It happens. That's why I would never choose a death sentence over life in prison if I sat on a case. Never. Who needs that on their conscience?"

Jess felt a hard lump in her throat. *Yeah, who indeed.*

Tom cut his chicken, stabbed it with his fork. Jess flinched. She could sense his ire.

"That's what I don't get about people, like this case I'm trying right now," Tom said. "They're all so quick to race to judgment, ruin a person's life. I can't understand why this jury can't see that this kid was just in the wrong place at the wrong time. Guilty of driving from a lot where a shooting happened to occur around the same time."

"He was driving pretty fast, like he was trying to get away," Jess said.

"He heard gunshots. Wouldn't you want to get the hell out of there?"

"Aren't there several witnesses who identified him?"

"Of being in the store, yes, of course. He was in the store shopping. He's on video. But that doesn't make him the shooter outside in the parking lot. Just because he's black and the shooter was black, and he was the only black person inside the store before the shooting doesn't make him the shooter. Who said the shooter outside was ever inside the store? Why would this kid need to rob someone outside the store when he was just inside the store purchasing items? The police didn't even find a gun. No residue on his hands. Nothing."

"Well, they didn't catch up with him until the next day, so he had plenty of time to ditch a gun and wash his hands." Jess took a long sip of wine, wiped her mouth with a napkin.

Across the table, Tom issued her a hard stare. "You sound just like them."

Jess sighed. Why was she antagonizing him? The last thing either of them needed tonight was additional tension. "I'm sorry, Tom. I was just playing devil's advocate, you know that's what I do." She squeezed his shoulder before she cleared the table, rinsed the dishes off in the sink. "He didn't want to take a plea bargain?"

"Second-degree murder, involuntary manslaughter? What's the difference? His life would be ruined, just the same." Tom sighed. "He's just a scared kid."

Jess stared out the kitchen window into a night sky filled with stars. A scared kid, just like Berman's son, sitting in jail and charged with a heinous crime he may not have committed. A scared kid, just like Mikael Kriskan was fifteen years ago.

It was almost unconscionable to think now what she'd done to get Kevin Ryland to change his vote. Maybe she did owe it to Kriskan to get a second chance. *KJ—do the right thing.* She shuddered. What in hell was she going to do?

CHAPTER 10

D imitry Romanov removed a slice of the freshly baked cheese pizza he'd ordered and slid it on the plate for the girl to eat. She happily dug in, wriggling and dancing in the red booth across from him as she licked sauce from her fingers. He'd bought her a coat, boots, and hat, and although it was a great risk to have her out in public, she was hard to recognize under all the gear. Plus, the pizza joint was a hole-in-the-wall and not in the nicest of neighborhoods, so few would expect a missing girl to be in such a place. Its location also served nicely for him to keep an eye on Kevin Ryland's duplex to see what the police were up to in their investigation while he made a few necessary calls.

"What time is it there?" he asked in Russian. On the other end of the line was Nikolai Petrovsky, his longtime friend and oldest client, leader of the Saint Petersburg Twelve. He was the reason Dimitry had come to Denver—to free his biological son, Mikael Kriskan, from prison.

"Two a.m. I cannot sleep," the man said.

"Then you've heard the news."

"The highest court denied him, yes. Now what can be done?"

"A plan is in motion."

"Nikov is on his way to States. He can help?"

Dimitry grunted. He'd never liked Nikolai's oldest and only legitimate, son, Nikov. He was selfish, spoiled, and without discipline, thinking and doing only what benefitted himself. Dimitry did not believe Nikov often had his father's best interest at heart, but his friend was bound to blood ties.

"Perhaps," he said. "But I remind you that you sent him here many years ago to find his brother and he failed. Had he succeeded then, I would not be here to clean up this mess now."

The old man grumbled. "I want my son. I don't have to tell you he would be of great use to us, to the Twelve, to Russia."

"I understand and I'm doing everything possible. I believe I have found a weak link, a way in with one of the jurors. The last one I spoke to told me a most interesting story."

"Good. I hope it is as you say. You sent a clear message?"

"The entire family, yes." He glanced at Bryn Berman, all smiles and pizza sauce. Nikolai would dislike the news that Dimitry had spared her, but he didn't need to know. If he discovered it, Dimitry would tell him he'd taken the girl only to make the case resemble Mikael's, since his sister's body had never been recovered. Nikolai would buy it, and it would be done. But it would not be the truth.

The truth was the girl reminded him of his own daughter, Viktoria.

Bryn Berman was just five, not twenty-two as his daughter had been, but she exuded the same innocence and sense of curiosity that his daughter had displayed during her lifetime. They were restless children, touching everything in sight and asking many questions. A bit rebellious, but little girls were little girls, and he'd always been able to charm them.

He hung up with Nikolai, focused on the girl. "You want ice cream for dessert?"

"Chocolate chip?" Her eyes sparkled like two shiny brown stones.

"Chocolate chip it is." He motioned to a server, ordered a scoop.

Bryn continued to wriggle and dance. "When can I go home?" she asked.

He glanced outside the window, watched the never-ending traffic stop and go at the corner light. The sun was getting low in the sky, casting a strange orange glow over everything.

Dimitry tried to smile. "You will be going to a new home," he said. "There is a special family waiting for you, in another country, far across the ocean."

"But why?"

"I told you. Your father and mother asked that I take care of you, should anything happen to them. And something did happen, honey. I'm very sorry, but you won't see your mom or dad or brother ever again."

Her contemplation was solemn as she studied her hands, counted her fingers. "Never?"

"No, sweetheart."

At one time his Viktoria had been this age, all dresses and curls and cherry-colored hair. Like Bryn, her eyes had always contained a special light, as if she knew a secret no one else did. It's what later drew many a man to her, to discover that mystery.

It only took one to beat it out of her.

Then he hooked her on the drugs that soon took her life. It had been Dimitry who'd found her in the barren hotel room, with veins like that of an old woman and the light taken from her eyes. Her death had killed what remained of his soul, and soon after, that of his wife, Inya. Reality proved too difficult without the light of her daughter.

The server brought the ice cream. The girl shoveled in a spoonful.

As she ate, he eyed the duplex across the street as the last police car departed for the day. He made a new call, this time to an associate. Again, he spoke in Russian. "Are the travel documents ready?"

"Yes. We will pick her up tonight, around nine?"

"Very well. You will not fly until it is safe?"

"We will drive to Kansas City, then fly to New York, then Moscow."

"So, it is done?"

"Yes."

He hung up and glanced at the girl with the curly brown hair. In less than two days, she would be safely tucked in a new country with little memory of what happened to her parents or older brother. And he would never see her again.

He picked up a slice of pizza, ate. Across the street, he saw a man walk down the sidewalk and eye Kevin Ryland's duplex. The police had left but a half hour ago, and now, his journalist friend, juror number four, had already arrived—Mr. Ethan Stantz.

Dimitry chuckled under his breath. "I thought I'd see you soon, my friend. Another curious one. Good boy. Now, go on in and do your job."

CHAPTER 11

E than approached the brown brick duplex two blocks from the state capitol building cautiously, making sure no police officers or detectives lingered nearby. He'd watched the activity at Kevin Ryland's place for most of the day and had identified members of Kevin's family, his parents and his sister. It was the sister now who stayed behind to go through Kevin's personal effects while his parents tended to the funeral and finances. Ethan wanted to speak with the sister and learn what the police had told the family, see if she'd possibly found any mention of the Kriskan case in the items inside.

He paced outside the property once, twice, waiting for Kevin's sister to appear outside the door of his apartment, the second of the duplex. When she did, he approached her and introduced himself. "I was a juror along with Kevin. I'm very sorry for your loss."

She thanked him, told him her name was Lynda, and to his surprise, invited him inside. At first, he wasn't sure he wanted to see where his old friend had spent his final moments, but followed her, knowing it was necessary. He couldn't help take an extra glance over his shoulder before he entered.

He couldn't shake the feeling that someone was watching him.

He shuddered as he crossed the threshold, a brief, biting cold gripping his bones. The hair on his arms and the back of his neck stood up as he caught sight of the loft where Kevin had taken his last breath. The image from the photo on Ethan's computer haunted him—Kevin hanging by a rope with the note taped to his chest.

The place smelled of disinfectant and chemicals that made his eyes water. A large stain of unknown origin remained on the carpet below the loft, and Ethan had to turn away. He didn't care to think about what bodily fluids the stain represented. Lynda took an empty box, one of many piled in the kitchen, and started packing glasses and dishware. She began to talk absently about her brother, all she loved and adored about him, her eyes still red-rimmed and swollen from two days of mourning. Ethan took a seat on a barstool and let her tell Kevin's story.

Kevin had just turned thirty-nine, an activist with a government job, whose main interests were politics and the environment. He didn't own a car but rode his bike to work daily, even in the snow, a premium ride that sat inside the back door and probably cost more than Ethan's first car. Lynda laughed at how her brother never had any food in the refrigerator, preferring to eat out at the local coffee houses and ethnic restaurants nearby. He liked to read, primarily history and nonfiction, which was obvious from the stacks of books lining the built-in shelves next to the fireplace. He wasn't much for sports but loved music, mainly alternative and rock. His perfect evening was spent drinking craft beers and engaging in a lively discussion of current events.

"I'm so sorry," Ethan said again. "You two were clearly close."

"Thanks. He was my rock. Which is why I don't understand what he did. He never showed signs of depression. Never said he was disturbed by the decision he'd made in the Kriskan case. I mean, he never wanted to talk about it, so maybe I should've picked up on the fact that it was bothering him?"

She looked to Ethan for answers. He didn't have any to offer.

"I just don't understand why he wouldn't have talked to me if it was haunting him so," she said.

"Did the police give any indication that his death maybe wasn't a suicide? Maybe somebody just wanted to make it look that way?" Ethan asked.

"They said only the autopsy could determine that and it could take upwards of a week, but all indications pointed to suicide. He did have some abrasions on his hands, as if he..." She choked back words, gathered herself. "As if he tried to climb back up the rope after he jumped from the loft."

Ethan glanced down at his hands, a heaviness like rocks on his chest.

"You think someone might've wanted to kill Kevin?" Lynda asked.

"I don't know. I'm just speculating. That note, *KJ—do the right thing*. He meant the Kriskan jury, didn't he? Did the police have any thoughts on that? Did they, or you, find any material or articles that Kevin had saved regarding the trial?"

She nodded. "Yes, quite a bit." She walked over to a small table near the couch, retrieved a stack of papers and printed articles, handed them to Ethan.

"He seemed obsessed with the appeals filed over the years and it appears he was investigating some things on his own. He has written notes of conversations he had with Kriskan's neighbors, the parents' coworkers. I have to tell you, he thinks you all made the wrong decision."

Ethan bit his lip. "That doesn't surprise me. Even during the deliberations, he was very vocal about the possibility that Kriskan was innocent of the crimes. At one point, we really thought we were going to come back with a hung jury, but a week in, he changed his mind. Something must've convinced him."

She grunted. "I don't know what that was, but," she said, tapping the stack of papers, "you might want to talk to Jessie Gaylord or David Foster. He mentions both in his notes and his comments are pretty nasty toward them. I don't know what happened on that jury, but I never knew my brother to be an angry man."

Ethan was surprised. He wondered why Kevin would be mad at Jess. The prosecuting attorney, David Foster, was a certifiable ass, so he could see that, but Jess?

Ethan regarded the stack of documents. There was too much to go through in a single sitting. "Lynda, I know you just met me, but would you mind if I took Kevin's research and read through it? If he was right about Kriskan, then I feel it's my obligation to do what he said, do the right thing. We owe him, and Mikael Kriskan, that much."

A tear came to the corner of one eye. She dabbed it away. "I don't know. I mean, those are his things. His handwriting."

"I can make copies and bring back the original documents. I promise, all intact."

She gave him a nice smile. "Okay, yes, that will be fine."

Ethan placed what he could in his backpack and carried the rest in his arms. He gave Lynda a hug, then took a taxi back to his loft. There, he grabbed a beer, sat down at his workstation, and began sorting everything out. Articles and op-eds from the internet, newspaper clippings, official transcripts of the appeals. He couldn't believe how much research Kevin Ryland had done on the Mikael Kriskan case.

He picked up a notebook, scoured the contents within. This was where Kevin had detailed his musings on the case. Lists and ramblings, pros and cons. The entries went back several years, to the time of the trial itself. As Ethan read through the pages, it didn't take him long to realize Kevin Ryland had committed a cardinal jury sin—he'd researched the case while serving as a juror. He hadn't stayed away from the media and internet as the judge had strictly ordered.

Ethan wondered if others had known about his research, including David Foster. And if so, why the prosecutor hadn't removed Kevin for juror misconduct in favor of an alternate. Ethan also questioned whether Jess knew, as she and Kevin had become close during the trial.

Why would Kevin Ryland have been so upset with Jess Dawson?

Yet, even though the research Kevin had done wasn't ethical, he'd discovered some interesting tidbits. For instance, a neighbor who'd told him of a bloody knife she found in her backyard days after the murders and gave to the police, though it had never been introduced as evidence in the trial. Kevin had left a question beside this testimony. *What happened to the knife? Was it related to the case?*

Another point of interest was the result of unidentified DNA discovered at the crime scene and a mention of one strand that was only a partial match to Mikael's.

Partial match Y strain, Kevin had noted. This one Kevin had circled and drawn a big black question mark over. *Matched Kriskan's male genome but remaining DNA contaminated or ??*

Ethan was deep into studying the material when his computer pinged—an instant message. He flipped up the laptop, stared at a new message from The Reaper.

"You found your visit interesting?"

A chill braced his spine. So, his instincts had been correct. Someone had been watching when he'd entered Kevin Ryland's apartment. And that someone was The Reaper.

"You believe MK is innocent now?"

Ethan hesitated, typed. "Do you?"

"Set him free."

"How? Appeals denied."

"Talk to Juror Five."

Juror Five? That was Jess. Again, pointing to Jess. "Why?"

"KJ—do the right thing."

A nervous buzzing invaded his brain. "If they don't?"

A long wait. "A juror will die every week until it is done."

Ethan's mouth fell open. He was staring at the words—the cursor blinking on the screen—when the entire conversation disappeared. He scrambled to retrieve the messages, searching his many inboxes, but just like that, they were gone. He had no way to prove the threat he'd just received.

"Damn." The prior buzzing in his head turned into full-on screaming. He brought up his blog, stared at the screen. He was glad he hadn't yet written of the connection between John Berman and Kevin Ryland the prior night as he'd originally planned because he had so much more to offer now.

He didn't know whether he should be excited or frightened, or both, only knew this was going to be big—locally huge but possibly national. A true journalistic investigation. Maybe he could uncover the truth about the Mikael Kriskan case, even set an innocent man free. Who knew? But he would have to play his cards very carefully and not reveal all he knew at once.

He would start by dropping the bombshell that John Berman and Kevin Ryland were jurors on the Kriskan case, then follow with the similarities between the cases. He'd include excerpts of Kevin Ryland's remorse and later, inquire about the unadmitted evidence and questionable DNA. He wasn't sure yet what to do with news about The Reaper, whether to inform the public or not, at least until he could find out more, learn who the man was and had proof of his existence.

He just hoped he didn't die in the process.

CHAPTER 12

Mikael Kriskan woke to visions of Anya twirling in a field of columbines. She was still just twelve in his dream, a girl with haunting dark eyes and fairy-tale hair. She approached him and offered one of the tiny flowers cupped in her hand, petals of periwinkle and ivory on a long green stem. A gift of peace, maybe, or a wish for good fortune. He started to ask her which it was when three loud bangs woke him.

He slid from the bunk, unaware of the time. Time was fleeting in prison, an element of unquestionable mystery. What difference did it make when you spent twenty-three out of the twenty-four hours of your day living in an eight-by-ten cell unaware of the changes of weather or setting of the sun? The only things that gave you any indication that time had passed was a serving of a meal or the changing of the guards. Even the definition of time in prison was different than that of the outside world. Doing time. Hard time. How much time until appeal? Strange that something so intangible would play such a large role in prison, for nothing tangible could make time stop its relentless tick toward inevitable death.

"What is it?" Mikael yelled, still rubbing his eyes. Suddenly, a white object with a screen appeared through the slot, a tablet of some kind. Mikael looked it over, confused. Death-row inmates weren't allowed time on such devices, so this was unusual. He took it, wondering what he was supposed to do with it. He saw the guard give a single nod through the window in the door before he walked away.

He sat back on his bunk, draped the covers over his legs. It was always cold in the cell. He could never get warm. He touched the screen and the device came to life, displaying a page with a single link. When he selected it, a headline to a blog appeared that caught his breath.

Jury foreman's death leaves others asking: Copycat, intimidation, or the real killer?

Mikael's pulse quickened as he began to read. First was a recap of the murder itself, a man named John Berman along with his wife, Alison. They'd been lured out of their bedroom, clubbed with a baseball bat, and stabbed multiple times. But what caught Mikael's attention was the information that the young daughter was missing and the police suspected the son of the crime.

An acidic taste erupted in Mikael's mouth. It sounded just like his case.

Then, a startling revelation—the man, John Berman, had been the jury foreman in Mikael's trial, and inside sources claimed that Berman and his wife were stabbed the same number of times and locations as Mikael's parents that cold winter night fifteen years ago.

Such began the writer's speculation of the events. *Copycat, intimidation, or the real killer?*

He started with the question of a copycat and whether Berman's son had, at some point, learned of and become infatuated with his father's time as a juror on the Mikael Kriskan case. The writer of the blog post speculated it didn't seem likely, as no friends or family could ever remember John Berman speak to his son about the case. His son's friends said Justin had only mentioned his dad's jury service once as a matter of passing interest—that his father had once been a juror on a big case that's now in the news. Justin was a lacrosse star at his high school, a participant in science and math clubs, and his social media accounts showed no indication of anything disturbing. Teachers said he'd never caused an ounce of trouble.

Nobody believed Justin Berman was capable of murdering his parents.

There was also the issue of his missing sister. The writer's sources indicated there was no evidence to suggest Justin Berman killed his sister and buried her nearby nor was there any evidence he drove her elsewhere in the family car. Investigators discovered no traces of blood in the car or trunk, none of Justin Berman's fingerprints on the steering wheel or dashboard.

In the writer's mind, that made the theory of a copycat by another perpetrator more likely. An outside party, one who knew John Berman had served on the jury. But who, and why?

Mikael read through the blogger's copycat theories: A stranger obsessed with the Kriskan case. An acquaintance whose real mission was to abduct the child, Bryn Berman. A friend of Mikael Kriskan's intent on getting Mikael an appeal or his conviction overturned. And finally, a suggestion that the murderer could be the true killer of Mikael Kriskan's parents, sending a message to the world that Kriskan was innocent as he neared execution.

Mikael kicked the blanket aside. Suddenly, he was hot. His heart slammed against his chest. How could this be? Who would do such a thing on his behalf?

It couldn't be true. Could it?

He skimmed over the writer's discussion of the various other copycat options before he focused on the second theory, where the story grew even more intriguing. The blogger surmised that Berman's murder could be a case of brute intimidation, that a friend or associate of Kriskan's was determined to get Kriskan's conviction overturned by threatening the lives of the jurors. He backed this up by revealing the death of a second juror, Kevin Ryland, the very day after Berman's. The writer stated that the police had not connected the deaths because Ryland's death initially appeared as a suicide and they hadn't known of their association—but he knew, because he'd also been one of the jurors.

Then he dropped the biggest bombshell. The writer claimed he'd been contacted by a man calling himself The Reaper, who'd threatened to kill a juror every week until they set Kriskan free.

Mikael nearly fell headfirst into the tablet. He couldn't feel breath reaching his lungs, couldn't grasp the meaning and consequences of what he was reading. More people were dying because of him. Yet, their deaths could raise questions about his guilt, possibly get him an appeal or get his conviction overturned completely.

How was he to reconcile such feelings of regret and hope?

The writer went on to elaborate further on Kevin Ryland's supposed suicide, alleging that—as they awaited autopsy and toxicology results—questions had already begun to circulate among the detectives as to whether the killing might've been staged. The detectives wouldn't speculate on what was causing their distrust, but the writer knew a strange note had been found attached to Ryland's body, a note directed at the Kriskan jurors themselves: *KJ—do the right thing.*

The writer went on to say that he'd discovered ample proof that Ryland had been extensively researching and following Kriskan's case for years and that evidence indicated Ryland now felt that he and his fellow jurors may have been wrong in their decision to find Kriskan guilty and impose the death penalty.

Regardless, the writer felt certain about one thing now—the governor should grant Kriskan a temporary stay of execution until the truth could be determined. A man's life was in the balance, and he didn't find it unreasonable that the police should reexamine the case for missed or new evidence. It was important to get it right, even if it meant overturning their conviction and ordering a new trial.

Mikael reread the words: *KJ—do the right thing.* His eyes watered. Somebody was trying to set him free, but who? Was it Ryland, the lone juror, or somebody else?

He pounded on the door for the guard. "Get me to a phone. I need to call my lawyer."

CHAPTER 13

Jess sat in the café reading Ethan's blog post for the twentieth time. Already more than one thousand comments had posted, and CNN, Fox, and the *Huffington Post* had picked it up. The Denver media was in a frenzy, trying to follow up on the theories and get comments from police, judges, and attorneys. But so far, nobody was talking. During breakfast, Tom had read the blog with great skepticism, but he'd cheered for Kriskan's possible stay of execution.

Jess, on the other hand, was scared out of her wits. Not just for the possible exposure that she sat on the jury, but for Ethan's revelation about The Reaper. Who the hell was he and who would he come for next? She could only hope the blog post would do the trick and give the man, whoever he was, what he wanted. She no longer cared about Kriskan's guilt or innocence—she just wanted a new trial so the responsibility of the case, and the potential for herself and her family to become a target, would fall to someone else. She wanted it all to go away.

Ethan had called multiple times this morning, asking her about The Reaper's comment—*Talk to Juror Five.* What did it mean, he wanted to know? Why did Kevin Ryland despise her so?

She watched her cell phone light up again with his number. Let it ring without an answer. David, too, had phoned three times, demanding that she contact him, but she couldn't bring herself to talk to him. She couldn't allow herself to discuss the time in her life she'd been *that* person. So, she sat in the back of the café, biting a nail, uncertain what to do.

She stared out the windows to the street beyond, met the gaze of the homeless man sitting on the steps of the venue next door. He was almost always present when she came to the café, holding a sign that said, *Veteran, Anything Helps, God Bless.* She wondered what his story was, why he hadn't or couldn't find a job. He seemed too young to be in such circumstances.

Her phone rang again. It was David. She took a deep breath. *I can't avoid him forever.*

She answered. He told her he was at the Oxford Hotel and needed to see her. He didn't sound like the regular David, calm and collected. He was unnerved, unraveling like an old rope. With reluctance, she agreed to meet him. Outside, she handed the homeless guy a five-dollar bill. It wasn't much, but if she could spend that much on a coffee, she could at least give that much to a homeless veteran.

She climbed the stairs to the second floor of the Oxford and was about to knock when she realized she could hear David on the phone inside. He was agitated, his voice raised a couple of octaves above his usual tone.

"The state is not going to slow down pursuing this execution. I don't care what anyone implies or what kind of crazy conspiracy theories they come up with, it's going forward."

She remained in the hall, wondering if this was a good idea, their continued meetings. With so much visibility on the case, with so many people seeking out the other jurors and wanting comments from the attorneys, they only needed to see a former juror with the prosecuting attorney to jump to all kinds of conclusions.

She heard voices behind her, saw a couple begin to ascend the stairs. She quickly knocked on the door. She didn't want to be seen here.

David opened the door and waved her in, his phone still to his ear, then closed the door behind her. No usual charming smile while standing in his boxers. No usual welcome hug and kiss. She could see the stress on his face, the former fine lines around his eyes and mouth now etched a little deeper, as if someone had shaded them in with a pencil.

He ran a hand through his hair and hung up the phone. "This case is going to be the death of me. I don't know who's going to die first, me or Kriskan."

Jess sat on the edge of the bed. "I know. I wish it would end."

"How come it took you so long to call me back?"

She gave him a crazy glance. "Do you really need to ask?"

He paced. "Has anyone contacted you?"

"Like who?"

"Reporters. Media. This crazy blogger, Ethan, your fellow former juror."

She studied him, saw how his fierceness and determination filled every pore. He was like a bull that had been teased and prodded one too many times.

"You know, Ethan may not be that crazy," she said. "Some of what he's saying makes sense. It's unlikely Justin Berman committed those murders. Someone is making a statement."

"Maybe, but that's not my case to try. My case was already tried and convicted."

"The jurors are scared, David. Two of them have already gone into hiding. I'm not sure what to do. I can't put Tom and Ricky at risk of some killer. I know how passionately you feel about Mikael Kriskan, but can't you give them what they want? Get a new trial with a new jury."

"Oh no. Not you too." He sighed. "We can't overturn a conviction and retry Kriskan because someone else believes—falsely, by the way—that a killer is out there to take out jurors and make a statement. Did you ever think that Ethan could be lying about this Reaper character? Or just conjuring up theories to get attention and make money? Or that some whack job is playing him into believing there is a conspiracy, when the reality is that Justin Berman killed his parents and Kevin Ryland committed suicide?"

He put his hands on his hips. "Come on, Jess. Do you know how many other 'confessions' we had during Kriskan's trial? Dozens. You can't listen to every form of crazy that comes along. You have to focus on the evidence, and you and the jury did that—the evidence said Mikael Kriskan killed his parents."

"There was evidence of someone else being there. Doesn't it bother you that his sister was never found? Maybe this someone else took the sister. Maybe this same someone else took Bryn Berman. Maybe we got it wrong."

David shook his head, refusing to acknowledge any weakness in his argument.

"Ethan said Kevin Ryland had done extensive research on the case."

David huffed. "Yes, we know that, don't we?"

"I mean even after the trial. A neighbor reported finding a bloody knife and giving it to the police. Why wasn't that presented at trial?"

"Because we already had the knife that matched the stab wounds, and a second nonmatching knife is pointless, and the defense attorney knew that."

"Kevin also found evidence of DNA that was only a partial match, not fully identifiable as Mikael Kriskan's, something called a Y strain match."

"Because the blood or saliva or whatever got mixed up with somebody else's. There was more than enough blood and DNA that was fully identified as Mikael Kriskan's." He threw up his hands. "I don't need to retry the case with you."

She shut up, turned away. He dismissed her questions just like the rest of the world, a little pat on the head and a *that's nice, Jessie.*

Why couldn't anyone take her seriously?

Apparently sensing that he'd offended her, he sat on the bed beside her and began to stroke the side of her face. "You know what, let's not talk about it," he said.

He leaned over and began to nuzzle the back of her neck, slipped his hand around her waist, drew her closer. He initiated a long, slow kiss. Backed away. Repeated. The next thing she knew, she was on her back with him on top of her.

"No, David, this isn't the time."

She tried to raise up, but he didn't stop. He pressed against her thighs, pushed her sweater up to reveal her abdomen, unbuttoned her jeans. Again, she objected. Again, he continued. It didn't take long to realize her attempts at stopping him were futile.

"Okay, fine," she said.

For the next hour, they got lost, away from the pressures of the case.

When he was finished, David slid into his underwear and got to his feet. He stood in front of the mirror, slid into his shirt, and began fussing with the cuffs. Jess sat on the bed, watching him.

He really did enjoy admiring himself. After he was done messing with the cuffs, he turned sideways to check out his ass, then slid into his pants one leg at a time. When that was complete, he rolled front and center again and ran his hands down his abs toward the waist of his undone pants. He buttoned the shirt from the bottom button up, popped his collar before adding his tie. He turned his face right then left, as if checking out which profile he admired best.

Jess felt sick. For two years, she'd watched this display and admired the physical specimen he was right along with him. Yet, today, she felt disgusted at his obvious self-absorption. She wondered what she was doing here and why she let him continue to use her.

I don't owe him anything, not anymore.

She pushed away the vomit that attempted to surface. She needed to get dressed and get the hell out of there, but she couldn't leave without trying to persuade him one last time to reconsider the case. She had to extract herself from this nightmare, from the guilt of Kevin's death, from the regret of what she and David had done. She had to start living right, be a good mom, a good wife.

Suddenly, in that instant, she wanted it more than anything.

"I know you don't want to discuss it, but I think you should get a new trial for Mikael Kriskan. I know you, like many in the community, admired and respected Kriskan's father, and you've made it your mission to see his son pay for his crimes, but you know the trial wasn't fair. It wouldn't have gone the way you wanted, not without..."

She pulled the bedsheet up to cover herself, feeling exposed.

He wheeled to look at her with eyebrows touching in the middle, the same menacing gaze she remembered from the trial. A bull who could gore his victim without forethought. "Without what?"

"You know what I'm talking about. I did it for you."

"You did it for a fix."

The slap of his words stung like a thousand bees. She felt the pain and humiliation surface and turned away. No matter how far she tried to distance herself from her past, it always found a way to come buzzing back. "I'm not proud of it."

"It is what it is," he said, turning back around and continuing to fuss with his tie. "His father was a mentor to me in college and I took a vow to get justice for his murder. And look, Kevin Ryland is dead now, and no one will ever know what happened except you and me."

"But, David, what if Mikael Kriskan really didn't do it? What if we got it wrong? I can't just sit by and send an innocent man to his death. I have some morals, you know."

He tucked in his shirt, pulled up the zipper on his pants, laughed. "Since when?"

A searing heat raced across her face and chest. She picked up a glass off the nightstand and threw it at him. It smashed against the wall, sending shards flying.

"How dare you. Don't you forget you're in this too. You sent that man to me. I have as much dirt on you as you have on me. Don't you forget that."

He lunged across the bed and shoved her back against the headboard, thrust his face to within an inch from hers. His skin was beet red, veins throbbing.

"Listen. You're not going to pursue this. You're not going to talk to anyone. Because if you do, baby, I will crucify you. I will expose you as the junkie whore you used to be, and I will bury you. You got it?"

He slammed the door as he left. Stunned by his outburst, Jess buried herself beneath the covers and cried. All the sweet talk and romantic gestures David had made to lure her into an affair, all his promises that she would never feel alone, and in one single threat to his world, she'd seen the real side come out in an instant.

CHAPTER 14

Jess left the hotel feeling more unsettled than ever. She scuttled back toward the café, wanting only to hide in the corner with a large cup of coffee. She needed to think, to figure out what she was going to do. David's threats had shredded her and any sense of security she'd hoped he would provide. She wondered if she should ask her stepmother for money and take Ricky and go into hiding until this ordeal was over. Or confess to Tom of her juror sins and get the advice she so desperately needed. Yet, how could she do that without exposing her affair with David?

Stinging tears ran down her face. *I sure know how to get myself in a mess.*

As she approached the café door, she didn't see the hand reach out and grab her until he tugged at her pant leg. "Got any money?"

Jess jumped a foot. The homeless man glanced up at her. She kicked at him and slapped his hand when he wouldn't release her. "Let go," she demanded. "Don't touch me. Why are you out here? You're always out here, begging. I already gave you money earlier."

He released her pant leg and hung his head. A couple of passersby glanced her way, frowned. She hadn't meant to sound so harsh, but he'd startled her, and she was much too easy to startle these days. She apologized to him as she ran through the door.

Once inside, she ordered the coffee then settled into the same back table where she'd been a few days ago with Ethan. So much had happened in that short time, she could barely remember life before Ethan's news, before the pending execution. She wondered if the rest of her life would be defined by this event, BE and AE. Before execution and after execution.

She set her phone on the table, ignored the two new calls she'd missed from Ethan, started to read the new posts to his blog. The theories, pleas for appeal, and calls for a stay of execution were escalating by the hour. A few minutes later she felt a presence, a shadow that swooped over the table like a large hawk. This was followed by a rich, musky scent emanating from the chair across from her.

Jess glanced up, went icy cold. The man who sat in front of her had the eyes of an eagle, hazel with a yellowish tinge, and a sharp, unwavering focus. His face was an interesting blend of flesh and bone, chiseled in a way that made you sit motionless until he commanded you what to do. He wore a wool sweater, black jeans, and a tan jacket that had seen better days. She didn't understand why he was seated at her table. She didn't like him being there.

"I'm sorry, you must have the wrong table," she said.

"I like it okay here."

His accent chilled her bones. She knew at once where he was from, having heard that same deep, foreboding dialect many times during the trial, as many a Russian testified both for and against Mikael Kriskan. She made a sudden move to slide out of the booth.

He gripped her wrist. "No, no. Let's talk."

It wasn't a request.

Like the rest of him, his hands were weathered, the look of years spent outside in harsh conditions. Below the table, he placed one of his much longer, stronger legs on the outside of each of hers, creating an extra barrier. He squeezed them toward each other, her legs in between, like a lemon in a juicer. He offered a thin smile at her obvious pain.

She winced, let out a small cry. She searched the crowd behind her unwanted guest, seeing if anyone had noticed her trouble. They hadn't. "Who are you? What do you want?"

"Just to talk."

"I'll scream. I'll call the police."

He grabbed both her hands, pressed. "That would be most unwise."

The pain left her breathless. Her eyes started to leak fresh tears.

He pried the phone from her fingers, began to search through her contacts. Jess wondered what he was doing when she got an answer. He turned the phone toward her to show her what he'd pulled up, a photo of Ricky. "A most handsome boy."

She grappled with his hands, wrestled his legs beneath the table, fear ripping through her heart. "You leave him alone." Her voice was unrecognizable, deep, throaty.

He swiped through more pictures—Ricky riding a horse, Ricky making a peace sign, Ricky tucked in his bed. "I have associates, it would be a shame what they would do to a boy like that."

His words were like a kick to the ribs, deflating her of breath. "You incorrigible bastard."

She had no doubt what kind of man she was dealing with now—Russian mafia or gangsters. He had seen things, done things, and she didn't want to know what they were. In that instant, she knew she was face-to-face with The Reaper.

Where is Ethan when I need him? Where is a police officer?

"We have a most odd dilemma, Jess Dawson, you and me. But I think we can help each other out. Your son, he is most important to you, yes? Well, my client's son is most important to him too. He wants him back. But fourteen years ago, you sat in a courtroom and made a most unfortunate decision. You condemned his son—his innocent son—to death."

"You don't need to tell me. I was there."

"Then how, may I ask, did you come to the conclusion you did?"

"We deliberated on the evidence. We decided he was guilty, that's it."

His eyes narrowed. "Is that so? Your friend, Mr. Ryland, recalls it differently."

She couldn't speak. Her throat felt dry and cotton-like, like someone had stuffed it with a rag. She didn't want to think about what had really occurred in the jury room or, most notably, outside of it. "No, he was guilty."

He jerked her across the table, drilled those eagle eyes into her pupils. "Guilty? You want to talk about guilty? You sit here, declare your righteousness, when just two hours ago you had the prosecutor's cock in your mouth. It's still on you, that smell. Like a two-dollar whore."

Jess felt the heat and color rush to her face, the shock of his words, so burning to her conscience. He might as well have backhanded her across the face or ripped the clothes from her body in public. Tears continued to blur her vision as she struggled for breath.

"Imagine my little stroke of luck, finding out one of my jurors is fucking the DA. At a hotel screwing another man, while your husband toils and takes care of your retarded son."

"He's not retarded." Her cheeks, forehead, burned. "I'm not a bad person."

"Who are you trying to convince? Me or yourself? Little Jess. Jess with the trust fund." He again squeezed her legs beneath the table. She struggled to pull away, her panic spreading like a raging wildfire. "You and I, we both know what happened on that jury. Don't play retarded with me, like your son."

She pulled and writhed until he clamped down and nearly crushed her hands. She had chosen the table farthest from the door for privacy. Now that seemed like a bad idea. There wasn't anyone in the café who could see what was happening.

"Easy. Take it easy. Don't be stupid, like your foreman and your friend. They fought me too and look what happened to them."

She stilled, all her energy disappearing with his words. Her mouth fell agape, trying to dissect his meaning, staring into his soulless eyes, into the eyes of a killer.

This man is John Berman's and Kevin Ryland's murderer.

He let out a deep-throated chuckle. "Yes. Good, I see that you understand. So, you know that I am serious. I have proposition for you. You and your son will not be hurt as long as you do as I say. You go tell the judge what really happened in that jury room, the hotel where you stayed. You get the conviction overturned. Then we both get what we want."

He turned her hands palms up, brushed his thumbs across them. "Look at you. Hands so soft. I can help you, Jess Dawson. Help you with money, with Ricky. Make life easy. That's what you really want, isn't it? That's what is best for girls like you."

He reached across the table and brushed a wayward strand of hair away from her face. She was certain she was about to pass out. "Girls like you, they just need to be taken care of. You do what is necessary, all will be paid for, the school, the medical bills."

"I don't think you understand. It's not that easy," she said.

She glanced up, saw those yellowish hawk-like eyes focus. "Not so complicated. Kill Mikael, kill your son. Save Mikael, save your son. Easy choice."

CHAPTER 15

Jess phoned Ethan and indicated she needed to see him asap. She needed a friend, an ally in this melee, and he was her only hope. When he learned of the truth, it was possible he would walk away from her, but she had to try. Ethan was smart and capable. Together, maybe they could find a way out of this mess.

The doorman at Ethan's building did a double take as she walked through the lobby. She didn't need to be told she looked like a train wreck, all dried tears and smeared makeup. The mirror behind the desk saved him the task. She kept her head down as she passed a couple getting coffee and two others conversing near a large art sculpture. Thankfully, she was alone in the elevator.

Before she knocked on Ethan's door, she attempted to pull herself together, but his candid look when he answered told her she hadn't done a very good job. "Jess, you're shaking. What's wrong?" He invited her in, took her coat, gave her a quick hug.

She walked to the far wall, looked out the floor-to-ceiling windows to the sparkling lights below. Ethan's loft was on the seventh floor, a corner unit overlooking lower downtown, or LoDo, as they called it. For a bachelor, he'd done well decorating the place, contemporary furniture and modern art, but his work consumed the place, magazines and newspapers everywhere.

She paced between the couch and the windows. "We've got a real problem. That man, the one who sent you those e-mails, I know who he is. He came to me, cornered me in the café."

"What? When?"

"Just now. Ethan, he's no joke. He's Russian. Like mafia or something."

"What did he say?"

"He threatened me. He threatened my son. He said if I didn't get Mikael Kriskan's conviction overturned, he would kill us both."

"Whoa. He actually said that?"

"Yes."

Ethan sat on the edge of a barstool for support, brushed his hands through his hair. "That's it, we have to go to the police. Warn the others."

"No. We can't. Before he left me, he adamantly warned me—no police. If I contact them, Ricky dies. If I let Kriskan die, Ricky dies. He said he wouldn't stop until all the jurors are dead."

"But he can't expect us to change anything. The verdict is in, the appeals are over, it's done." His voice was an octave higher, reflective of his concern. Jess wondered what he'd sound like when she told him the rest of the story.

"Oh, Ethan." She collapsed on the couch, wrapped her head in her hands. "I have something to tell you. What you were asking me about. It's not good."

He took a deep breath. "Okay. This is about Kevin Ryland, right?"

"Yes, and more. Much more." She pulled at her long sleeves until they covered half her hands. Chewed what nails remained. She couldn't force herself to look at him.

"Ethan, I have done some really stupid things in my life. I haven't always made good choices, and fourteen years ago, I was just...a different person, you know?"

He raised from the barstool, joined her on the couch. "We've all done dumb things, Jess. Sometimes, I look back and wonder how I ever made it to adulthood."

She nodded, forced a smile. Of course, he would be nice. Ethan was nice. Just like Tom. But everyone had their limits. "One of the very worst choices I made was doing drugs. My ex, Ricky's father, he used, and he got me into using. For nearly a decade, I was a heroin addict, Ethan."

He scooted back a nudge, immediately looked at her arms even though they were covered. That's what everyone did when she told someone, some strange auto reflex.

"Wow. I never would've guessed. But you got clean. You beat it, right?"

"Yes, eventually, but when I served on the jury, I was using, almost daily."

"I guess that's not something you can offer up during jury questioning."

She chuckled. "Hardly. My addiction wasn't a problem during the trial itself since I could use when I got home at night, but when we were sequestered, I only brought a little with me. I was so afraid I'd get caught and I didn't think we would be there more than a couple of days. Day one, day two, it was tolerable, but when we got to day five, Ethan, I was so sick."

He seemed to recall back to the time of the trial, nodded. "Right, I remember but...oh my God. You didn't have the flu. You were in withdrawal?"

"I was a train wreck."

He pulled at his beard. "Okay, but what does your heroin habit and your withdrawal have to do with Kevin? And the trial?"

She took a deep breath. This would be the difficult part. Confessing one's sins and exposing your soul was a hard thing to do. She sat up, turned toward Ethan so their knees purposefully touched. If she was going to reveal all, she might as well do it as directly and honestly as possible.

"This is where it gets bad. Somehow, David Foster, the prosecutor, he learned about my condition, and he was worried, really worried that my...illness was going to result in a hung jury or a mistrial. You may not know this, but I later learned that Mikael Kriskan's father was one of David's favorite professors at DU. He was the one who encouraged David to go into law in the first place. So, to say David Foster was passionate about winning that case and getting justice for his friend was an understatement.

"Anyhow, David sent someone to approach me one night, outside in the garden when I went to get some air and the court attendant was away. That someone offered me a deal—in exchange for a guilty verdict and a vote for the death penalty, he would get me a fix."

Ethan paled. His eyelids fluttered like the wings on a bird. "The prosecutor sent someone? He's the one that got you a fix so you could finish deliberations? Holy shit."

"Hold on. It gets worse. I told him my vote wouldn't matter because you and Kevin Ryland were also holding out for not guilty. He told me to convince you otherwise."

He crinkled his brow. "That's why you came to me that night and talked me into changing my vote? Not that it took much convincing. I was much more on the fence than Kevin. But him, how in the hell did you convince him?"

She turned back toward the window, wishing she could skip this part. She could hear the Reaper's burning remarks repeat in her head. *It's still on you, that smell. Like a two-dollar whore.*

"It's true. Kevin was much more difficult. The courier told me to do whatever it took, you know, so I did." She glanced at her lap. Even after all these years, the shame remained, hanging on her body as much as the clothes she wore. "I slept with him and I planted heroin in his room."

And there it was, laid to bare, like her soul, just like that.

Ethan put both hands on his knees, lowered his head, shook it very slowly. She could only imagine the emotions he was wrestling with—betrayal, anger, despair.

She put a hand on his shoulder. "Before you judge me, understand that I was out of my mind, Ethan. Withdrawal is a dark and terrible journey, and an addict will do anything—absolutely anything—for a fix. David Foster knew that and used me and my addiction for his advantage. Not that I'm trying to shun responsibility. Believe me, I know what I did was wrong—morally, ethically, and legally. But I was young and stupid, and I didn't think about the consequences of my actions."

Ethan took off his glasses and rubbed his eyes, as if it might help erase the new image of Jess he now saw, preferring the one he believed her to be before. "Jesus, Jess. Jesus." He got up on wobbly legs, walked the length of the living room, arms crossed, unable to meet her gaze.

Probably deciding whether to throw me out or not.

"I apologized profusely to Kevin afterward," Jess said. After the courier confronted Kevin with the research he'd done and the heroin in his room, he threatened Kevin with charges of juror misconduct and drug possession and distribution. With those charges, Kevin would have lost his government job along with any chance he ever had of running for political office, which was his dream. So, he yielded. I tried to convince him that I'd only slept with him because I wanted to and that leaving the heroin was an accident, but he knew better. He gave David Foster what he wanted. But he never forgave me."

Ethan looked like he was about to be sick. His skin was the color of applesauce, his posture humped like an old woman. He hung on to the back of a chair. "This is bad. Oh, Jess, this is bad. You have to go to the judge who presided over the original case or file an affidavit or something with the court and tell the truth. The Reaper doesn't even matter. Mikael Kriskan didn't get a fair trial. David Foster tampered with the jury. I mean these—his actions—they could open up appeals for other cases he's tried and won. It won't be just Kriskan who goes free. Every other defense attorney who's lost a case to him will file for an investigation into jury tampering and misconduct during their own trials."

Jess gripped the arm of the couch, trying to steady herself, but she couldn't stop trembling. It was as if her entire body had undergone electric shock therapy, and the waves continued to course through her body. *This has to be the absolute worst day of my life.*

"It would ruin his career for sure," she said. She thought about David's words to her earlier in the day, how he would bury her if she said anything to anyone. After his actions today, she didn't give a damn about his career, but she did care very much about her safety and her son's, and she feared the lengths David might go to intervene in her coming forward as much as the Reaper's threats if she didn't. Not to mention what it would do to her already teetering marriage to Tom. So, how could she talk? David would make her out to be a liar, he would go unscathed, and she would lose her marriage and possibly custody of Ricky if Tyler's mother got involved.

"I know you don't think very highly of me right now, Ethan, and I don't blame you, believe me. I'm not a saint. But I don't know if I can go up against David Foster. He holds a great deal of power in the city and he will deny everything, and with his reputation against mine, I don't know if a judge will believe me about the courier."

"Of course, they will. Why wouldn't they?"

She sighed. She really hated herself right now. "Because for the past two years, I've been having an affair with David Foster."

Ethan groaned. He leaned over the kitchen island, covering his ears and closing his eyes. "You know, maybe you should be telling this to a priest or something."

"I don't think the church would have me," Jess said. She recalled how she'd felt the first time entering rehab, how her father had wiped away tears unaccustomed to his face and her stepmother had clicked her tongue and rocked back and forth, a silent accusation of Jess's irresponsibility and the shame she'd brought upon her father. She never thought she could feel any lower than at that moment. Now she knew better.

"Look," she said, "I don't know if I can explain how or why I ended up having an affair with him, because I know on the surface, David Foster seems like a self-indulgent prick."

"David Foster is a self-indulgent prick. He used you, Jess, and he still is, just for other reasons. Why would you let him do that to you? Why would you even be attracted to him?"

She glanced away. These were questions she'd asked herself many times. How and why she'd ever become involved with David Foster. Did she believe that in some strange way, she owed him for helping her out? Or was she just gullible to a man's attention? Or was it as her rehab counselor had repeatedly told her—that she kept seeking out ways to dull the pain of losing her mother while simultaneously punishing herself believing she was responsible for her mother's death? She honestly didn't know.

"Okay, yes, he did use me, I admit that. Yet, in a weird way, he saved me too. Because after the trial, I realized that I had to get clean. I had to get away from my ex and get my life on track. Granted it took me another eight years. I went to rehab three times until I succeeded. I had Ricky and I married Tom, and life was good. But then I gradually learned of Ricky's difficulties, and my father died, and the money ran out, and my marriage began to struggle, and I looked for another out, another save."

"David Foster to the rescue." Ethan swung his head. "Ah, Jess."

Jess wrapped her arms around herself, squeezed. She wanted to curl inside herself from the inside out, hide for eternity. "I know, I should be in a psych ward."

He stood up straight again, took a deep breath. "No, you're not crazy. You just need to start believing in yourself. You're a strong woman and you need to stop letting others, particularly men, run your life. You need to stand up, face your struggles, own it."

She held his gaze. She thought he actually meant it.

"I do," he said, reading her thoughts. "You don't need an out. Don't let people tell you you're weak and fragile, because you're not. You overcame heroin. You were a single mother with an autistic son. You persevered and finished school. You're stronger than you think. We all are."

Jess felt her eyes grow moist. She thought he might just be the most forgiving person she'd ever met. In her experience, it was a rarity to hear someone try to lift you up instead of tear you down.

Ethan grabbed two beers from the fridge, handed one to her. He paced for two minutes before sliding onto a barstool. "Okay, so at least we know where things stand.

It is what it is. The question is, what do we do now? Tell me, was there anything else this man said I need to know about?"

She took a long pull on the beer, happy to be discussing anything but herself. "Yes. That his client was Mikael Kriskan's father and he wanted his son back. I'm assuming he meant his real father in Russia, but he never mentioned his name."

"Right, Kriskan was born in Russia. It was his adoptive parents here who were murdered. But who is his real father and how did the man find Mikael?"

Jess could see Ethan's wheels turning.

"And why would he go to these extreme lengths to get his son back now after he gave him up for adoption as a child? To be willing to kill others to get him back? There has to be something bigger at play here," Ethan added.

"It's above my pay grade, which isn't much, since my pay is zero," Jess said.

"Did this Reaper give you a name of any kind, drop a hint about where in Russia they were from?"

She shook her head. "Not that I can remember. I was kind of shitting my pants."

"Okay, I can start digging into Kriskan's background, see what I can find on his real father. But, Jess, what are you going to do? Do you want to tell your story, or not?"

She finished off her beer, stood, and brushed herself off. Ethan was right. It was time she stood up. Stop feeling sorry for herself. Take charge, make good decisions.

"Maybe. First, I'm going to go talk to Mikael Kriskan's attorney. Because, before I can make a decision, I need to know one thing. I need to know if Mikael Kriskan really killed his parents or not."

CHAPTER 16

J ess climbed the stairs to the tan stone structure that used to be a historic church and now doubled as office space for various attorneys and nonprofit organizations. Oddly, she'd been in the building before. One of the nonprofits housed in the building was a support group for former addicts and meetings were commonly held in the basement. She'd attended one or two times but never found the group format that helpful. She preferred digging a hole and burying her past addiction than continually rehash her time as a heroin user.

Nick Whelan's office was on the second floor. Jess gave a phony name to the receptionist and took a seat on a worn wine-colored leather couch with gold studs. Whelan came out moments later, his hand extended. Not to her surprise, he squinted when he saw her, sensing familiarity. He checked the name with the receptionist, frowned, but let it go and led her into his office. The area was oddly angled, as if cut from whatever remaining space they had in the blueprint, with two windows staring out onto a patch of grassy lawn and a flagpole.

"Mrs. Smith, is it? You're not Tom Dawson's wife? I feel as if we've met before."

"Yes, I am." She shook his hand. "Jess Dawson. I'm sorry about the fake name. I didn't want any record of me actually being here."

Nick Whelan studied her. A thick stubble covered his chin and his light-brown hair looked like it hadn't been combed in days. That, or he'd been pulling it out in patches trying to figure out how to get his client clemency. "Why is that?"

"Because I'm not just Jess Dawson. I was also juror number five on the Mikael Kriskan jury."

His eyes grew wide. "Oh."

He thumbed through stacks of paperwork on his desk until he found what he wanted. Did a double take between the paper and Jess. "Jess Gaylord. Now Jess Dawson. How about that?"

She frowned. "I thought the jury members' names were sealed."

"Not for the defense attorneys. They get your name and your address."

She raised an eyebrow. "Great."

"I guess you're not feeling too comfortable given what happened to John Berman and Kevin Ryland."

"That would be an understatement."

He moved a couple of the stacks, folded his hands on the newly created space on top of his desk. "So, what can I help you with, Jess Dawson? It's not every day I get a visit from a juror who sentenced my client to death."

She tightened her lips. He had no idea how right he was to be angry. "As I understand it, you're Mikael Kriskan's appeals attorney, and now, the post-conviction appeals have run out. I admit, I haven't kept up with all the details—let's just say I wanted to put as much distance between myself and that trial as possible—but Kevin Ryland apparently did stay on top of appeals, and Ethan Stantz has filled me in on the research Kevin conducted. You've done just about everything to get a new trial— present new evidence, question the ability of the original defense, that sort of thing."

"Yes, among other tactics."

"What about juror misconduct? Would that get Kriskan's conviction overturned and provide the DA with an opportunity to retry the case? Theoretically, what would happen to a juror who, say, didn't exactly follow the judge's orders?"

His eyes narrowed. "Do you know of such an instance?"

"Just, theoretically."

He raised his chin. She could sense his distrust. "Okay. Theoretically, it would depend on the severity of the misconduct. Something like a discussion among a couple of jurors without everyone present or researching the case on the internet could result in removal from the case, but that's long past possible. Something more serious, like lying on the jury questionnaire, or knowing a witness or officer involved in the case might force a retrial, but those type of things normally come to light far earlier than now."

She nodded. Scolding taken. "But still no charges against the juror? Let's say the misconduct was even worse than lying on the questionnaire. In fact, let's just say it was severe misconduct. Egregious, even." She cleared her throat. "What would happen to such a person?"

He leaned forward, wrung his hands. "Maybe you could give me an example?"

"No, I can't. Not yet."

"Okay. Would it have changed the outcome of the trial?"

Jess took a deep breath, tried to keep control of her nerves. Beneath the table, she could feel her legs trembling like gelatin. "Yes."

The blood drained from Nick Whelan's face. He cleared his throat. "Well, then, I'd say that juror has an obligation to come forward in the name of justice, and I'm sure a certain defense attorney would do what he could to eliminate or reduce any potential charges." He spoke the last few words extra slowly, to make sure she understood.

He cocked his head. "Can I ask? What does Tom think of your...situation? Has he offered any advice?"

Jess glanced at her lap. "Mr. Whelan, my husband doesn't know that I served on the Kriskan jury, and I need to keep it that way. He's not a fan of capital punishment, as you know."

Nick scratched his head, leaving a new tuft of brown hair to stick out behind his right ear. He pursed his lips, put his hands together in the prayer position. He didn't seem to know how to respond.

Jess played with her purse strap, thinking about what she was about to ask of him, how he would react. "I'm sorry to put you in this position, Mr. Whelan, but before I decide what to do, I need to know the truth about Mikael Kriskan, whether he murdered his parents and younger sister. Do you truly believe he is innocent? Do you think we, the jury, made a mistake? I mean, the evidence, it seemed compelling at the time. The blood all over his hands and clothes. His bloody shoeprints all over the house. The lack of drugs in his system."

He stood, poured himself a cup of coffee that smelled hours old, offered her a cup. She declined. "I understand, Jess, I do. The prosecution made its case, and the defense, at the time, they didn't. I know it must've been very difficult for you to make such a decision, especially against such a young man. I want you to know that, okay? I do understand."

He sat back down. "But I have spent the last decade poring over the evidence in this case—to the point that I can see the photographs in my sleep. I see every drop of blood on his hands, his clothes, his face. The stab wounds, I know the angles and the depth. I've read and reread the autopsy and toxicology reports, or lack thereof, studied all the charts and graphs, and yes, I've come to believe in his innocence."

He abruptly stood. "Let me show you something. Do you mind?"

He rounded the desk and swiveled his laptop so she could see the screen, brought up photos from the original crime scene. The first four were of Mikael Kriskan's hands and forearms, front and back, two close-up, two more distant. Jess felt herself recoil seeing the images again, part of the evidence she'd worked so hard to forget, the constant parade of charts, diagrams, and details of blood and dead bodies that long-ago summer in court.

"You see this area?" he asked as he pointed. "How the forearms are splattered in blood as well as the fingers and knuckles, but above and between the tops of the fingers are not? Also, here, how a strange blotting of the blood exists on each wrist? I've had multiple blood-spatter experts take a look at these photos and run various analyses, and while some still stated they believed the patterns were consistent with him holding the knife, a few others disagreed, and one in particular, provided me with an explanation that I believe is accurate."

He pushed a button on the laptop and a simulation began, an animated computer model that started with Kriskan's mother and father sitting by the wall with Mikael kneeling in front of them. A fourth figure entered the simulation and knelt behind Mikael, then wrapped his arms around Mikael's from the back and secured his wrists and hands within his own. Jess watched as Mikael's animated head lolled from side to side, as if he weren't awake.

"Wait. Stop," Jess said. "Why is his head moving like that? Are you saying Mikael isn't conscious here? That he has no idea what's happening?"

Nick hit pause. "Correct," he said. "I believe he was drugged, as he stated, and as I attempted to argue unsuccessfully on appeal. I know toxicology didn't come back with any trace of unusual substances, but that's not uncommon with GHB substances. Toxicology doesn't pick up GHB drugs unless the blood is collected early after the crime. The body chemically breaks down GHB drugs, like Rohypnol or ketamine, within hours.

"Let's say the crime occurred around midnight as detectives estimated. Mikael doesn't wake until the next morning, spends an hour fumbling around wondering what the hell happened, finally calls the police. They immediately take him into custody and spend ten hours interrogating him before they take his blood, hair, and saliva samples. What is that, eighteen, twenty, hours? Way too much time. I believe that's why the toxicology report didn't test positive for GHB."

"Rohypnol, that's like a date-rape drug," Jess said.

He nodded. Selected play on the laptop again. Now the figure behind Mikael dragged him forward and positioned him so he was hovering over his mother. He placed the knife between Mikael's hands, but it was the figure's hands that were in control as he began stabbing the victim. Imaginary blood spatter landed on Mikael's shirt, face, and arms, matching the patterns in the photos.

Goose bumps crawled across Jess's flesh. She pulled the sweater she wore tighter around her. Just seeing the act in simulation made her blood freeze.

Up came a detailed close-up of the images side by side, real photos versus computer generated, emphasizing the missing spatter on the upper fingers where the other figure had interlaced his own fingers, and the two matted spots near each wrist.

Jess sat back, stunned. "This was never presented at trial."

"No. This expert only put it together a few years ago. I presented it for appeal, along with the GHB argument. No go."

"But why? Mr. Whelan, if that had been presented at the original trial, that would've constituted reasonable doubt in my opinion."

"I believe you. Unfortunately, to the judges, it's one theory in a sea of hundreds."

"One theory that might be correct," Jess said. "You think with this case being a death-penalty case, they'd want to make damn sure they got it right. Just like I want to."

Jess sat motionless, feeling the rise of frustration and desperation while staring at the computer screen before her. She turned to Nick Whelan. "Can I speak to Mikael Kriskan? Can I visit him?"

Nick cocked his head. "It would be highly unusual for a juror to go see the man in jail the same said juror sentenced to death. That might even qualify as misconduct."

Well, then, they can just add that to my other considerable charges.

"But the decision has already been rendered. I mean, nothing he says or does now can impact my, or other jurors' decisions, so what could be the harm?"

"True, I guess. But it could raise an eyebrow, suggest potential earlier juror misconduct. Maybe the defendant and the juror knew each other at the time of trial, that sort of thing. Maybe the juror always felt the defendant was not guilty but was intimidated into a guilty verdict and now feels remorse."

He was fishing. "Nice try," she said, offering a small smile.

He crossed his arms, sighed. "Do you know something about the trial I don't, Jess?"

"Yes. No. Maybe." She fidgeted. "I can't say yet. First, I need to know if Mikael Kriskan is truly innocent. I want to talk to Mikael Kriskan."

CHAPTER 17

Dimitry Romanov leaned against the brick wall of a building across Seventeenth Street, waiting for the dashing, brash district attorney to leave his office for the evening. David Foster was often the last to leave, to be the lone man walking to his car in the parking lot late at night. Three times a week he would cross over to the athletic club first, work out and shower, then head home, where his wife would meet him at the door. His wife was a fine-looking woman, a woman of sharp angles and tailored clothes. Most different from Jess, in her oversized sweaters and hair in a ponytail. Perhaps that was the basis for his attraction. One elegant for show, one wild and free. One Arabian, one mustang.

As soon as Dimitry saw him exit the revolving doors, he headed across the street. The sun was sinking low behind the mountains, casting orange and pinkish hues across the western skies. It was warm for a winter day, mid-fifties, and while snow covered the peaks, a thick brown haze lined the foothills. Surrounding him, skyscrapers towered, their office lights glowing. A horn or two honked at unknown annoyances, all desperate to race from the concrete jungle so they could get to the highway and spend another hour in bumper-to-bumper traffic trying to get home.

He did not understand Americans.

He approached Foster as he unlocked his car, the lights flashing twice. An Audi, black, sleek, the kind of car that leaves an impression. "Mr. Foster, could I have a word?"

The man turned, sized him up. His suit, too, was styled to make a statement, a fine, silky gray fabric that left no question about its price tag. "Do I know you?"

Dimitry took a step closer. "No. But we have mutual acquaintances."

He could tell his accent gave the man pause. "You're Russian."

"You don't like my country?"

Foster opened the car door, put his briefcase inside. His eyes, wary, aggressive, never left Dimitry. "I don't have an opinion either way, but I don't think we have anything to say to one another." He slid inside, started to close the door.

Dimitry stayed just behind the rear bumper. He didn't think David Foster would have the guts to back over him. "Tell me, Mr. Foster, does your wife know? About your mistress?"

He watched as Foster sat unmoving behind the wheel, bowed his head. Dimitry could imagine the many thoughts rushing through the man's head right now, how he'd like to jump from the car and punch Dimitry in the face. Foster swung his feet back out, stood, straightened his suit coat. Took three steps toward Dimitry. He wasn't scared. He was pissed off. "What do you want from me?"

Dimitry shrugged. "Just to have a word."

A large sigh. "Then speak."

"You tried a case a few years ago. A case of great interest to my client. You charged his son with an act he didn't do. You pressed for his death, yet he's innocent."

Dimitry didn't know whether Mikael Kriskan was, in fact, innocent, but he thought it likely. He'd used the fourth man scenario presented on appeal to kill Berman and his wife, because it appeared to be accurate and because he knew it would create many questions about Kriskan's guilt. But who knew? Perhaps the kid did actually kill his adoptive parents. He was his father's son, after all, a man Dimitry had seen gut another man simply because the man had beaten him at a hand of poker, so perhaps the apple didn't fall from the tree.

"Mikael Kriskan was charged with killing his adoptive parents. He had a fair trial, an adequate defense, and a jury of his peers found him guilty and sentenced him to die. Had there been evidence to the contrary, I'm sure the defense would've presented it and the jurors decided differently."

Dimitry chuckled. So smug, this man. He sharpened his gaze. "You think trial was fair? I think Mr. Ryland felt differently. So much despair, he was found hanging from rope. So sad for a man to harbor such guilt from a trial that was so fair. So free of any, say... misconduct on jurors' part, or on the part of the prosecuting attorney."

He took pleasure as Foster's face began to twitch.

Dimitry took a step closer, enjoying the view. "And to think now, here is that very prosecutor sleeping with one of the jurors on the biggest case of his career. It would be a shame for media to learn of such a thing. A most unfortunate event."

"I wasn't sleeping with her during the case. It was many years after."

Dimitry shrugged. "Maybe, but media may not believe so much. Public is very quick to blame. Might be grounds to overturn the conviction. Nothing you would wish, no? Or perhaps, Mr. Foster, you can think of another way to get our client set free."

"Look, whoever you are, whoever you represent, Mikael Kriskan is not going to be set free. He's already exhausted all of his post-conviction options. The best he can hope for now is clemency and a life behind bars."

Dimitry looked out at the skyline, now harboring shades of deep purple. "With new information, perhaps new evidence, that could change. Perhaps the exposure of what Mr. Ryland knew that made him so guilty. Something to get conviction overturned. Otherwise..." He pulled a few photos from his inside pocket, showed Foster the pictures of he and his Jess. "Hmm?"

Foster turned a deep shade of red. He put his hands on his hips. "Is this a shakedown? Is that what this is? You're treading on dangerous ground here. You're trying to influence a district attorney. I could charge you with attempted bribery, corruption."

Dimitry laughed, causing Foster's skin to grow even more fiery before Dimitry lunged. Foster raced for the door of the Audi but he didn't make it. Dimitry had him pinned in an instant.

He grasped Foster's tie and collar and twisted until he could see the man's neck muscles strain. "I don't care much about your laws, Mr. Foster. American laws don't apply to me. I follow Russian law. Russian code. You got that? Do you?"

A subtle nod.

"I don't care what you have to do. You figure out a way to set Mikael Kriskan free or I will do it for you."

He released his collar and shoved him against the car. Issued a firm punch to his gut for good measure. David Foster buckled. He did not look so impressive now.

As Dimitry walked away, he issued one last statement. "Your wife is very lovely. I hope she stays safe. And you, as well, Mr. Foster."

He disappeared into the shadows, leaving David Foster crumpled in a heap on the pavement.

CHAPTER 18

E than stared at the screen, watching the conversations unfold, the theories getting wilder by the day. He was horrified, and yet, fascinated, by the way the human mind sought to make sense of a world they didn't understand. Some were crazy, far-out theories, but others displayed hints of truth. He read a couple. *Did Mikael Kriskan take the fall for his evil little sister? Did she really kill their parents?* The next one. Was *Mikael Kriskan in a satanic cult? Did he give his sister to the cult to sacrifice?* And the next. *The Russians are promising payback to the jurors that sentenced to death one of their own. They will all die.*

Ethan sat back, thinking the last one might contain the most elements of truth. Since Jess's revelation about the man who'd cornered her in the café, Ethan had been afraid to leave the house or even speak to strangers in the lobby of his own residence. Instead, he'd hunkered down and thought how best to approach his next blog post, whether to discuss The Reaper, the man's threat to Jess and his purported involvement in Berman's and Ryland's deaths, or just leave it alone.

The last thing he wanted to do was make the situation even more dangerous, especially until he knew exactly who and what they were dealing with.

He searched through some of the other threads, posted thanks and replies at random. Sent warnings to a couple of posters about their harassment of others, their use of offensive, bullying language. He noticed one of the commenters, MexHatMan, and knew instantly that was Emmanuel Perez, one of the other original twelve jurors.

Ethan had warned him along with the others, and Manny had been none too happy to hear about the man who called himself the Reaper. Manny believed their fellow jurors had been murdered by that man, and he had no intent of being his next victim. He told Ethan he was going into hiding until this whole mess was over.

Others, too, had spoken of their grave concern, including the retiree, Hazel, who planned to contact the district attorney's office and express her concern. She felt that each of the remaining jurors should be assigned protection, although Ethan knew that would be a long shot in a police department stretched thin already. A couple of others, like libertarian Gerald Fowler, expressed no fear at all, indicating he'd be happy for the Reaper to try and come get him. He kept a shotgun in nearly every room of his house and would welcome the opportunity to use Colorado's "Make My Day Law" to, well, make his day.

Ethan wondered how long the Reaper would give Jess to make a decision before he would act on his threat to kill another juror. He also speculated about who would be next.

He jumped at the harsh rap on his door, expecting no one. Shutting his laptop, he slid from the barstool and tiptoed to the door, glanced through the peephole. Two men, one African and one Caucasian, stood outside in the hall. Although they were dressed in civilian clothes, Ethan was certain they were police. He'd been very specific with the doorman—no visitors without calling him first—so they had to be of some importance to get by him.

"Who is it?" he shouted.

"Detectives Walker and Rouche, Denver PD. We need to speak with you."

Detectives? "Show me your badges."

They did as he instructed, pulling out their credentials and holding them up to the peephole. Ethan unlocked the deadbolt and sized them up. Walker, the African American, towered over his Caucasian counterpart, Rouche. After the introductions, Ethan cleared a path for them to sit in the living room.

"I take it you know why we're here," Walker said. "Your blog has created quite a stir in the community." His hands, the size of oven mitts, folded over each other.

Ethan nodded. "I mean, yeah, I guess. I thought it was important to let the public know of Berman and Ryland's relationship. That maybe their deaths were more than coincidence."

"Not something you cared to discuss with the police first?" Walker asked.

He glanced at their stern faces, first one, then the other. Walker's nose was as wide as any Ethan had ever seen. Rouche had bad skin and the jowls of a bull mastiff. "I mean, I did, in a way, talk with the police."

Walker grunted. "Care to provide names?"

"No. I wouldn't have sources if I gave up journalistic integrity."

Walker raised an eyebrow, glanced at his partner. They both smirked. "So, that's how you see this...your operation? As journalism?"

Ethan cleared his throat. He could feel his face redden. "Yes. It is. In the twenty-first century, anyone can create their own online news. I've worked hard to create a niche site."

"You make money from this operation, Mr. Stantz?" Rouche asked, joining the conversation. "I mean, looks like you're doing okay for yourself. LoDo loft. New furniture. Pricy art. What's the rent on this place?"

"I make do. I run paid advertising on my site. People who want to reach my readers."

Rouche picked up a stack of articles Ethan had printed from the internet, glanced through them, no doubt looking for anything illegal. "I suppose Berman's and Ryland's deaths have given you a little revenue boost. Increased ads, recognition by the big dogs, CNN, Fox News."

Ethan hesitated, unsure of their intent. He shrugged. When they remained quiet, Ethan began to sweat. Was this some police intimidation tactic to get him to stop writing the blog?

"How did you find out about the circumstances of John Berman's death? In particular, the number and locations of the stab wounds inflicted on the victims?" Walker asked.

"I told you, a source."

"A source who knew Berman was a juror?"

"No. A source who knew I was a juror and frequently wrote about the Kriskan case. Apparently one of the detectives on the scene recognized the similarities right away."

"That would be me," Walker said. "Fifteen years ago, I was rookie cop stationed to keep curious onlookers away from the Kriskan crime scene. Now, I'm the detective. But I didn't tell anyone of my suspicions."

Ethan shrugged. "I don't know what to tell you."

Walker's gaze hardened. It might as well have been a dagger he used to stab Ethan, so viscerally Ethan felt it pierce his chest. "You sure you didn't know about it because you were there?"

"Excuse me?"

"As a juror on the case, you would know, maybe better than anyone, the location and number of stab wounds Mikael Kriskan's parents received that night so long ago. You would know how Kriskan lured them into the living room from their beds, surprised them with a baseball bat, taped their hands and feet. You would even know what concoction of drugs were discovered in Kriskan's system afterward, might even be able to put together the same little cocktail for John Berman's kid."

Ethan's shoulders tensed. "There weren't any drugs discovered in Kriskan's system," he shot back. "That was one of the reasons we convicted him. He couldn't have slept through all that, his parents' screams and struggles, while they were murdered."

"Well, you would know that too since you were a juror," Walker said.

Ethan couldn't believe his ears. "Are you really accusing me of murdering John Berman and his wife right now? Because I can't believe what you're implying. You must be pretty desperate."

Rouche interrupted. "Kevin Ryland's sister said you came to the apartment after his death. That you asked a lot of questions and left with his research into the Kriskan case."

"Yes. I wanted to know why he left the note."

Rouche and Walker exchanged another glance. "Oh, that's right. You knew about the note too. Knew even what was written on it. Let me guess, another source?" Rouche said.

"As a matter of fact, yes," Ethan said.

"Convenient," Walker replied.

Ethan was growing uncomfortable with this line of questioning. The thin layer of dampness beneath his T-shirt brought chills. "What are you insinuating? That I killed Kevin Ryland too? I made him jump from his loft? You guys are unbelievable."

"Perpetrators often like to revisit their crime scenes days after the crime," Rouche said. "Maybe you thought you'd pay the sister a visit, see if anybody suspected Ryland didn't commit suicide. See if the police had asked questions about you."

Walker leaned toward Ethan. His considerable weight shifted forward, causing a loud pop in the spring of the couch. "You have a lot to gain from John Berman's and Kevin Ryland's deaths, don't you, Mr. Stantz? Money, notoriety, maybe a future book deal? How do we know you haven't planned this whole crazy thing out? People do funny things to get their names in the papers."

"They don't murder people," Ethan said.

"You'd be surprised," Rouche said. "And this Reaper character, what a story. How do we know he's real? You have proof of these messages he sent you?"

Ethan put his hands on his hips, tried to keep his demeanor. They really considered him a suspect. He scratched at his beard, shook his head. "Oh my God, this is insane. Look, the Reaper is real. I haven't published anymore about him yet, but just two days ago he contacted another juror directly. Cornered her in a café and threatened her and her son's life if she didn't work to get Mikael Kriskan freed."

Walker frowned. "We've received no such report. What's her name?"

"I can't tell you that. This man, he was Russian, and he meant business. He was adamant about not contacting the police, no law enforcement of any kind. I mean, just you two being here could be endangering her life and mine too."

The two men studied him, still seemed unconvinced. "The messages?" Rouche asked.

Ethan clenched his teeth, bit hard. Cursed himself for the thousandth time. *Why didn't I take a screen shot as soon as I received the messages?*

He shook his head. "No, they were timed out. Disappeared after a minute. No traces of them on my account. He knew what he was doing."

"Another convenience," Walker said. "Do you have alibis for the evening of January tenth and January eleventh of this year?"

"You're serious? Really?"

They were. They were deadly serious.

"Let me check my planner." He grabbed his laptop, opened it up. A ping and a message popped up. Ethan gasped.

"Back off the Kriskan case now, Ethan Stantz. Or you will end up like John Berman—dead."

He turned it toward the detectives. "Still think I'm kidding?"

CHAPTER 19

Jess met Nick Whelan at his downtown Denver office at nine the next morning. As usual before she'd left, she'd watched Tom feed and dress Ricky, then load him in his car seat for the short trip to school. Yet, this time she'd watched in earnest, sensing a love and longing not felt for a long time, wondering what her life would be without either of them, and thinking how much better it could be with a little more money and a good nanny. She didn't know how she was going to pay for his school for the remainder of the year, or all the other bills. They were at least a month behind on utilities and credit cards and past due notices were starting to pile up. For every day for the past two weeks now, she'd made certain to get home and get to the mail before Tom did so she could shred the notices without his knowledge. With the intensity of his latest case, she didn't want to burden him with the status of their debt. She wanted him to concentrate on winning. If he won, maybe he would entertain a new, better job offer.

But if he didn't, then what? She thought about the Russian's words, how he could make her life easier, take care of things. Money in exchange for her testimony. If she wanted, she could tell Nick Whelan the truth today, have him set things in motion for her to talk with the judge. Maybe it wouldn't be that bad. Maybe she could testify against David and any charges against her could be dropped. Her life might be hell for a while but it would all be forgotten after a time. They could take the money, move to California or Oregon. Start anew.

She sat in traffic and laughed at herself, living in such a fantasy. *Still being the old me, looking for the easy way out.* Nothing good came easy. Hadn't she learned that yet?

Once downtown, she parked in one of the open pay lots and walked the two blocks to Nick Whelan's office. The streets were unusually empty for a weekday morning. On the first block, she only passed an old man with rheumy eyes reading a newspaper on a park bench and a construction worker with a jackhammer breaking up a sidewalk. At the next block, she scanned the men leaning against a concrete wall blowing hot breath on their hands as well as several people waiting for a bus, wondering if the Russian was anywhere nearby. If she was lucky, he would see her with Kriskan's defense attorney and believe she was about to tell the truth.

She entered the door to the old stone building but didn't get far. Nick Whelan met her halfway up the stairs. "Follow me, the car's just around the block."

They headed back out into the cold. The day was unusually gray, not one of the prized three-hundred-plus sunny days per year Denver boasted of when drawing business and industry to the region. But Jess didn't mind because it fit her mood. She was on her way to see Mikael Kriskan at the Sterling Correctional Facility, where Colorado's four death-row inmates were housed.

"You sure you still want to do this?" Nick asked.

"Yes. I need to know. I need to hear his story."

"You still won't tell me what's going on?"

"I can't. Not yet." She glanced across the street, behind her toward the convention center, in front closer to civic center park. The heels of her boots clumped along the pavement.

"You seem jumpy. Want to tell me why?"

"Can't tell you that either."

"You know I'm really going out on a limb here."

She glanced at him, his young but haggard face. "I know you are and I appreciate it. I promise you, it will be worth your time."

They climbed into his SUV, a late model Acura MDX. Unlike David's car, this one wasn't all high polish and spotless. Full of boxes and briefs and fast food bags, this car looked like it belonged to a hardworking attorney.

"Do you live in here or what?" Jess asked.

"Sorry." He cleared everything off the passenger seat and added it to the rubbish in the back. "Sometimes it feels like I live in it, I tell you. Too many trips to Cañon City, where most of my clients end up."

Jess fastened her seat belt and nodded. "To tell the truth, I thought all high-risk prisoners were kept in Cañon City. I was surprised to hear Mikael was being kept in Sterling. I mean, of all places."

Nick pulled the Acura from the curb. "Death-row inmate number one filed a lawsuit a few years ago stating that the Cañon City property didn't have proper outdoor exercise space to meet his constitutional rights. I'm not making that up. He won. So, all four death-row inmates were moved to the Sterling Correctional Facility, where there's more adequate outdoor space."

Jess shook her head. "The legal system baffles me."

They departed downtown, headed northeast on I-76, settled in for the two-hour drive.

"Let me ask you something," Nick said. "Guy walks into a movie theater and kills twelve and injures more than seventy people. Two jurors—two people selected out of thousands summoned across an entire county—say they aren't comfortable committing to the death penalty, and the guy gets life in prison. But one guy is accused of killing his adoptive parents and possibly his sister, although there is no definitive proof without a body, and that man gets death. No lone juror holds out for life. How does that happen?"

Jess turned away, feeling the rush of guilt flood over her. Frame after frame of flat brown landscape and open prairie covered with splotches of snow flashed by the window. "I don't have an answer."

That wasn't true, of course. She did have an answer, just not one he would want to hear. "I would've voted for the death penalty on the movie shooter. I know that doesn't make it better."

"That's why I dislike Colorado's system," Nick Whelan said. "It's all random. Dependent upon the jurors that get picked and not a classification of the act itself. Any act of murder that a prosecutor determines to be *especially heinous, cruel, or containing depraved conduct*. Who gets to determine that? It's a chance lottery on the jury picked and whether the verdict is unanimous or not. That's why I fight against it every single day."

Jess stayed quiet, listening to the tires hum against the grooved pavement of highway. She thought about how it never should've come down to this, Mikael Kriskan facing an actual execution day. She remembered the day the jury had disbanded, how Ethan had tried to excuse any late feelings of guilt with news that death-row inmates didn't actually ever make it to the execution chamber in Colorado. Most sentences ended up appealed and changed to life in prison or were stayed by the ever-more liberal leaning population.

So how had this one, Mikael Kriskan, made it all the way to the execution? Especially when, as Jess knew, their jury had contained not just one but two not-guilty verdicts to start. There never should have been a unanimous verdict.

And now the Russian knew as well.

The closer they got to Sterling, the more Jess was sure they'd traveled too far and ended up in Nebraska. So much prairie and desolation lined the highway, the landscape was like the backdrop of an apocalyptic movie. A place where the wind was constant and you could see two miles in any direction.

She thought about the old joke, how Colorado and Kansas had fought over who owned the territory east of the front range and Colorado lost. She had to admit, it was a great place for a prison.

As they pulled up and parked, he said, "Listen, don't forget your name."

"I know, I know. Linda Richards, your new junior attorney."

THE FIFTH JUROR

He handed her an ID. She stepped out of the vehicle into the whipping wind and Jess had to turn her back to the biting cold. Nick Whelan offered her a second coat for shelter as they made their way toward the front doors. Near the entrance, her knees began to grow unsteady, like loose legs on an old piece of furniture. She'd never been on the inside of a prison, not even the city jail, and just walking in the door and seeing the guards armed with guns made her long to flee, sensing her own loss of freedom.

It only proceeded to get worse as they were led deeper into the facility, past studded metal doors and security, where her person and belongings were checked and x-rayed. She felt her heart thud in her chest as the female guard patted down her legs and thighs.

She couldn't help but wonder if this was what she would face if she told the truth. Inspections and pat downs, and intrusive scrutiny. She didn't think she could spend a single day in this place without losing her mind.

Once through security and approved for entry, Nick turned and motioned for her. "Follow me. Stay close."

He didn't need to ask twice. This wasn't a place she wanted to be left alone. She scurried to catch up with him.

In-person visitation of death-row inmates was limited to legal counsel only. Friends and relatives were only allowed to speak via phone between a plexiglass barrier. Since Jess and Nick were there on legal business, they were placed in a private room slightly larger than a postage stamp where a guard stood watch. As they waited for Mikael to arrive, Nick hugged a large file folder between his arms, containing much of what he'd accumulated on the case the past ten years.

Oddly, he looked every bit as nervous as Jess felt.

Her heart pounded as they sat and waited. She thought how few people ever saw what it was like in here, isolated to a cell with nothing but a toilet and bunk, all but a single hour of the day. No time with others. No conversation. No contact. Just day after day with your own thoughts and fears, and no hope.

How could anyone ever hope to spend the rest of their life in such a place rather than to flee the pain through death?

Maybe they'd made the right choice for Kriskan after all.

Antsy, she cracked her knuckles and waited. It would be interesting to hear Mikael's thoughts on the matter.

CHAPTER 20

As soon as the door to the room opened and Jess saw Mikael Kriskan, her heart buckled. He no longer looked like the same young man, not young at all. By her calculation, he would only be thirty-four, the same age as herself, yet she swore strands of silver lined the temple above each of his ears and brown spots mottled his skin, like aging fruit. His eyes, previously a stunning gray, the color of a dolphin, held no more brightness than two street puddles. Fourteen years might as well have been forty.

He shuffled across the floor in arm and leg irons, waiting for the guard to lock him to the table. His eyes twitched as he sat, never leaving Jess. She recalled how his IQ had been discussed in detail during the trial, topping 140, and saw that level of intelligence working right now. She often saw the same grinding glimpses from Ricky, typically while solving a puzzle or telling a story in such detail you knew his mind didn't work like everyone else's.

Mikael finally turned his attention to his attorney. "I thought you said you were bringing a new assistant?" His gaze shifted back to Jess. "You're no assistant. I remember you. You put me here." His voice still held a hint of Russian dialect from his early childhood.

"Listen," Nick said. "We may have a real break in your case. "Jess came to me with some news. You know two of the jurors who participated on your trial have died recently. And now there's been some additional...activity. Jess asked to speak directly with you."

"What type of activity?"

She glanced up, looking into the accusing eyes of a dead man. "I was visited by someone, a friend of yours. A friend who said he works for your father."

A shadow crept across his face. "I have no friends, and my father is dead."

"I think he meant your biological father. The man who came to see me? He was Russian."

Mikael raised his chin. Jess noticed his jaw clench, the skin tighten by his temples. Beside her, she could sense Nick Whelan stop breathing. This was the first he was hearing the news as well.

"He said your father is very interested in gaining your freedom. That he and his associates will do"—she hesitated, cleared her throat— "well, most anything, to gain your freedom. I may have some information that could help in that endeavor so you can get back to Russia and be with your father, but first, I need to know the truth."

He cocked his head, issued a wayward smile. Beneath the gesture, she could sense his anger. "Truth? You want truth?" He laughed, as if it were the funniest thing he'd ever heard. "As a wise man once said, it is a sad regret to have searched for truth and settled for an answer. The truth does not matter here, not in American justice."

Jess bowed her head. "I understand what we have put you through. I'm sorry."

"You understand? You?" He swept his cuffed hands across the table, looked her up and down.

She glanced at the fine fabric of the clothes she wore, the three-carat diamond ring on her finger, and instantly understood how ridiculous that had sounded. She, with her life of privilege and luxury, born in the United States, with plenty of access to food, clothes, and education, along with the freedom to be, or do, as she wished. What could she possibly understand about what he'd been through—taken from his home country at a young age and thrown into a culture he didn't understand? Then, convicted of his parents' murder and spending fifteen years behind bars.

"I know this isn't related," Jess said, "but my mother was Russian too. Well, Ukrainian. Her name was Katerina. My father met her while she was staying with her sister in Denver." She wrung her hands, took a deep breath, tried to push the image of her mother draped face-down on the bed, an open bottle of sleeping pills spilled beside her, that instantly filled her vision. "My mom, she committed suicide, when I was eight."

She felt a darkness descend, as it always did when she thought of her mother. It crept around and enclosed her in a suffocating embrace until she feared it would squeeze her to death. "I may not know what you've been through in here, but I know what the loss of a mother at a young age does to a person. That's what I wanted to say."

He studied her, his eyes never flinching.

He issued a slight nod. "It rips out your soul."

The pain she always tried to push away infiltrated her heart. The struggle of betrayal, the anger at her mother's weakness versus the guilt that Jess, as a rebellious child, may have played a part in her mother's decision to take her own life, battled, as it had countless times before. *Didn't she love me? Didn't she love my father? Why weren't we enough?*

"Yes, it does," she said.

"I watched cancer consume my mother," Mikael said. "It literally ate her alive. I can't explain it any other way. At times I would sit with her and parts of her leg would pulse, like the disease was crawling and growing beneath her skin. It is most vicious in its pursuit of death."

A shudder rippled up Jess's spine. Most vicious in its pursuit of death. Just like Mikael's friend, the Russian, and what he would soon do to Jess and her son if Jess didn't do as he wanted.

"I wanted to talk to you about your parents. At the trial, you made the choice to not testify. You didn't defend yourself. That always bothered me. Why?" Jess asked. "Why didn't you get on the stand and tell your side of the story?"

He blinked several times. "I cannot remember. My memories are vague of that night. I went to bed early to listen to music. I fell asleep with my headphones on. I don't know what time it was. When I woke up, I was in my bed covered in my parents' blood. And that of my Anya."

He choked as he said the name of his younger sister. He hung his head.

Jess felt a tug of empathy. "I remember during the trial when the prosecutor went after Anya and your relationship with her. At one time, he tried to suggest that maybe you had sexually abused her and when your parents found out, you tried to cover it all up. It was the only time I saw you get emotional. Even now, I see your feelings for her. But I never believed the prosecutor was right in his allegations. I don't think you would ever harm your sister. I think you were her protector."

Mikael Kriskan turned his face away from her.

"Tell me that I am right," Jess said. "Tell me you didn't kill your parents."

"Why are you doing this?"

"I want to do what is right. If the decision we made was wrong. Was it?"

He sat quietly, studying his hands.

"Your father wants you to come home," Jess said.

"Home?" he said. Mikael laughed in a manner that made Jess's bones feel like they'd been ripped from their sockets. It was a deep, dark laugh, full of despair.

"Home? Russia is not home. Not for me. You do not know where I come from. What kind of people, those they call my family, what they do. These are not good people. You have no idea what they would make me do. Life of hell."

Nick interjected. "But, Mikael, you wouldn't have to go back to Russia if you don't want. You're an adult and an American citizen. You can go back to school, finish your degree, move on with your life. They can't make you do what you don't want to do."

More laughing. "Oh, you Americans, you don't understand how the rest of the world works. They could, and would, most certainly make me return to Russia. My mother warned me many times about my father and his associates before she died. The only time I met him, I was a child, and it is not a pleasant memory. My mother saved my life by coming to America. It wasn't easy for her to do. She took a great risk.

We left Russia for a very good reason. If it is true what you say, that it is my father who has come for me, then I must say no."

Jess didn't understand. "But why? I can help," she said. "I can make it right. You'll go free, you'll…"

"There is no freedom when you spend your life running. Always looking over your shoulder." He leaned across the table, his eyes locked on hers, his tired, blemished skin rigid. "Look. You want absolution? You're forgiven. But you let me die." There was no sign of any indecision now, only a directive, a certainty. "You. Let. Me. Die."

"But, Mikael," Nick said again, reaching for his hand.

"*No!*" he shouted. He raised his shackled hands above the table and slammed them down. His leg irons rattled against the table legs. "*No, No, No!*"

The guards fled into the room and quickly had each of his arms within their grasp. He wriggled and writhed, lunged at Jess. Spittle flew from his lips. "You do right. You let me die. You let me die!"

CHAPTER 21

Jess was relieved when she arrived home to an empty house. Although Nick Whelan had cranked the heat to high, she hadn't been able to stop shaking during the entire drive back to Denver. Nothing helped. Not a hug. Not a warm cup of coffee. Because her trembling wasn't due to the winter chill. It was the repeated sounds of Mikael Kriskan's shouts. *You let me die!* She didn't think those words, and the desperation in his voice, would ever leave her head.

Nick had pleaded with the authorities to speak with Mikael privately after his outburst, but the warden had denied it. Instead, four guards had arrived to drag Mikael down the hall and throw him back into his isolated cell. On the way home, Nick had repeatedly slapped the steering wheel and mumbled under his breath, not understanding for the life of him why his client didn't wish to be set free. He looked like a man who'd awakened to a bad dream only to discover it was true.

With Tom and Ricky still out of the house, Jess decided to take a moment and just breathe in the silence. To say that it had been a trying day and week was a gross misrepresentation. She placed her purse and keys on the kitchen island, took off her hat, coat, and gloves. Before the oblong mirror that hung to the side of the hallway secretary, she tousled her hair and placed a hand on each cheek. Her skin was so pale, her eyes so fearful, she didn't even recognize herself.

She collapsed into her favorite chair, a soft blue rocker with a matching ottoman. She'd spent many an hour in the chair nursing Ricky as an infant, additional days rocking him asleep or comforting him after one of his outbursts or seizures. It was a miracle it didn't show any more wear than it did, just a few scratches on the arms and a faded line of cushion where the sunlight often hit it from the window nearby.

She closed her eyes and focused on her breath, let the small sways back and forth try to calm her nerves. Yet, no matter how hard she tried, the thoughts that held her mind hostage wouldn't leave. If she didn't go to the judge and tell her story, then she and Ricky and the other jurors would die at the hands of the Reaper. If she did go to the judge and he overturned the conviction and set Mikael free, then she could be facing David Foster's ire and sentencing Mikael Kriskan to death all over again at the hands of his father and his associates. Not to mention wreck her marriage and potentially her son.

What the hell am I going to do?

Just then, she heard the sound of the garage open and Tom's car drive in. Two minutes later, the door flung open, and Ricky appeared, running through the house with a drawing in one hand and crayons in the other. One shoe went flying, then the other, and he dropped his coat and hat in the hall. Tom followed, dutifully picking up each object as Ricky stripped it from his body.

Jess pushed up from the chair and kissed Tom on the cheek. She noticed he looked worn, his clothes limp on his body, his hair sticking up at odd angles. "You look like you've been in a street fight."

"That's an apt description. Court was brutal today."

She wrapped her arms around his neck and planted her face against his chest, where he smelled of a light sweat. She glanced up into his soft, steel blue eyes, and wondered why his easy-going style hadn't been enough for her in the past. Did she secretly believe she didn't deserve him and so purposely set out to sabotage her relationship with him? It was almost like she wanted to be treated badly. As if in her heart, she believed she deserved punishment.

"Maybe we can just skip dinner and go upstairs?" Jess said. "Get some cuddle time?" After the day she'd had, she just wanted to feel safe in the arms of a man who truly loved her, not one who pretended just to satisfy his own needs.

He seemed surprised. A light smile crossed his lips. "Yeah?"

She kissed him, felt a heat stir within that had been missing too long. They embraced a second time, until Ricky interrupted.

"That's gross." He climbed onto the barstool next to the kitchen island. "Mom, look what I drew for you today." He tugged at her shirt. "Mom, look."

She backed away from Tom, slid a finger down his abdomen. "I'll get his dinner. Be up later." He disappeared and was already loosening his tie as he went upstairs.

Jess fixed a quick box blend of macaroni and cheese and spooned out a dollop of applesauce onto a plate while she oohed and awed over Ricky's drawing before displaying the work proudly on the refrigerator. The pictures and colorings were multiple layers deep and covered the entire door.

For once, Ricky ate without trouble. No complaints of macaroni that was too mushy or cheese sauce that was too runny. She sat across from him on the island and watched him chew, her heart aching for him. He'd already been through so much at such a young age, she would do anything to protect him from any future harm.

When Ricky was finished eating and the dishes were done, Jess turned off the lights and double-checked the locks on the doors before ushering Ricky off to bed. Once he was tucked in, she entered the master bedroom and closed the door until only an inch remained open. Tom was already beneath the covers, his bare torso resting against the headboard.

She moved playfully across the room, detached the magazine from his hands, tossed it aside. Slid the glasses from his face and placed them on the nightstand. She straddled him above the covers and leaned her body into his. They kissed for several minutes before Tom's hands moved beneath her blouse.

As he started to nuzzle on her neck and she ran her fingers through his hair, they both jumped at the sound they'd become all too familiar with—Ricky's headboard knocking against the wall.

They couldn't untangle themselves fast enough.

Ricky was having a seizure.

Jess fled first, followed by Tom. "Grab the medicine," he yelled.

She sprinted to the bathroom, flung open the medicine cabinet, fumbled with pill bottles, inhalers, and boxes of over-the-counter drugs. Several fell from the shelf and across the vanity. After locating the correct bottle and a clean oral syringe, she raced back to the bedroom. There, Tom had already checked Ricky's mouth for any food or obstacles, placed pillows all around him, and turned him on his side. His little body rocked and kicked, unaware of what was happening.

She filled the oral syringe with the anti-epilepsy drug to the level indicated and waited for the seizure to stop. They couldn't give him anything while he convulsed.

"Come on, Ricky, come on, baby," she pleaded. "Open your eyes. Come back to us."

As she watched him writhe, unable to do anything to stop it, she felt the tears—and the guilt—surface. Every time Ricky went through one of these, fault clawed at her, wondering if her former heroin use had affected Ricky's development in some way. Even though she'd entered rehab immediately upon learning she was pregnant, she didn't see how injecting a chemical of unimaginable power into your veins wouldn't affect early prenatal development. Her doctors had repeatedly told her it wasn't likely, but that would never satisfy her because she would never believe it to be true.

It was the worst feeling in the world, to believe that because of your actions your child was suffering. That was a special kind of pain, a unique kind of hell.

Finally, the seizures began to ease, and Ricky settled into place. As he began to utter sounds and his little hand ran over his sleepy eyes, Jess sat him up and administered the oral dosage. For days after a seizure, he would be exhausted, confused, and irritable, not understanding why his brain didn't cooperate with the rest of his body.

She scooped him up in her arms and stroked the back of his head. Tom spoke gently to him, reassuring him that he was okay, that he was safe. But as they comforted him, all Jess could think of was that they were lying to him.

Ricky wasn't okay, and he wasn't safe, because once again, his mother's previous actions had put her family in harm's way.

Holding Ricky, with Tom by her side, she realized just how much she had to live for, so much to appreciate and love. They didn't need the money or the nanny or any of those other things to make the family she wanted. They just needed each other.

And in that moment, Jess knew, she had to fix this. She had to do whatever she could to correct past transgressions and make it right.

KJ—do the right thing.

CHAPTER 22

Mikael sat on his bunk late into the night, thinking heavy thoughts. Somewhere down the corridor, he could hear the slow tapping of an unknown object against bars, the distant laughter of the guards. He glanced at the four walls surrounding him and felt them closing in, like one of those carnival fun houses. Since Jess Dawson had come to see him, he couldn't get her out of his mind. She had come to him on a mission, wanting to know his truth, but in the midst of the conversation, her revelations about the man who'd come to visit her had disrupted his ability to think rationally. She, along with the writings of the blogger, had revealed a disturbing truth—the Russians had found him. His mother had feared they would come for him someday. But the man or men who were murdering and intimidating others on his behalf were not men he longed to keep company with— they were of his father and his associates, an organized group of men known for tactics of a nature he could not comprehend, men who lived to harm and torture at will.

How could he ignore his mother's warnings at the hands of his own freedom?

He choked back the dire despair that now encompassed him like a blanket. All previous hope he'd felt after reading the blog, that little ray of light that had swept over him for the first time in nearly a decade, had darkened in an instant. His father wanted him to come home, and Mikael could only imagine the real reasons why— certainly not because he loved and missed his son. If that had been the case, his father never would've forced his mother from the country in the first place.

No, Mikael didn't believe he would be any safer in Russia now than he'd been as a child. His mother had taken him and fled for good reason.

He lay down on the bed, stared at the chalk stars he'd created on the ceiling. He missed his mother, his time snuggled with her on the couch, the high pitch of her laugh, the way her eyes twinkled. He recalled the day she'd told him she had cancer, how she'd muted the television and patted the seat of a chair, indicating for him to come and sit. Then, holding his hands, she'd spoken of her disease and also of her previous life, time cornered by a dangerous man, the father she never named but he'd briefly met. She stressed to him that he must never seek to find him, promise to never step on Russian soil. She hadn't planned to inform him until he was older but it was of special importance for him to understand now, at this young age, because she wouldn't be around much longer to protect him.

In that moment, the flashes of cartoons in the background seemed surreal against the gravity of her words. Bugs Bunny, Wile E. Coyote, the Road Runner, and death. Even now, just the mention of those old cartoons brought his mother to mind and the glowing look of strength on her face. No fear for herself, only resolve for his future.

Speak to no one. Trust no one. Especially the Russians. If they come for you, run, hide. Never return.

He often wondered, in the many options he'd considered over the years, if the Russians could've been involved in the death of his American parents. The brutality of the killings was certainly of their nature, but he couldn't understand why they would've chosen to leave him to take the fall for his parents' murders rather than kill him too. Or, why instead of taking only Anya, they hadn't taken them both. And since it made no sense, it didn't seem likely.

Yet, there were times he dreamed of an accent and saw flashes of images he didn't understand, and he speculated if the images were truly of a dream, or a reality of what had taken place that winter night so long ago.

He curled onto his side, pulled the covers over his shoulders. Jess Dawson again entered his thoughts. She was pretty, near his age. He remembered her sitting on the jury, appearing disinterested at times, as if she were dreaming of faraway places. So, he couldn't help but question what she was doing here now, if her growing conscience was real or due solely to intimidation.

She'd stated she might have information that could help in his release, but what could that possibly be? And would he want it anyway, his conviction overturned and possibly facing a new trial? The initial trial had taken an enormous toll on him. No sleep. Horrible, powerful words accusing him of doing the most despicable things. Day after day of endless persecution, the sideways glances of the judge and jury.

The relentless pursuit of the prosecuting attorney—a man Mikael despised.

At times, Mikael imagined leaping from his chair and cutting the man's throat.

And why not? He was telling lies, so many lies.

Did they know what it was like? To sit there and listen to such things and be accused without being able to defend yourself?

Innocent until proven guilty. American bullshit.

Listening had been bad enough. To add the actual images—photographs of his dead parents, close-ups of stab wounds and blood spatter—and parade them around the courtroom as if they were items to be admired, that was quite another.

He recalled watching the prosecutor hand the photographs to the jurors for further examination and seeing Jess Dawson flinch at the images and quickly pass them to the juror seated next to her before wiping her palms on her pants, as if trying to remove their stain from her hands. Afterward, Mikael had briefly met her gaze, and her eyelids had fluttered and she'd turned away.

In that moment, he remembered how he'd wanted to scream at her, at all of them, inform them how the images the prosecution presented were of equal shock to him. He wanted to shout that if they felt repulsed, imagine how much more revolted he was, to wake and see such a thing with his own eyes. To smell the musky copper scent of death, feel the slime of blood on his hands. To see it all and yet, not remember a thing.

Imagine. Imagine it.

He groaned in the dark, reliving the torment. Soon it would all be over. He had made the right choice, for everyone. He no longer wanted to stare into a void of nothingness and writhe in an emotional grave. He no longer wanted to dream of Anya among fields of flowers only to wake to her renewed death. He no longer wanted hope dangled in front of his nose like a steak outside the cage of a starving dog only for it to be thrown to the well-fed wolves.

He wanted, simply, to die.

CHAPTER 23

Jess paced Ethan's apartment, updating him on her previous day's conversation with Mikael Kriskan. She'd woken him early but brought a large cup of his favorite coffee as a consolation. Like her, he looked like he'd endured a late night of his own, his hair unruly, face unshaven, and dark circles beneath his eyes. "Ethan, the man would rather die than be released into the custody of his biological father. I mean, what does that say?"

Although she'd added a shawl over her turtleneck, leggings, and boots, she still couldn't shake the chills of the prior day. A long night with Ricky tucked in her arms hadn't helped. She'd been surprised to find him energetic enough this morning to go to school but had informed the teacher to call immediately if he appeared to be struggling. "Mikael was afraid. I mean, genuinely afraid."

Ethan wrapped his wire frames around his ears and tightened them. "Well, to be honest, I think I can understand his hesitancy," he said. "I've been doing some digging and I've discovered some things—disturbing things. Come, take a look."

Gaining her interest, she joined him on the couch and sat. Strung out on the coffee table were prints of articles and photographs. It appeared his multiple late nights had been spent conducting research and lots of it.

"In trying to find Mikael's biological parents, I started with his adoptive parents and worked backward. I knew there had to be connection between them and his biological parents somewhere, so that's what I set out to discover."

He sorted through the items on the table, selected a couple of photographs, pictures of Mikael's parents in younger days along with an article from the *Denver Post*.

"Malcolm Kriskan and Ruth Loft were third-generation Americans, but they both descended from the large influx of German Russians to immigrate here in the early 1900s. These were Germans who settled along the Volga River and the Black Sea in western Russia after Catherine the Great invited Germans to settle in the sparsely populated western region in exchange for no taxes and free land. At the time, the

Germans were suffering through war, starvation, high taxes, and religious intolerance, so many of them were tempted by Catherine's offer and relocated to Russia. For many years they enjoyed the benefits and a stipend from the government equal to about fifteen hundred dollars per person at the time. Not a bad deal, right?"

Jess nodded.

He handed her the article he'd found detailing such events.

"But when Alexander the Second came to power, he withdrew the special benefits and stipend, and eventually, famine drove those same German Russians to immigrate to America and guess where many of them ended up? Right here, in northeast Colorado. They took up sugar beet farming and set up new homesteads around Sterling. So many came here, in fact, that at one time, the German Russians were the second largest ethnic group in the state."

Jess quickly read over the article. "Learn something new every day."

"I researched Mikael's adoptive parents' ancestry and luckily it's well documented because of their history. Yesterday afternoon, I made several calls. Nobody I contacted was surprised to hear from me. Apparently, since my blog post, they've been bombarded by the media. I found them all talkative, but it was Mikael's aunt Miriam, Malcolm's younger sister, who proved to be the most informative."

He stopped for a large gulp of coffee. She could sense the caffeine beginning to work, Ethan's energy and enthusiasm gaining momentum.

"According to Miriam, Malcolm and Ruth had trouble getting pregnant so turned to adoption. They had many connections to other German and Russian communities across the country and Mikael became available after his mother, a Russian immigrant from Saint Petersburg, died in Detroit. Those that knew his mother spoke of the urgency to get him placed with an American family so the boy would not have to return to Russia, as he was not yet an American citizen. His mother was very adamant before her death that he must not return to his father's family. Now, hold that thought, because it's important, and we're going to circle back to it."

"Got it," Jess said.

"So, Malcolm and Ruth flew to Michigan and met the then ten-year-old. They said he was bright and very polite and after a couple of days of discussing it over with family and friends, they decided to take him in. Because he was already ten, they kept his first name but changed his last to their own, that being Kriskan, of course. Two years later, surprise, Ruth got pregnant when they'd stopped trying, and they had a child of their own."

"Anya," Jess said.

"Right. I know I'm repeating some things we knew from the trial, but I want to make sure I don't forget something."

He circled the coffee table, looking for something else of note. "Now, just like she was during the trial, Miriam was fervent about stressing that Mikael loved being a big brother to Anya, and Anya idolized him in every way possible. She also reemphasized that Mikael adored Malcolm and Ruth. Unlike other kids, he preferred the company of his family over his friends. Even while in college, he came home nearly every weekend to visit."

"I remember her testifying to that at the trial as well," Jess said. "That even on the weekend the murders happened, he was home with them on a Saturday night versus out with college friends."

"Right, and she was a credible character witness until your pal David Foster brought forth another family friend that tore apart her testimony with theories about Malcolm's strict upbringing and that Mikael only came home every weekend because Malcolm demanded it."

Jess sighed. "I remember that too."

"And we knew his IQ was off the charts, in the range of 140, but here's what we didn't know." He handed Jess a series of articles, one again from the *Denver Post*, others from his high school and college newspapers.

"In high school, Mikael won several state and national science competitions, mostly involving engineering. He possessed one of those minds that could envision how items could be constructed and work. Miriam said one day he was shooting rockets and the next he was building robots and mini cars. He built Anya a motorized bike and a flying Barbie."

Jess raised an eyebrow. "A flying Barbie? Wow."

"She liked superheroes apparently." Another sip of coffee. "Miriam said Mikael gorged himself on science and history books the way most kids eat candy. He couldn't get enough of them. Lived at the library. So, it's probably no surprise that Mikael Kriskan became an inventor at a young age. And not just little stuff. I mean, he owned at least a dozen patents."

He handed her several new documents, blueprints with lines, measurements, and notations Jess couldn't make heads or tails of. But the photo left no doubt to what was being detailed. "Drones?" she asked.

Ethan nodded. "And not just any drones. Check it out. The one you're holding is a drone with eyesight and automated weapon technology. Seek out and hunt your victims by drone, let them fight the wars for you."

"Whoa." Jess looked over the design. Just thinking about such a war—based on machines that could seek and destroy—made her shudder. It was the stuff of a sci-fi movie. She put the blueprints down, not even wanting to touch them.

"You get what this means, right?"

Jess shook her head. "Other than he's a genius?"

"No. It means Mikael Kriskan isn't just some Russian's son. Mikael Kriskan is an asset."

Jess felt her heart stutter. An asset. As in, someone the Russians would like to get ahold of to work for them and their government. Or someone a criminal organization would like to nab to create machines they could use against their enemies, possibly even sell them to other organizations or foreign countries.

She thought of the way Mikael had described his father.

These are not good people. You have no idea what they would make me do.

No wonder he didn't wish to go free. And now she was certain they couldn't set him free. They had an obligation to not let the man fall into the wrong hands. Not just for Mikael's sake, but for the entire world's.

Jess circled the living room trying to wrap her head around the information. Her cheeks and lips felt numb, like she'd been at the dentist for hours. Shock, perhaps.

God, was there no way out of this endless mess?

"This is terrible, Ethan. There's no way we can give a man his freedom who might be exploited to do harm on the world. And yet, if we don't figure out a way to grant him his freedom, this Reaper character will kill all of us."

"I hate to tell you, but it gets worse."

"Worse?" Her voice was high-pitched, near frantic. "What can possibly be worse than our potential death?" An uneasy laugh escaped her throat.

Ethan took a deep breath. "I think I know who Mikael's biological father is."

He sorted through the stack of documents again, laid down a head shot of a man with a heavily scarred face and lifeless eyes. "Meet Nikolai Petrovsky. Nickname, The Butcher of Saint Petersburg."

Jess's blood went ice cold. She sat back on the couch, fearing she might pass out. She didn't even want to touch the photo, fearing some death curse would come with it. She scooted back away from it, as if distancing herself might make her less of a target. "How did you find him?"

"Miriam had the name of Mikael's biological mother. His mother changed her name when she first arrived in the States, but it wasn't hard to trace her back to her original visa, and from there, I searched for her associations in Russia. I found her parents, and Mikael's birth certificate, and from there, a single people-finder site listing her possible relationship to Petrovsky."

Ethan was revved up now, circling the coffee table and grabbing different documents and handing them to her to make his various points—like Sherlock Holmes on acid.

"Her name was Helena. Her parents were a seamstress and iron worker by trade, and they lived in Saint Petersburg. Helena dropped out of school and worked as a bartender in a club I can't pronounce, but what translates as the *Big Dipper*. The club is known for its criminal element, has mob ties, most specifically to a group known as the Saint Petersburg Twelve. I located several articles detailing crimes that occurred there and guess who is one of the Twelve?"

"Let me guess. Nikolai Petrovsky," Jess said.

"Bingo."

Jess looked over many of the articles. They were all written in Russian or variations thereof. "How did you read these? It just looks like Egyptian hieroglyphics to me."

"Google Translate. It's not perfect, but you get the gist. The translations are stapled to the back of each of the articles."

Jess scanned one after another. She was amazed by how much information Ethan had gathered. She knew that in his time as a blogger, he'd become adept at researching the internet—even tapping into the depths of the dark web when he needed—but this was brilliant. "How did you get Mikael's birth certificate? That couldn't have been easy."

He raised an eyebrow. "Don't ask."

"I thought you didn't hack."

"I don't," he said, pushing up his glasses. "I just, um, occasionally cross boundaries."

Jess sat back, took it all in for a moment. "The father is listed as *Unknown* on the birth certificate. So how do you know the father is Petrovsky?"

She wanted the father to be someone—anyone—other than the man in the photo.

"Because..." Ethan thumbed through additional photographs. He selected another headshot, slapped it down on the coffee table. "Look familiar?"

Jess gasped. "Is that Mikael?" She picked it up, examined the face. "No, wait, it's not, but..."

"Meet Nikov Petrovsky. The brother from another mother. Safe to say they both resemble daddy, don't you think? Nikov is five years older than Mikael. His mother is Lenova Portina Petrovsky, Nikolai's wife, and the daughter of another mobster, who is also one of the Saint Petersburg Twelve. Get the picture?"

Jess slapped her cheeks to get the blood to return to them. She again stood and walked the length of the room, back again. What the hell had they gotten themselves into? A genius asset? Drones? Russian mobsters? She wished for the thousandth time she'd never stepped foot on that jury.

"Oh, this is starting to make sense, and not in a good way," Jess said. "Nikolai has an affair with the pretty young bartender, Helena, gets her knocked up, tries to keep it a secret. But maybe word gets out, and his wife, Lenova, is none too happy, and neither is her father. Maybe they threaten to kill Helena or tell Nikolai to get rid of her."

She turned. "Mikael said his mother told him they were in great danger because of his father. At the time, I thought that was because he—the father—was the danger, but Helena might've fled Russia because she and Mikael weren't just targets of Nikolai's but of Lenova and her father's associates."

"Right, which brings me back full-circle to that statement I wanted you to remember. How Helena was so adamant that Mikael be taken in by an American family and not returned to Russia. Because it would be death for him. Maybe not at the hands of his father, but because of his father."

"If Nikolai was intent on killing him then, why care about his son now?"

"Well, I think we know the answer to that. Somehow, he found out about his son's brilliance. But he also learned his son is in prison and awaiting execution, so he sends this Russian to come and get him out, by any means necessary."

Jess nodded. "And because Nikolai has discovered his son is a master engineer with a genius-level IQ, he can convince the Twelve not to harm him should Mikael return to Russia and work for the organization."

"Correct." Ethan took a momentary pause, although his foot continued to jitter. "So, there's one thing left." He walked over to his workstation, gathered up several more items.

"What are those?" Jess asked, joining him.

"Photos of known associates of Petrovsky's. I thought you could look through them and see if you recognize the man who approached you in the café."

Jess's hands shook as she took the items. She flipped through photo after photo of men with hardened stares and dull eyes. High foreheads, no foreheads, cheekbones, no cheekbones, jowls, dimpled chins. When she landed on the next photo, she instantly knew it was him. She would never forget his eyes or the chill of the words that escaped those lips.

Kill Mikael, kill your son. Save Mikael, save your son. Easy choice.

She turned the photo toward Ethan. "That's him."

Ethan grabbed it, looked at the back. "Dimitry Romanov? Shit. Not good. He's one of Nikolai's crew. A position known as a thief-in-law. I think it means he's like a made man." He let out a breath and brushed a hand through his hair. "Well, at least now we know who we're dealing with. I'll find out everything I can about him tonight."

Jess walked over to the wall of windows overlooking the early morning light of LoDo. Outside on the streets below, people bustled by, completely unaware of the predicament facing the two people seven stories above them.

She envied their ignorance.

"I don't know where to start, Ethan. If Mikael Kriskan is innocent—and I'm beginning to believe he is—I can't live with letting him die. But if I can tell my story, convince a judge, and get his conviction overturned, I can't live with turning him over to Russian mobsters either. There must be a way to save him without doing the rest of the world harm."

Ethan joined her. "Well, do you know where we can get some money? We need to seek out Dimitry's associates and gather intel, and, well, information is expensive."

CHAPTER 24

The next morning, Jess was on her way to meet her stepmother for brunch and a conversation about money when she saw the black Audi following her and flashing its lights. *David. Damn.* She felt a hint of electricity brush the fine hairs on the back of her neck and arms and realized it was no longer excitement to see him, but fear. After their last encounter, after his damaging words, she wanted to stay as far away from him as possible. The phone next to her buzzed, him calling, but she kept driving. She didn't think he would follow her all the way outside downtown Denver and the extra miles to Cherry Creek, but he did.

She swung into the open lot of the nearby mall, waited to see what he would do. Surely, he wouldn't do anything stupid, not in broad daylight. The last thing either of them needed was to be seen skulking around with one another when they were both under such a spotlight.

He pulled behind her and blocked her in.

She flung open the door of her SUV. "What the hell? What do you want?"

He raised his hands slightly. "Just to talk. Get in."

"I have an appointment. Move your car."

"It can wait. Get in."

Growling, she glanced around to make certain no one was watching and slid into the passenger seat. He backed up, pulling into an empty space away from the busy street. David appeared ready to try a new case, dressed in a navy suit and tie, his dark hair freshly trimmed and touched up with a spot of gel. His cologne permeated the interior of the car.

"Listen, I'm sorry about our last...encounter, but I needed to tell you something. I was approached by someone, a Russian, who knows about you and me, about us."

"Dimitry," she said. "Yes, I've had the pleasure."

An incredulous look crossed his face. "You know him?"

"I didn't. Not until yesterday. Ethan did some research and I saw a photo. He's Russian mafia, David. He's what they refer to as a thief-in-law. He's connected."

Just saying the words caused a chill to pass over her.

"Okay, tell me everything," David said.

Jess took a deep breath and told him of her encounter with the man, the crushing of her legs beneath the table, the threats to Ricky and herself. "He said the most horrible things about Ricky. Implied the things his colleagues would do with a boy like that. He didn't say what Kevin Ryland had told him but it was clear he knew something. And David, he insinuated that he'd killed Kevin Ryland and John Berman. I'm certain he's also the same man who messaged Ethan Stantz saying he would kill one jury member every week until Mikael Kriskan was set free."

David stared at her as if he couldn't believe the words coming from her mouth. As if she spoke in a foreign language his ears were unaccustomed to hearing. His face twisted into a variety of shapes as she explained Dimitry's demands.

He shook his head. "This can't be happening."

"But it is. It very much is. What did he say to you?"

"About the same, but not in so many words. He threatened to leak our involvement to the media. Said no one would believe the affair only started later, that it never influenced the case. And he's right. Of course, he's right."

"It would tear Tom apart."

"It would end my career."

She wanted to roll her eyes. David, as usual, was only interested in himself. She again wondered why in the hell she'd ever felt drawn to such a self-absorbed man. And yet, in the back of her mind, all she could hear was a voice say... *Takes one to know one.*

"This can't get out. It can't," he said, massaging the back of his neck.

"Can't you tip the police to Dimitry? Put them on his trail? Have them look for evidence of his involvement in Berman's and Ryland's deaths? He's a very dangerous man, David."

"I don't know. Maybe, but what good would it do? If they find and catch him, they might lock him up, but he made it clear to me the evidence he has, photographs of us together at the hotel, will still go to the media. Then what? We're finished anyway."

She felt sick. "He has actual photos? Did you see them?"

He seemed embarrassed. Nodded. "They're not good. He's got us going into the room together."

She studied him. "Okay, but we could say we were meeting to discuss the old case. I mean, don't you care about justice even a little? For Berman and Ryland? John Berman initiated that guilty verdict and Kevin Ryland gave you what you want—not that you offered him much of a choice. You owe him."

"He broke the law. He researched the case."

Jess felt her jaw drop. "*He* broke the law? You can really sit there and say that with a straight face? You should've gone to the judge and had us both removed and replaced with the alternates and you know it."

She poked him in his chest. "No, *you* broke the law. You used me and my addiction as leverage. You saw an opportunity, and instead of taking your chances with the alternates, you decided to get two firm votes of guilty. So, don't sit there and give me that self-righteous look."

He flashed her the same menacing glance as in the hotel room before turning away.

"I don't think you understand, Jess. If what I did to help you—provide you with an illegal substance, and admittedly, set up Kevin Ryland—got out, that wouldn't just mean overturning the Kriskan case. It could jeopardize every case that I've tried and won since. Countless murder cases, assaults, kidnappings. Not good, Jess. I've put away a whole lot of bad people, and all of them could get a new trial if the judge thinks I may have influenced other jurors, hell, even slept with other jurors, to win cases."

"Have you?"

He wheeled, a dark sneer on his face. "Very funny."

She shrugged. "How would I know? I know what you did to me. Why not others?"

"Because, like you, I regret what I did. You may not believe it, but I do. I was young and ambitious and I hated Mikael Kriskan for taking away such a gifted professor that had offered him a decent life, and I knew winning that case would break my career wide open. If it had resulted in a hung jury or mistrial, who knows what would've happened. I might have been stuck with crap cases the rest of my life. They don't give you big cases if you can't win them."

Jess shook her head, grunted. "Sorry, but you're right, I don't believe you. I don't think you feel bad about what you did at all. You made that pretty clear with the words you spoke to me the last time I saw you. I don't think you care one bit about what you did to Kevin Ryland or what now happens to me, or Ethan Stantz, or any other juror."

She glanced out the passenger window, watched two women leaving a nearby department store with oversized shopping bags. A sudden darkness overtook her, as if a cloud had blocked out the sun. She didn't know why. It's not like she ever believed David Foster had loved her, but at one time, she'd thought he would've at least protected her, cared if she was sick or in danger.

Now, she knew better.

She felt pity attempt to surface, forced it away. "Look, the only way I see to get out of this is to find new evidence of Kriskan's innocence and slip it to Kriskan's appeals attorney. Get Kriskan's conviction overturned and if your office wants to try him again, then that's your call. At least his fate won't rest on our backs. Dimitry can't come after us if Kriskan gets a new trial."

She turned toward the driver's seat. "Nick Whelan believes the only way to prevent Kriskan's execution now is if compelling new evidence comes to light. So, make some up if you have to, David. It's the only way."

His dark face whipped toward her, deep lines framing his forehead. "What? What did you say? You've spoken to the defense attorney about this?"

He grabbed both of Jess's arms and shook her like a rag doll. "What are you trying to do? Ruin me? Us? Maybe you don't care about your future and reputation, but I care very much about mine."

"Stop!" she yelled, a sudden terror once again swelling in her at David's hands.

"David, stop, or I'll start screaming." She writhed and slapped at his arms and face until he came to his senses. She curled away, already feeling the swelling—knew bruises would appear later that night. "You son-of-a-bitch. I should have you charged with assault."

She grabbed the door handle, flung open the car door.

He reached across the seat and gripped her arm to prevent her from leaving. "I swear to you, if you do anything to fuck up this case, I will…" He bit his bottom lip, punched the dash with his other hand.

"You'll what? How dare you threaten me, after all you've put me through. Don't you forget, I could ruin you. So, let me set you straight, you lay a hand on me again, or anyone I know, I will make sure everything that happened between us gets released to the media and personally handed to Nick Whelan."

He huffed. "Resorting to threats the same way as your friend Dimitry?"

"You want to bury me? You'd better be ready to dig your own grave first."

"There's no proof I sent that man to you. None. It will be your word against mine."

To his surprise, she shoved him back in his seat. "You really want to take that chance? Get on board, David. Find something to use to charge Dimitry Romanov with the murders of John Berman and Kevin Ryland and find a way to prove Mikael Kriskan is innocent so I don't have to come forward with my story."

"Jess, I can't. Because he's not."

"Find a way, David," she yelled. "Find a way, or I will."

She slid from the car and started to slam the door when she poked her face back into the car one last time. "Oh, and this? Us? This is done."

CHAPTER 25

Still shaking from her confrontation with David, Jess rubbed her sore arms and walked across the street to the restaurant where her stepmother was waiting. Barbara had agreed to meet her at this particular location, claiming it was close to an appointment later in the day, but Jess knew the restaurant was one of her favorites, a place where her friends and acquaintances frequented and the staff knew her well. Jess was well aware of why Barbara had really selected the place, knowing if the two of them got into an argument, there would be plenty of people on hand to rescue her, poor Barbara, from the evils of the selfish stepchild. The tactics weren't lost on Jess. Her stepmother always had to surround herself with an army of allies and money, a barrier between herself and reality.

It was warm for a midwinter day, the sun shining brightly and melting what remained of the last snow. The sidewalks and streets were dirty with the remains of sand and salt, the cars buzzing by still coated with the thin white residue of the same. The local boutiques and restaurants she passed were decorated with posters advertising upcoming Valentine's Day and restaurant-week promotions, the last thing on Jess' mind.

When Jess entered, the hostess recognized her and led her to a table near the front window. As soon as Barbara saw her, she waved and smiled, a large, fake, overdone stretch to ensure that everyone would see how pleasant and accommodating she was to her dead husband's child. The light silver-blue sweater and platinum necklace and earrings she wore matched the January landscape—Barbara always dressed with the seasons in mind.

She and Jess exchanged a hug and a Hollywood kiss before she sat. Outside on the street, afternoon shoppers drifted by, all thin, all attractive, most wearing sunglasses and toting handbags that cost more than the monthly rent.

As soon as Jess removed her own glasses, Barbara puckered her lips, turned serious. "Jess, hon, have you been crying? Your eyes are puffy."

Jess sighed. She'd hoped the extra makeup she'd applied directly on the top and under her eyes after leaving David would've done the trick, but apparently it wasn't enough. "Just not getting enough sleep these days. Between Ricky's issues and recent news, I just can't shut down my brain at night."

Barbara cocked her head. "News? What news?"

Jess momentarily thought about telling her about the developments in her former case, but it wasn't worth the effort. Jess knew she'd just view it as Jess whining about yet another issue that didn't really matter. Plus, she needn't remind her of the case on the outside chance Barbara spoke with Tom. "It's nothing, never mind."

Barbara motioned for the waiter to pour Jess some wine. Her stepmother's glass looked like it had already been refilled at least once. "You should try melatonin, dear. Knocks me right out."

Jess cast a fake smile. *Yes, that's all it would take. Melatonin. And maybe not having a Russian mobster threatening to kill me and my family.*

"Well, maybe this will make your day better," Barbara said. She held up a little blue bag with an arched handle. "A little something for you from Hermès. I know how you like their bracelets."

Jess opened the bag to see a four-inch blue box. Inside was a shiny silver bracelet dangling with plaid Scottie dogs. Tactic number two. Get the girl a gift to make it harder for her to be unpleasant. And damn it, it was cute.

Jess smiled. "Thank you. It's adorable." She sighed. "I do miss my baby." Jess's mother had owned two Scottish terriers, and her father had bought Jess a pup shortly after her mother died, hoping it would provide comfort. Jess had named her Lucy and the dog had become her best friend. Jess lost her during her freshmen year in college.

"You should think about getting another one."

"I don't know. I'm not sure how Ricky would do with dogs."

Barbara frowned, straightened the napkin in her lap. "How is the boy doing?" she asked, seeming genuinely concerned—except for the lack of using his name, of course. Jess had never understood why her stepmother had insisted on referring to Ricky as "the boy" and not mentioning his name, as if he were some object instead of a human being. It was even more annoying than Barbara's insistence on continuing to call her *Jessie*, although Jess had asked her time and again to call her *Jess*. It felt like she did it purposely, as a way to continue treating her like a child.

"Well, that's partly what I wanted to speak with you about. Ricky has been having these seizures. They're very frightening."

Barbara placed a hand on her chest. "Seizures? My goodness, you never mentioned that before. That's terrible, honey. Is he okay?"

"He seems to be, but he's fatigued for days afterward. They really take a toll on him. And the doctors don't know what's causing them. They want to run more tests, but..."

She swished the wine in her glass, hating that she had to play this part. "The tests are very expensive, and Tom's insurance won't cover them. They said they're experimental, so they consider it alternative therapy."

Jess shook her head, disgusted. She glanced up and saw Barbara's twisted lips, the slight wrinkle to the left of her nose. The woman knew what was coming.

Jess sighed. "Barbara, you know I hate to ask. I do. I wish Tom and I made more money. I wish the insurance companies weren't assholes. And yes, I wish I had done a better job of spending my inheritance wisely. But Ricky's medical bills have far surpassed anything I expected. I'm two months behind paying for his school as is, and he needs to at least finish out the term. You know I wouldn't ask if it were not for Ricky. He's Dad's only grandson."

"Jess, hon, he needs the special school. They have the right teachers, the right tools. What will you do after the term is up? You can't place him in public school."

Jess shrugged. "I know, I do, but I may not have a choice. The reality is, I have to go to work to keep him there, but so far, I haven't found a job that pays enough to cover the school and someone to watch Ricky until I get home. It's a losing battle. Tom says he is willing to look at other job offers once his current case is done, but right now..."

Right now, I need to keep Ricky and Tom alive, and that means paying a bunch of sleazy Russian mobsters for information. So please, won't you help?

"Right now, you're all I've got," Jess said.

She glanced out at the affluent shoppers again, brushed her hair back from her face. "You know, I used to listen to people argue about health care and how expensive it is, and I used to think, why don't they just get insurance?"

She looked at her stepmother, laughed. "What an idiot. I had no idea of what the real world was like. None of us do."

Barbara played with her platinum necklace, perhaps feeling suddenly aware of her wealth, Jess's reference hitting a little too close to home. "Oh, Jess, this is so dark of you. You're so down. Your father would never have wanted this life for you. Living paycheck to paycheck." She swilled a large gulp of wine. "He had such high hopes for you." She sighed. "So did I."

Yeah, Jess could see how much it was tearing her up. She'd always suspected Barbara secretly delighted in her screwups so she could turn to her father and issue a little *I told you so.* "I don't know what else you expect me to say. I can't pull sunshine out of my ass."

Barbara snapped. "Don't talk like that. We're in a public place. Have some manners." She sighed and grabbed her pocketbook, making a show of it. A not-so-subtle gesture, as if she were proving to all her nearby friends the truth of what she'd told them to expect—the girl would ask for money again, just wait.

She clicked a pen. "How much this time?"

Jess cringed at the emphasis she placed on "this time," as if Jess made begging for money a daily habit. She bit her tongue, trying to keep her fury at bay. "Ten thousand."

Barbara rolled her eyes. "Goodness gracious."

It was always like this between them, a subtle shifting of politeness laced with undertones of bitterness. Shades of Barbara feeling slighted by the time Jess's father had spent fussing over Jess rather than herself and her own daughter, Andrea. Feeling insulted by the interruptions in time, travel, and finances inherent when one had children from a previous marriage. Jess, on the other hand, feeling like Barbara was an outsider who was stepping in to steal away her father's time and affection, resenting the woman for replacing her mother, illogically blaming her for her mother's death. They rarely had a conversation where there wasn't the ghost of her father sitting between them.

Barbara's frown was the deepest Jess had ever seen. It even looked real. "I know it's a lot of money, but think of it this way, you'll be that much closer to being done with your obligation to me. Once the trust is gone, it's gone."

She slammed her purse on the seat. "That is not how I see you. Why do you insist on fighting me? I promised your father I would look out for you, just as he did, and I'm trying, Jessie, I'm really trying." Her eyelids fluttered as she patted her neck, as if her blood pressure had risen.

"I'm sorry, Barbara. I'm clearly just under a great deal of stress."

Barbara killed off the remaining wine in her glass. "I know you don't think so, but I understand stress. I'm not immune, you know. Since your father passed, I have to take care of everything. These house repairs, always something you know, a pipe or the furnace, or new flooring. And these finances, well, I have Walter to help, but your father was involved in some most confusing business investments."

Jess nodded. Walter had been her father's financial advisor for thirty years. Jess was pretty sure she'd rather be dealing with the likes of such first-world problems rather than what she was going through, under threat of death or time in prison for juror misconduct, but she refrained from commenting. "I'm sorry you've had to deal with so much," she said.

Barbara handed her the check. "Now, can we just have a nice lunch?"

CHAPTER 26

Money, check. Now, for the next hurdle. How to find Dimitry Romanov and locate his associates? How does one stalk a man who's stalking you? This seemed a losing exercise. Even now, as Jess was thinking of how to follow him, he was likely lurking nearby, watching her from someplace down the street. She walked the few blocks back to her car, considering her options.

She could hire a private investigator but guessed that would be expensive. She could place a GPS device on his car but she wasn't even sure the man had a car. At times, she wasn't even sure he was a real man. He seemed more like a ghost, appearing from the shadows whenever he wished.

Outside the mall, on the street corner facing busy traffic, she noticed a panhandler asking for money among stopped cars. She felt her eyes narrow, got a lightbulb of an idea. Maybe she couldn't afford a PI, but she might be able to hire someone else. Someone who could blend in various places, someone not affiliated with any of the jurors or attorneys in the case.

And she thought she might know just the man for the job.

She drove back downtown, fighting the glaring winter sun sparkling through the bare trees that lined both sides of the road. Runners and cyclists occupied the bike paths that ran along the creek bed, enjoying the warmer day. Once back in LoDo, she parked the car, got out, and glanced around for any sign of being followed before heading out.

As she approached the café, she took out a five-dollar bill and a scrap piece of paper, scribbled on the back. In case Dimitry was watching, he would only assume she was giving the man money, nothing out of the ordinary. When she reached the corner, she could see him—the army vet—dressed in a dull-green T-shirt and brown jacket, his sign perched in front of his legs as he sat on the bottom step of the venue next door. Unlike other downtown businesses, the place had never ushered him away or complained to the police.

He flinched as she bent down to greet him, as if she might strike him or say something rude or mean. He was probably used to such things. Instead, she handed the man the money. He took it and started to say, "Thank you," when he saw the note attached and read.

She slowly glanced up at her. It was the first time she'd ever met the man's eyes. They were green, with flecks of brown, like her own. "Thirty minutes?" she said.

A subtle nod.

She stopped in the café for an iced coffee, then headed back the other direction. At the small, dark diner, two blocks away, she slipped in through the back door—just in case Dimitry was watching—and waited. Sure enough, he arrived on time.

He approached the table with great hesitancy, as if she were setting a trap. Parked his backpack on an extra chair, looked at her with immense distrust. Jess introduced herself, asked his name. "Brett."

"Hi, Brett. Good to meet you. You're probably wondering why I asked you here today."

"The note said you have a job?" His voice was deep, a baritone.

Jess nodded. "I do, yes." She looked at the nearby waiter, motioned him over. "Do you want something to eat? Please, get whatever you want."

He didn't even look at the menu. Just asked for a bacon cheeseburger, fries. Extra pickles. "What do I have to do?" he asked.

"Like, PI work, surveillance. You can do that, right?"

"I'm a veteran, ma'am, I can do a lot of things."

She paused at that, felt like an ass. Just because he was homeless didn't make him stupid. Of course, he could do things. He'd likely seen and done things the likes of which Jess couldn't fathom. Every time she watched a war movie, she wondered how men and women could put themselves in harm's way so willingly, contemplated the mind-set it must require. To be so selfless, then come back to a country full of people who only cared about themselves. It had to be hard. She couldn't imagine how hard.

"Brett? Why are you homeless? Don't you have friends, family?"

He glanced at his hands, picked a nail. Jess noted they were surprisingly clean but heavily scarred. "In Texas, yes. But...I made a mess of things when I came back. Angry, you know, at the world. At the government. At the people. I can't, I don't...fit in."

She took a deep breath. "What about other vets? They must understand. Can't you get help there?"

He nodded. "Some, yeah. That's where I get most of my meals and an occasional cot, but they always want me to talk about it, and I'm not ready."

When his cheeseburger arrived, he looked reluctant to dive in, although she could practically see the drool on his lips. "No, please, I've already eaten. Dig in. Enjoy."

He bit into the meat, chomped, gave a thumbs-up to the waiter. The waiter, an elderly Asian man with cloudy eyes, returned the gesture before returning to mop up tables with a dishrag. "So, what about this job?"

"Before I begin, I'm going to tell you a story, and if you repeat this to anyone, I'll deny everything. Plus, they'll think you're crazy anyway, because it's, well...pretty crazy." For the next forty minutes, she told him about the trial, about John Berman's and Kevin Ryland's deaths, about Mikael Kriskan and Dimitry Romanov. Then, as a side dish, she told him of her affair with the prosecuting attorney and the fact that she used to be a heroin addict. By the end, she wasn't certain if she'd hired him to do PI work or become her therapist.

Using a napkin, he cleaned off his fingers one at a time. To her surprise, he chuckled, his eyes twinkling. "Damn, and I thought I had problems."

Jess smiled, laughed along with him. It actually felt good, to shake her head and slap her forehead and realize how ridiculous it all sounded. But she had to admit, telling someone of it, all of it, brought relief. "Oh my God, I can't believe I just told a total stranger my life story."

She sat back in the chair in the dark little space, examined the man across from her. "We never know what's really going on with someone, do we? Never really know what their true story is, their hardships and struggles."

He shook his head. "No, we don't. And truth is, most people don't want to know." The waiter removed the empty plate from Brett's side of the table, asked if he'd saved room for pie. "Chocolate?" he asked.

"I'll have one too," Jess said.

"Okay, so tell me about the benefits of this job. Is there pay involved?"

"Cash, and a hotel room for as long as you need."

"I'm in."

Over dessert, they plotted their course of action.

CHAPTER 27

Dimitry Romanov sat in the LoDo cigar lounge, smoking a hand-rolled Dominican blend and drinking whiskey. He saw Nikov Petrovsky the moment he walked in the joint, striding in like a pimp at a whorehouse. He wore a long wool coat and red scarf and had his blond shoulder length hair smoothed back with a touch of grease. "Well, well, look at what the cat dragged in."

Nikov smirked, tugged at his gloves one finger at a time. "Mr. Romanov, most good to see you too. What brings you to this particular part of the world?"

Dimitry exhaled a thick line of smoke. "Looking after your father's interests, as usual."

Without being invited, Nikov pulled up a chair to the side of Dimitry, took off his coat and scarf. "Then I should thank you, as my father's interests are my interests."

He motioned for the server as he sat. The woman who came over, a brunette with full lips and big tits, stared at Nikov as if he were a delicious steak or fine wine she'd like to devour. Nikov returned her interest with a full-body examination and a wink. He took out a hundred-dollar bill. "Take care of me?"

She giggled, charmed by his thick accent. Brushed the tips of her fingers across his as she took the money. "Most definitely."

Nikov admired her wriggle as she returned to the bar.

Dimitry studied Nikolai's son, a man nearing forty with dark gray eyes. The man's pupils were not unlike his own, thin and distant, revealing a numbness to pain and an impassiveness to suffering. Maybe they had that, and a few other things, in common, but Dimitry did not like Nikov Petrovsky. He was nothing like his father, a hard, calculating man who demanded loyalty and respect yet knew how to return it as well. Nikov was impulsive and reckless, and often took risks that put himself and others in danger simply because it suited him. His main work consisted of trading stolen art and antiques, brokering between sellers and buyers, but Dimitry knew the man's best talent was spending his father's money. A playboy who spent more time skiing, driving race cars, and whoring around than pursuing any gain for father or country. Dimitry often questioned Nikolai of his unmovable trust in his son, as many of Nikov's friends were the sons or cousins of his father's enemies, and of the Twelve, but Nikolai would dismiss it with a wave of his hand. Yet, Dimitry knew—Nikov Petrovsky was a man who would kill his own father in his sleep if it meant more money in his pocket.

"You came to see your brother?" Dimitry asked.

A crooked smile. "Ah yes, my brother, the killer. He with screw loose." He tapped his temple. "Prone to such acts of rage. Such violence." He growled like a rabid dog.

"You came to help?"

"What? Is there something I can do? Somebody's legs I can break?" He settled in the broad, leather chair with gold studs, rested his arms on each side like it was a king's throne. The sultry brunette returned with a fresh cigar and a glass of whiskey. Nikov sniffed it and studied the fine roll of the wrap before the brunette bent over to light it, allowing Nikov a proper view of her cleavage.

Nikov took several puffs, continuing to stare down the woman's shirt. "Very nice."

She blew out the match like she was blowing him a kiss. Nikov returned the gesture before turning back to Dimitry. "Tell me, old friend," Nikov said. "Why is my father so interested in my brother's return? When he is nothing but traitor to our country?"

Dimitry exhaled a long, loose trail of smoke. "He is not a traitor. You know your father had no choice in the matter. The woman had to leave, along with your brother. Lenova would have it no other way."

"As it should be. Why does he care so much about a bastard child?"

"Because it is his bastard. And the boy is a genius. He can make your father a very wealthy man. You should remember that, given your...interests."

"My father is already a wealthy man. And I don't care to share my inheritance with a crazy bastard. What is it they say, a thin line between insanity and genius."

Nikov downed the whiskey, motioned for another. Wiped his hand across cracked lips. "In American Bible, there is story about prodigal son, no? He spends all his inheritance on wasteful things while the other son remains home, faithful to his father's wishes. But the first son shows up, and his father wants to throw elaborate party, welcome his son home. Return to father's favor while other son is dismissed." His eyes grew dark. "Well, not in my world, old friend, not in my world."

Dimitry felt a heat burn across his chest. He wanted to reach across and strangle the little punk, teach him a lesson in respect. He peered at the spider tattoo on the back of Nikov's hand, that with four heads along with the words—honor, respect, loyalty, family. How could he burn such a message upon his skin when he knew nothing of the words' meaning? He had taken the nickname Spider because that's how he liked to think of himself. To bring his victims to his lair, trap them, then race in to kill and devour as he wished. "So, you are jealous, is that it?"

"No, just...the man is not my blood, not to me."

The burning grew. "You jackass. Mikael is your brother. A genius that can bring many good things to Russians. Build things of great power. What is it you do, Mr. Nikov? Put on art display? Trade some Russian dolls."

Nikov's eyes flashed a deep hatred. "You'd better be careful there, Dims."

Dimitry leaned toward him, challenging him. "What will you do? Hmmm?"

"I still have my father's ear."

"You fool him, but not me. He sent you here to help free your brother but if you are not here to help, stay out of my way. If you are here to help, then do something other than play with your cock."

He and Nikov locked eyes for several moments before Nikov broke it, chuckled. "Mr. Romanov, always playing hero, aren't you?" He blew smoke to the ceiling, watched it drift in hazy circles. "So, what do you know? How do you attempt to help, to get my brother free?"

Dimitry sat back, drank. "Things are in motion," he said, offering no details.

Nikov leaned toward Dimitry. "I hear the foreman of the jury met an untimely demise. And then another juror hung himself from his loft. Most unfortunate." Nikov said, his eyes again flashing.

Dimitry scanned the room, checking out the crowd, ensuring no one was overhearing this little bastard who didn't know better than to speak of such things in public. Most were young men, in their twenties or thirties, like Nikov, with crisp clothes and bearded faces, all huddled around mahogany tables discussing the world's issues. Near the fireplace, a man in a camouflage T-shirt and jeans briefly met his eyes before returning his attention to his own cigar. The man's jaw was slightly off-center and the muscles in his neck were thick, like that of boxer. For some reason, Dimitry took a liking to the man. He was built like a fighter and had scars, and a man with scars was usually a man who'd earned them.

"Yes," Dimitry said, "most troubling. Guilt is a weak man's nicotine."

Nikov grunted. "And what of this other juror, the blogger? He's trying to get my brother a new trial, a stay of execution. He now believes my brother might be innocent. All your doing?"

Dimitry shrugged. "It is good for the cause."

Nikov cracked his knuckles, glanced back at the bar where the waitress with the big tits was now flirting with another guest. "Tell me, old friend, do you think my brother killed his parents?"

"Doesn't matter what I think. Nikolai wants him free. It is my job to get him free."

Nikov nodded. He stood and placed a hand on Dimitry's shoulder, leaned over to speak near his ear. "Good luck. I think you are going to need it." He tugged at the cuffs of his sleeves.

"Where are you going?" Dimitry asked.

Nikov nodded toward the bar and winked. "I'm going to go play with my cock, as you suggested. See you around, old friend."

CHAPTER 28

Jess, Ethan, and Brett met at Ethan's loft, all entering the building at different times so they wouldn't be seen together. They huddled around the kitchen island, each with a beer in hand. Jess listened anxiously as Brett brought her and Ethan up to date.

After following Jess for a couple of days, Brett had picked up on Dimitry, and had since been his constant shadow. Dimitry had given him a good once-over in the cigar bar but Brett didn't think the man suspected he had a tail of his own. He now knew Dimitry was staying in a private residence near Governor's Park and drove a black Ford pickup. He socialized very little, preferring to stay in the shadows. Without a car of his own, Brett had been unable to follow him during times he left downtown, but they all suspected he was keeping an eye on the other jurors.

"It's been more than a week now, so he may be looking to keep his promise," Ethan said. "Seeking to make another statement by killing another juror."

"Hasn't everyone gone into hiding by now? I mean, except us?" Jess asked.

Ethan shook his head. "Not Gerald Fowler. He's willing to take his chances. Not Saku or Fred either. They have businesses to run. And Libby Allen, well, she's just too stubborn."

"We need to get you a car," Jess said, looking at Brett. "I'll line one up today."

"Get one with tinted windows," Brett said. He continued to tell them what else he'd learned about the man, how he mainly stuck to dark places, dive restaurants and bars, had a penchant for cigars.

"The most interesting person he met up with was at a cigar bar here in LoDo. Looked like a real player. Your guy clearly knew the man, but I got a sense he didn't like him very much."

He scrolled through the phone Jess had purchased for him. "The pictures aren't the best, because I couldn't make it obvious that I was taking photos, but I think you could find him by the tattoo. See it there? It's a spider, a four-headed spider. Above each knuckle is a different head."

Brett enlarged the photo until only the hand filled the screen. Jess and Ethan looked over his shoulders.

"Honor. Respect. Loyalty. Family." Ethan read and glanced up. "Shit, I know who that is. That is Nikov Petrovsky, Mikael's half-brother. He goes by the nickname Spider."

Jess stood back. She felt her heart tumble. "Half-brother? Great, now we've got two thugs to deal with?"

"It appears so," Ethan said. He shook his head. "From all accounts I've read about him, he's one temperamental son-of-a-bitch too. In Russia, he was suspected in the murder of a man just because the guy spilled a drink on him at a bar. He's also mentioned on the FBI's watch list."

"What for?" Brett said.

"Ties to the Russian mob operating here in the States, like the others, but as for specifics, I don't know. I'll do some research, see what other details I can find out."

"I could tell he was a hothead," Brett said. "At one point, I thought he and Dimitry were going to get into a fight. Their conversation got heated. Had a little stare down before Nikov backed off."

Brett took a long pull on the beer. "As a side note, Nikov is a real ladies' man. Since Dimitry headed back to his rented condo after the cigar bar, I decided to double-back and follow Nikov to his hotel. He was met at the door to his room by two women. One redhead, one brunette."

He swiped through more photos, showed them a picture. "Could be prostitutes, but they're also possibly girlfriends. Both of these girls have full-time bodyguards. A couple of beefed-up Russians who are clearly associates of his."

Ethan took a gander. "Damn, those are some burly dudes."

Jess glanced at the women, instantly felt sorry for them. "Poor girls. Probably his sex slaves. Can't leave without permission. That, or he hired them to be his girlfriends while he's in town, maybe from one of those pricey escort services."

She did a double-take at the redhead, sensed a familiarity. *Probably nothing.*

"I did a story on one of those services while I was at *Westword*," Ethan said. "Police busted it up after a five-year investigation. They ran into a whole lot of resistance trying to get arrests. And no wonder, the client list apparently contained some of Denver's most notable and wealthiest judges, police officers, athletes, and politicians. Come to find out, the woman running the whole thing was a suburban housewife with four kids. Still to this day, the list hasn't been released."

"Sounds like a cover-up," Jess said.

"Wouldn't surprise me in the least if he hired them," Brett said. "He's a piece of work. Before he left the bar last night, he banged the waitress in the bathroom."

Jess groaned. "Classy. Sounds like we need to keep track of him, though. I mean, what the hell is he doing here? Is he here to help Dimitry? Now we have to watch out for him too?"

"I'm on it," Brett said.

Jess examined him. It seemed hard to believe that the guy standing in front of her was the same man she'd avoided previously on numerous occasions outside the café. This guy who spoke in a baritone, humbled by two tours in Iraq and one in Afghanistan, whose intelligence was beyond his years. Who used to sit out on the sidewalk on a cold, blustery day holding a sign and begging for money.

But no more. Ethan had already taken such a liking to Brett that he'd offered his guest bedroom to him as a place to stay as long as needed.

"You know," Brett said, "I was thinking. Dimitry keeps physical tabs on you both, but what are the chances he's listening too? It might be worth me getting my hands on some equipment and sweep this place just to make sure. Your house too, Jess."

Jess raised an eyebrow. She hadn't even considered that Dimitry could've come to her house, let alone inside it. The thought instantly instilled terror, especially for Ricky. The three of them glanced around the apartment, as if the whole place might be bugged.

"Out of curiosity, have you seen any evidence that Dimitry is keeping tabs on David Foster too?" Jess asked.

Brett shook his head. "I haven't seen an encounter between them. Dimitry is very careful about who he approaches. As opposed to Nikov, who seems not to give a shit. In fact, he seems to seek out confrontation. He knows quite a few people in the area. In particular, at the Diamond Cabaret. I followed him there last night and it was almost like he was a regular. Flashing money and luring the girls. He and another man there also nearly got into a fight. He also seemed to know Nikov and disliked him immensely."

Ethan finished off his beer. "Did you get a picture?"

"No, too dark inside the club not to use a flash. But he also appeared to be Russian and had a whole army of friends with him."

Ethan walked to the kitchen, grabbed three new beers out of the refrigerator, twisted off the caps. "Hmmm. The enemy of my enemy is my friend. That may be where we need to start."

Brett appeared to think it over, nodded. "Good idea. Ballsy, but good."

"Wait," Jess said. "The enemy of my enemy?"

"If I'm your enemy and Brett is your enemy, then that makes Brett and I allies. We get together to help each other defeat you."

Jess sipped. "Right. Warfare and battles and all that. So, what? We're going to just walk up to some Russian guy and introduce ourselves and expect him to trust us and us him?"

She watched the two men drink, study each other, subtly nod their heads. "Yeah, I think that's exactly what we're going to do," Ethan said. "Want to be my sleazy, hot date to a strip joint, Jess Dawson?"

Brett frowned. "How come she gets to be your date? What about me?"

Ethan rubbed his beard. "Come to think of it, you would look good in a thong."

Suddenly, they got lost in the moment and started laughing. Who would have thought a few weeks ago that a woman sleeping with the DA, a blogger from the city, and a homeless vet would be hanging out enjoying a beer and plotting against Russian mobsters?

Jess made a resolution that this time together wouldn't be their last. If they made it through this, she owed it to them both. For Ethan's forgiveness and Brett's trust.

For the next hour, the three forgot about their troubles and relaxed. Because they all knew that around the next corner awaited a fight, maybe even a war.

CHAPTER 29

Two nights later, Brett called Jess from a club downtown. In the background, a DJ was screaming over a pulsing beat. Brett had to shout over the music. "Our frenemy is here. Can you come? Ethan is on his way."

Jess glanced back from the bathroom at Tom, half asleep in bed, his book hanging at a weird angle. It was already late for them, eleven p.m. They'd tucked Ricky in more than two hours ago. Just a few nights before, Tom had questioned her extra hours away from the house during the past several days, and he hadn't seemed happy about it. What possible excuse could she make to leave now, at such an hour?

My stepmother is the emergency room? No, he would eventually speak with her and discover it wasn't true. *A friend was arrested and needed bail?* No, he could check on that too. Maybe she could just tell the truth. *Sorry, dear, but I have a date with a Russian mobster.*

How had her life become so ridiculous?

"I'll see what I can do," she whispered and hung up. She thought again. The only friend that would cover for her would be Catelyn. She owed her a couple favors anyway.

She went to Tom, shook him awake. "Hon? Hey, sorry to wake you."

He moaned and shut the book, placed it on the nightstand. "What's wrong? Is it Ricky?"

"No, it's Cate. She called me, crying, upset. I couldn't understand a word she said. I think I need to go over there, see what's going on."

She was already out of her bathrobe and sliding into jeans before he could object. She layered a couple of camisoles and overlaid them with a sweater. Slid into boots but grabbed a pair of low heels and hid them under her arm. She could remove the sweater and the boots later in the car. It wouldn't be the best of club outfits but it would have to do.

"Cate? That girl's a load of trouble. No telling what's she got herself into," Tom mumbled. He rolled over and turned out the light. "Good luck."

Jess glanced at herself in the mirror, raised an eyebrow. *Not as much trouble as your wife, I can guarantee that.*

Downstairs, she grabbed her purse and keys, texted Brett from the car. "B there in 20." As she drove, she texted Cate to cover, got a reply. "No Prob."

Outside the club, she applied her makeup, changed into the heels and removed the sweater, tousled her hair. She ran to the entry, thankful there wasn't a line outside waiting to get in. The bouncer didn't bother with checking her ID, just waved her in. It had been a few years now since anyone had bothered to check.

Inside, the bass pulsed with bright flashes of color—*boom, boom, boom.* From a nearby corner, Ethan appeared and took her arm. She could barely hear a word he said. "Follow me," he yelled.

Holding on to the waist of his jeans, the two began to move through a pack of scantily clad bodies writhing on the dance floor. The music was pumping so loud, the vibration passed through the floor to her feet. Jess squinted as the lights rotated and flashed while she wound through women and men in shades of red, blue, and green, all staring at her as if she were an exotic drug. A few purposefully squeezed against her, a reminder that things hadn't changed much in the years since she'd frequented such places.

When they reached the other side of the club, free of the bodies, she brushed herself off, straightened her clothes. "That wasn't a good time. I think I was sexually assaulted."

"Sorry," Ethan said, "but the guy we want to talk to is at a table in back surrounded by his friends."

"Don't you mean *comrades?*" Jess said. She glanced over her shoulder at the man sitting in the middle of a corner booth, two women on each side of him. To the side stood three other men, two who appeared to be acting as his guards, the other busy flirting with yet another woman. The man in the booth wore a black turtleneck and expensive shoes and watch and hid his eyes behind slightly tinted spectacles. "He doesn't look like a man you can just approach."

"No. Let's get a table nearby."

They found a string of empty tables near the back wall not too far from the bodyguards. Jess sat so she could see the corner and the man they wanted to speak with. A cocktail waitress approached, and they ordered a couple of drinks. "Where's Brett?"

"At the bar. It's better he's not seen with us."

"So, what's the plan?"

"Did you bring the money?"

Jess nodded, waving her clutch.

"Pull out a hundred and set it on the table. Let's get the guard's attention."

Jess did as he instructed, tucking the bill under a glass so half would dangle off the edge. It blew in the breeze from the vent above, waving at the guard like a flag. Ethan checked out the two men, saw them whisper to one another. He let a little time lapse before he subtly nodded toward them. Jess held her breath as one of the beefy men approached.

He was six-foot-five and weighed at least three-hundred pounds. He leaned on the table with his hand over the hundred. "You need something?"

"We would like to have a word with your associate."

"Concerning?"

"Nikov Petrovsky and his...family."

The man's dark eyes deepened into slits. He scooped up the hundred and returned to the other guard. They exchanged words before the other guard, slightly smaller but thick through the neck and shoulders, approached the man at the table. Jess watched as the guard whispered in the man's ear, pointed over his shoulder at her and Ethan. The man leaned forward to see around his friend, squinted at them for a minute before giving a single nod. The guard motioned them over after he dismissed the girls seated at the table.

"Here we go," Ethan said.

As they took a seat at the man's table, Jess's nerves fired like bands of twisted electric wire. She tried hard to appear cool, all the while trying not to throw up. Even behind the spectacles, his glare was ice. He never took his eyes off her.

"You are friends of Nikov's?" His accent was thick, like half his tongue was glued to the inside of his mouth. He emphasized the word "friends" as if he might kill them if they said yes. The rotating white lights from the dance floor splashed across his face.

Ethan quickly responded. "No, no, definitely not," he said. "No friend of ours." Ethan introduced himself, then Jess. They did not shake hands.

The man grunted. "That is for best. He is not good man."

"Then, you do know him, yes? His...family? Mr...."

The man hesitated. He didn't seem like a man who would readily share information about himself, but he must've decided they were harmless. "Volkov. Alexai Volkov. And yes, I'm familiar with Nikov Petrovsky. He killed my father. Someday, I hope to return the favor." He tipped back his drink, finished off the amber liquid. "But you didn't hear it from me."

Jess and Ethan exchanged a glance.

What the hell were they getting themselves into?

"What do you want with such a vile man?" Alexai asked.

"Right now, information. Nikov and one of his father's associates, Dimitry Romanov, are both in town, and have threatened us if we...don't do certain things for them."

His brow furrowed. "Romanov? He is here as well?" He seemed to chew on that. "That could explain some things. Tell me, what is it they're demanding?"

"Do you know of Mikael Kriskan?" Ethan asked.

The man removed a small metal case from his pocket, took out a toothpick, began to clean his teeth. Jess took note of a single gold tooth. "Yes. I met him few times as a child. My parents knew his father and mother. They were good people."

Jess and Ethan again shared a glance. *Getting more interesting by the moment.*

"Are you aware of his relationship to Nikov Petrovsky?" Ethan asked.

Alexai spat in his empty glass. "I am. It is well known in our community, but not to be spoken of—but you, how would you know such a thing? And why?"

Ethan cleared his throat. "Let's just say, we have a vested interest," he said. "We know Dimitry is here because he is intent on getting Mikael Kriskan set free. Even though he killed his adoptive family, and possibly his younger sister, his father wants him returned to Russia."

"No, Mikael no kill his family," Alexai shot back. "You are wrong." He pointed a finger at Ethan. "Let me tell you something. Mikael was a good son, a good friend. He loved his family. He was loyal. If I knew who committed this heinous act against his family, I would kill them myself."

He pounded the table with his fist, sending the glasses jumping.

Jess flinched. Once again, like so many others who'd grown up in the community with Mikael and his parents, he defended Kriskan and vouched for his innocence. What, Jess wondered, did they all know that the defense had missed during the trial?

"Do you believe he killed his family?" Alexai asked, moving forward like he was ready to take them out. From the corner, Jess saw the three-hundred-pound guard take note of his boss's action.

Jess held up a hand to the side of beef heading their way. "No," she said. "We don't think Mikael killed his family. Maybe once upon a time, but not now. See, we also believe in his innocence. And initially, we thought Mikael would be happy to hear that his father and brother were here trying to get his conviction overturned, so he could return home to Russia. But..."

"What?" Alexai asked.

"Mikael would rather die than return to Russia. He wants nothing to do with them."

Alexai considered her words. He removed his spectacles, revealing a deep scar under the left eye. "Yes, well, that is understandable. Mikael is brave man."

"He's afraid his father's associates will make him build bombs," Jess said.

"Yes?" Alexai turned to the nearby server, waved the empty drink in his hand. The woman dashed for the bar. "He is probably right. They would have him make killing machines. Robots and drone assassins."

Jess felt her eyes widen. "You know this? This is certain?"

"Among other things."

The waitress was back with not one but two drinks. He tipped her and waved her away. "See, many in Russia believe a new kind of war is coming. One that involves more machines than humans. They need to keep up with American technology. Many in my home country, they are working hard to distract you Americans, and they are doing a good job. They create propaganda to divide you, so you turn on each other like rabid dogs. Instead of embracing your likeness, you divide based on your differences—the color of your skin, religion, politics. In time, you will be so busy killing each other you won't see the true enemy when she comes for you. That's how Russia wants it too, believe me."

Jess stared at the man. Though the club was near melting with all the bodies inside, a cold chill crawled along her back and arms. Given the current political state, he couldn't have uttered truer words. "So, you understand why we can't let that happen. Can't hand him over to his father."

"You would rather let an innocent man die?"

"No, that's why we're here, Mr. Volkov. That's where you come into the picture," Ethan said. "We want to help Mikael, but we can't do that with Dimitry and Nikov planning to intercept him once he is released."

Alexai took a drink. "So, you are asking me to kill them?"

Ethan recoiled. "No, no, God no, that's not what I meant," he said, chuckling nervously under his breath. "Just information. Something we can use as leverage against them, maybe proof of illegal activity they're involved in, evidence we can take to authorities here to get them arrested or make them leave the country."

Alexai seemed to think that over. He studied them, drank more.

"Even if you could do such a thing—get them out of the picture," he said, passing a hand in front of them. "What superpowers do the likes of the two of you have to free Mikael Kriskan? Why do Dimitry and Nikov threaten you anyway?"

Ethan sighed. "Dimitry has threatened to kill a juror on the case every week until Kriskan goes free. We think he's killed two already, including the foreman and one other juror. It could be any day now that he goes for another," Ethan said. "We can't let that happen."

Alexai Volkov rolled the ice cubes around his glass, took a long swill. He still seemed to be sizing them up. Just the vapors from the amber liquid damn near made Jess pass out. "Why should I trust you?"

"Because..." Jess said. "We're two of the jurors. If we don't get Mikael free, we're going to die. And so is my son. Please, we need your help."

CHAPTER 30

Mikael woke to the sound of death-row inmate number three banging on the door of his cell and screaming obscenities in Spanish. He did this at least once a month in his crusade to convince others of his innocence, but Mikael knew he was not innocent. Anything but. He often laughed about the women he killed, spoke to himself about the details of the crime when he thought no one was listening. Mikael was listening, and Mikael understood Spanish. He also could speak Russian, French, Italian, and Chinese. The countless empty hours here gave him time to absorb books like fine wine, the only good that had come from his solitary life.

He'd also learned to code in five different programming languages, studied the majority of the world's religions, and was pretty sure he could breeze through a master's degree in psychology if ever given the chance. But that would never happen. All of his new skills would never matter now. They would die, right along with him.

He missed designing drones and rockets most of all. During his prison time, he'd formed numerous new ideas, desperately wanted to draft the designs and create prototypes. He'd designed his earliest drone prototypes thinking how they could help the world, assist police and military to patrol thousands of miles of unsecured border, or seek out and destroy enemy compounds and ammunition warehouses without any loss of life. Drones and machines could be programmed to do many things. But he didn't want them to become a new kind of evil, used by governments or mobsters as secret assassins.

As with all things human, they took everything intended for good and made it evil. So, it had been since the beginning. If you gave a man a gun to hunt, he soon turned it on another man. If you gave him a knife to carve, he soon plunged it into the chest of his enemy. If you gave a man an apple, he would soon poison it and hand it to his brother. Such as it was with mankind.

A knock on the door. "You have a visitor," the guard said.

"Who? I'm not expecting anybody."

The voice from the other side: "I'm not sure, but the warden granted his request to see you. Said he's your family and has traveled a long way."

The back of Mikael's neck prickled. *What if it is him? The man that Jess Dawson spoke of? What if it is his father?* He had no desire to see them, any of them. Just the thought of them brought a coldness upon his heart.

"I don't want to talk to anybody."

"No? You'd rather sit here by yourself?"

Mikael sighed. He thought for a moment, had to admit he was a bit curious.

He slid from the bunk. What harm could it do? They couldn't physically hurt him in here, not with so many armed guards around.

He got up, put his hands through the slot, waited for the cuffs. Stepped outside the cell, awaited the leg irons. He shuffled between the guards, across the long walkway where he could see the low-risk prisoners playing cards and roaming freely in the common area. Many of them give him a nod, a gesture of goodwill. He returned it.

Instead of the private rooms they used for attorney-client privilege, they led Mikael to the noncontact visitation area, a room containing a row of plexiglass cubicles that allowed prisoners to see and speak to guests but have no physical interaction. Here, unlike the attorney rooms, they weren't required to lock him to the table. There wasn't anywhere he could go.

He thanked the guard as he left, took a seat in the end unit near the far wall. The area here was in need of a good cleaning and repair, the tiles on the floor broken and chipped, the plexiglass filmy and scratched. He didn't want to think how many hands had gripped this phone.

He glanced through the window to the man on the other side, a man who instantly gave him pause. In many ways, he looked like Mikael, with dirty-blond hair, a round face, and dimpled chin.

A strange vibration hummed within his chest. They could be related but the man couldn't be his father—he wasn't old enough.

He glanced over the man's fine wool coat, the cashmere scarf, polished shoes. His hair was styled and gelled, nails manicured. This was in contrast to Mikael in his orange jumpsuit, his face unshaven and hair uncut.

Though he couldn't explain it, a fireball of hatred erupted from his very core.

What kind of man comes to visit another stuck behind bars dressed in such privilege? Not a good man. Not a righteous man. Only evil.

They stared at each other through the glass until Mikael picked up the phone. As the other man followed, Mikael took notice of the tattoo on the back of his hand, a spider with four heads, one for each knuckle. Out of nowhere, something flashed in Mikael's mind, all at once white and brilliant—the man's face and that tattoo.

But where, and when?

Mikael felt his mind wrangling with the images, trying to fit them in their proper place, like pieces in a jigsaw puzzle. Had he known this man back in Russia as a boy? Had he been part of the community back in Detroit? Or was it right here, in Colorado, sometime much more recent? He thought it had to be the latter because of the tattoo. Kids didn't get those kinds of tattoos.

The man finally spoke. "You looked perplexed, my brother. Is there something I can do to help?"

His accent was dripping of discontent. "Do I know you?" Mikael asked.

"You do not remember?"

"I'm not sure. You look familiar."

A cynical smile, one that Mikael did not like, as if this man were playing with him.

"Drugs can wreak havoc on the mind. Make you lose your memory," the man said, tapping the temple of his head.

Mikael felt his eyes narrow. He did not like the man's inference. He'd never taken drugs. "No drugs for me. They weaken the mind."

"Yes, I understand you are a man with much intelligence, brother."

"How do you know?"

"Word on the street."

"Why do you keep calling me brother?"

The man laughed, a deep-throated, husky sound. "Because I am, Mikael. I am your brother. My name is Nikov." He leaned closer to the plexiglass. "My father is your father. He sent me after he heard of your...situation."

Mikael grew cold. So, it was true. They had found him.

"My father is dead. If you're referring to the donor who gave me life, why would he send you? Why should he care what happens here—to me—when he didn't care of my birth or my mother?"

More laughing. Nikov pointed at him. "You know, that is valid point. I have asked him same thing. Many times. You are bastard child, it is true. Not of his wife, my beautiful mother, but a Russian whore. And yet, he sends me for you."

He shrugged, as if it were a great mystery he didn't understand.

Mikael's blood went hot, as if his veins had been shot with gasoline. His saliva tasted of copper, a bitter blend of blood, family, and revenge. He wanted to punch this man in the face, wipe that smile from his face. He knew he should call for the guard before he exploded, yet, he wanted to learn more.

That tattoo kept speaking to him. Something about that tattoo.

"To do what? Get me out? Are you the man responsible for the foreman's death? You are the one who intimidated the woman juror? She told me about you."

His eyes flashed, as if maybe Mikael had told him something he didn't know.

"A juror? You spoke to a juror? What did she want?" Nikov asked.

"The same thing as our father, my freedom. And I will tell you what I told her—I don't want out."

His brother's eyes narrowed. "Who is this woman? A juror trying to set you free? Tell me more. Maybe I can be of assistance, help her help you."

He rapped his fingers on the desk, the words *honor, respect, loyalty, family* tapping out a hidden directive. Mikael saw his eyes shift subtly and thought he shouldn't utter another word about Jess Dawson. He did not know this man's true motives but sensed he might be here for reasons that were anything but helpful.

"I don't think she needs your kind of help."

Nikov chuckled, continued to tap those fingers.

They exchanged a stare for a cool minute.

Finally, Nikov nodded. "I understand. You don't trust me, and you know what?" His smile faded, as did all other former false impressions of civility. "You shouldn't."

He leaned closer to the glass. "My father insisted I come here to speak to you, and now, I can say I did. But, brother, if I told you I was here to help set you free, I would be lying. Because what I really came here for was to tell you the truth—I don't want you to be free. Our father is a very powerful man, and when he dies, I alone will gain control of his empire. An empire I don't care to share with my bastard brother."

He motioned for Mikael to come closer to the glass as well. Mikael didn't want to comply, but he felt compelled. "The truth is, I came here to make sure a certain job I started many years ago gets completed."

His unsympathetic eyes fixated on Mikael and he grinned, slowly, as if to seal his words' intent. Again, an image flashed in Mikael's mind, that tattoo, that hand, gripping his own hands from behind his back. A raising and lowering motion, blood squirting, again, and again, and again. He felt the knife drive down into his father as if he himself were being stabbed, all while he could do nothing, say nothing, to stop it. And in that moment, a towering weight came crashing down, and Mikael knew— he was staring at his family's killer.

He flew back from the window, only to see his brother laughing once more.

"Ah, I see there is some remembrance now, yes?"

Mikael clenched his fist, pounded it on the glass. Spit ran from his lips as fury filled his heart. For fifteen long years, he had battled with the dreams and the demons and the doubt of having possibly killed his parents, and now he knew for certain it had not been him but this man, his own blood, his own brother.

"You? You bastard. I will tell all."

Nikov shrugged. "Who will believe you? What will they do? I live far away, in another country, a country with no extradition."

Mikael struggled to breathe, thinking about how much this man had taken from him, from his parents, from his Anya. First, his father had stolen his and his mother's right to his Russian family and heritage, then his brother had snuck into this country and robbed him of the same in his new American life. And for what? For fortune and position.

"What did you do with my sister? With my Anya?"

His brother grinned again. And it was a malevolent grin, an enjoyment at Mikael's desperation for knowledge. Mikael's anger exploded like dynamite. He slammed the plexiglass with both fists. "What did you do?" he shouted.

He had never hated anyone so much in his life.

A guard started toward him but Mikael shook his head.

Nikov smoothed his sweater. "You know, I have most amazing girlfriend. She is young woman now. But I have to tell you, she likes the drugs, and like you say, they make her mind weak. No memory. Like most, she will do most anything for the fix. Truly, most anything." He raised and lowered his eyebrows many times. "You know what I mean?"

Mikael curled into himself. He thought he might vomit. It was everything he could do not to hurl himself through the plexiglass. His Anya. Poor Anya. She'd probably endured worse in the past fifteen years than he had, trapped with this miserable man.

"Oh, wait, I bet you never even felt a woman that way, huh? My brother?" Nikov said. "So good. So soft, and those lips. Make a man explode between his legs."

Mikael clenched his fists, undid them, clenched again. Every muscle in his body went rigid. He glanced through the window and into his brother's eyes.

The wrath inside provided an answer to a question he'd often asked himself— whether he had it within him to kill a man—and now he knew the answer. "If I ever get out of here, my brother, I am going to kill you."

Nikov leaned in to whisper. "There is only one problem. You are already dead."

CHAPTER 31

Jess was busy flipping pancakes when her cell phone rang. Ricky ran through the kitchen flying a paper airplane, his latest obsession all things planes. Tom was adjusting his tie in the mirror and gathering his things, preparing to leave earlier than normal. She glanced over at the phone and was surprised to see the caller was Nick Whelan. She waited until she kissed Tom goodbye and fed Ricky before she returned the call.

"I don't know what's going on, but Mikael wants to see you."

"See me? Why?"

"I told you, I don't know. But he sounded very upset. Can you come?"

She glanced back at Ricky. "I'll be taking my son to school shortly. Maybe I can arrange for someone to watch him this afternoon?"

"Great. We'll leave as soon as you get here."

She quickly dressed, got Ricky ready with only a minor struggle. While she drove to his school, she called a friend and arranged for her to pick Ricky up that afternoon and watch him for the extra hours it would take to return from Sterling. Then she left stern instructions with Ricky's teacher that no one, absolutely no one, was to pick Ricky up except her friend. The teacher nodded, said she understood.

Since her run-in with Dimitry, Jess had experienced nightmares about him lurking near Ricky's school, watching him on the playground, snatching him in an instant. She hated leaving him even for a moment. She knew the teacher thought she'd lost her mind walking him into class every day and informing her who would be picking him up, but she didn't care. She wanted to know he was in an adult's custody at all times.

An hour later she met Nick Whelan, and they suffered the long drive to Sterling once again. They spoke little along the way, both wondering what had transpired to cause Mikael to be so upset. The plains passed by in a never-ending shade of beige fields, life still hibernating for the winter.

They endured another round of security, the intrusive pat down. Awaited Mikael.

He entered the room like an angry bull, threw himself in the chair, awaited the cuffs to be attached to the table and the guard to step outside. "I had a visitor."

"Who?" Nick asked, alarmed. "When?"

"Just yesterday. This man comes here, says he is my brother. He comes to rub his privilege in my face. He tells me he is not here to help but to finish the job he started many years ago."

His neck pulsed, a single vein throbbing beneath his jaw, as if it might burst at any moment. "He tells me he has taken my Anya and made her into a junkie whore. His whore."

He slammed a fist on the table, causing the chains to rattle and Jess to flinch.

Nick placed a hand on his shoulder, trying to calm him down. It didn't work.

"I wanted to kill him. I wanted to reach through the glass and rip out his heart. I know now. I know. It was him. He murdered my parents."

Jess gasped. "What? Who?"

"He has a tattoo of a spider with four heads. I remember that tattoo now. I have flashes of memory of him holding my hands from behind." He nodded at Nick. "Just like you told me. I know it is him. I know now for certain what I always knew—I did not kill my parents."

"You're talking about Nikov Petrovsky?" Jess said.

"You know him?" Nick asked, looking as incredulous as David had the day she'd told him about Dimitry.

"No. I know of him. He met with the man who threatened me, Dimitry Romanov. But..." She glanced away, confusion clouding her mind. "But that doesn't make sense. Dimitry is threatening to kill a juror every week unless we help set you free. I thought Nikov was here to help him."

"No," Mikael said. "He's not here to help. He's here to make certain that I die. To protect his inheritance. To keep honor in the family. To keep the bastard child from his father."

"Wait a minute," Nick interrupted. "Who is making these threats?" he asked Jess. "Killing a juror every week? I thought that was something the blogger just made up."

Jess shook her head. "No, it's true. It's all true." She bit her lip. Anxiety infected her and spread like a virus. She wondered if Dimitry had any idea that Nikov was the one truly responsible for Mikael's parents' death. It wouldn't seem so, as that could be a death sentence for Nikov—his father wouldn't be happy to learn it was his son who'd caused his brother's incarceration and death—if it was true.

"If we get Nikov's DNA, you can have the evidence retested, right?" Jess asked, wheeling toward Nick. "A judge will surely take Nikov's words as a confession, and post-conviction DNA testing is a right of death-penalty convicts, right?"

Nick rubbed his chin. "It is, but we've already covered all the post-conviction options. The trial court judge has already issued the death warrant. I have friends who would be happy to run a DNA test, but we'd obviously have to get Nikov's DNA first. Without probable cause..."

"The conversation is probable cause," Jess said.

"Yes, possibly," Nick said, "depending on what was actually said. The conversation should've been recorded in here but unless he outright confessed, a judge may not think much of it. I'll have to hear it first. Still, if there is something there, a positive DNA match would lend credibility that Nikov was present during the time of the murders. Proof that Nikov was in the country at the same time would also help."

"And Anya? You said he has her?" Jess asked Mikael.

"Yes. He tells me he has her in his possession. My Anya is alive." He wiped away a tear. Seeing his grief, Jess felt her own pain. The mother in her wanted to reach out and take away his agony. The juror in her wanted to issue the biggest apology of her life and promise him she would make this right.

She'd never felt so responsible for a situation —and a desperation to fix it—in her life.

"If Anya is alive, we could find her and she could testify," Jess said to Nick. "I wonder why she hasn't come forward and told someone?"

"Stockholm syndrome, maybe," Nick said.

"No, he's got her," Mikael said. "He's holding her, like a slave. He has men watch and control her. Keep her drugged. That's what they do. I know."

He met Jess's gaze. "You know."

Jess's heart sank. She did know. She recalled how, just after her mother's suicide, her father had attempted to explain her mother's depression to Jess. He'd told her about meeting her mom for the first time, how she'd come to America under the impression that she would work as a personal assistant to a wealthy businessman, only to be forced into prostitution and hooked on drugs. Years later, she'd escaped, but not without permanent damage. He'd often talked of her eyes, so drawn and sad, and her body and soul fragile, like that of a porcelain doll.

Yet, at the time, all of her father's talk had just made Jess more disgusted of her, for thinking her mother weak and learning the truth about her past. The irony wasn't lost on Jess when, years later, she sat in a rehab of her own, struggling to overcome many of the same obstacles as her mother.

"We have to go to the police with news of this Nikov and Dimitry," Nick said.

"No, we can't," Jess said, too hurried.

Nick turned to her. "What? Why not?"

"You've read Ethan Stantz's blog. Dimitry Romanov is the Reaper. As I said, he's the one who threatened to kill a juror every week until Mikael was set free. If we go to the police, he'll kill us all. He's already threatened me and my son."

"What?" Nick said, his eyes huge. "You only told me this man came to you urging you to help set Mikael free. You didn't tell me he threatened you. You're saying all of Ethan's blog is true? This Reaper character is real? This is massive juror intimidation. He could be responsible for John Berman's murder."

"I have no doubt he's responsible for John Berman's murder and likely Kevin Ryland's as well," Jess said. "He all but confessed it to me. But if we go to the police, there will be more bloodshed, and Nick, he'll come for my family. I can't risk that."

"The police can protect you, the others as well."

"For how long? Forever?"

She stood from the table, her nerves frayed, like strands of rope pulled apart.

"Without solid evidence, even if the police locate Dimitry and Nikov, they won't be able to hold them," Jess said. "Not without some kind of evidence of wrongdoing here in the States or a link to the current or former cases. But..."

She bit a nail. "There may be another way to at least apply pressure—Ethan's blog. If he outs Dimitry and Nikov publicly and tells of the crimes they're suspected of here and abroad and include Nikov's comments to Mikael, that would alert the police to seek out evidence in Berman's and Ryland's crime scenes and also notify Dimitry of Nikov's true intentions."

"Then the police will come to you anyway, or at least Mr. Stantz. What's the difference?" Nick asked.

"The difference is, strangely enough, that by exposing them—especially Nikov's partial confession—we would be demonstrating that we are doing exactly what Dimitry wants of us—attempting to get Mikael set free. By providing another suspect, we are giving the governor a reason to issue a stay of execution and the police to take another look at the murders while also doing ourselves a favor by making everyone aware of Dimitry's and Nikov's separate intentions."

"You're playing a dangerous game," Nick said.

"You'll have a whole lot of pissed off Russians, I'll tell you that," Mikael said. "There are plenty in my community who believe in my innocence. Now they will know. They will hunt Nikov down like the dog he is and get justice."

Nick shook his head. "You could be starting a local war."

Jess turned and stood steadfastly. "Yeah, well, they started it first," Jess said. "And we're running out of time." She thought she saw a flicker of admiration toward her from Mikael, gratitude that she was standing up for him.

Nick ran his hands through his hair. "Well, you're right about that. Maybe this will at least be enough to cast doubt on Mikael's conviction and get a temporary stay of execution. That would give us all time to sort this whole thing out, locate this Dimitry and Nikov, get his DNA tested."

Nick stood. "I'll get to work on it." He gathered his notes, filed them back in his briefcase. He shot a look at Jess. "And on the way back to Denver, you're going to tell me everything you know about these guys and the threats they've made to you and the other jurors. No more secrets."

As Jess started to follow Nick out, Mikael grabbed her hand. His eyes danced from side to side, pleading. "Will you do something for me? You know Nikov. Find him. He will not be far from Anya. Please, find my sister."

CHAPTER 32

E than brewed a fresh cup of coffee, the strongest he had in the house. The aroma filled the apartment, calmed him a little. Sunshine cast through his eastern-facing windows, adding warmth to the place. He'd stayed up all night writing his latest blog, and the words at times had left him frozen. In it, he was naming names and making accusations, and he knew the moment he hit that publish button, he was going to be a marked man. The last warning to back off the case ensured him of that. But if it was the only way to get a judge or the governor to grant a temporary stay of execution until they could collect and test Nikov's DNA, then so be it.

He reached over to the mouse, moved the cursor, and clicked.

The headline appeared: *Russian Mobster Confesses to Kriskan Killings*.

Ethan proceeded to recap highlights of the case before he outed Nikov Petrovsky and his comments to Mikael Kriskan. "I learned yesterday that Mikael Kriskan had a visitor, a man claiming to be his biological half-brother. Nikov Petrovsky, or Spider, as he likes to be called, is a well-known member of the Kazen mafia in Saint Petersburg, Russia, and has been seen around the Denver area for the past two weeks. Nikov is the son of Nikolai Petrovsky, a Russian businessman suspected of many crimes, including racketeering and murder, and one of a fringe group known as the Saint Petersburg Twelve."

He went on to detail Nikov's taunting of Mikael regarding his father's money and a confession that he was not in Denver to help his brother but to, quote, "make sure a job he started many years ago gets completed." He ended with Nikov's response to Mikael's plea about the location of his sister, Anya, that Nikov may have in fact taken the girl and forced her into a life of prostitution and drugs.

Ethan sipped his coffee and read through all the details that followed, as if he were one of his subscribers reading the words for the first time. He'd tweaked it countless times over the course of the night, but he still wanted to make sure he'd included all the items he'd wanted. Nikov and Nikolai's suspected crimes in Russia—check.

Nikolai's history with Mikael's mother—check. Mikael's adoption and his mother's dying wish for his protection—check. Mikael's IQ, designs and patents owned, reasons his biological father now wanted his return to Russia—check.

It was a pretty damn good story, if he did say so himself.

He left no stone unturned for Dimitry Romanov either. Ethan told the readers how he'd learned of the man's name after another juror had identified him from a photograph on the internet as the man who'd cornered her in a café and threatened her and her son. Ethan was also certain he was the man who'd sent him messages and identified himself only as the Reaper, a man Ethan believed was responsible for the murder of John Berman and his wife. He insisted police should dig further into Kevin Ryland's death as well, as Romanov admitted to the female juror that he'd had prior contact with Ryland before his death.

But he couldn't write a story without tossing in a conspiracy discussion, so to mix things up and add some conflict, he openly wrote about questioning whether Dimitry knew of Nikov's involvement in the original Kriskan murders, and whether his father knew Nikov's true mission was to harm—not help—his biological brother. He thought perhaps that if the Twelve were that interested in gaining Kriskan's freedom, they might not take kindly to one of their own trying to kill him instead.

He ended it all by demanding a judge or the governor to issue a temporary stay of execution for Mikael Kriskan until Nikov Petrovsky's DNA could be collected and tested against the evidence. He reemphasized the strands of DNA discovered at the Kriskan crime scene, previously identified as a partial Y strain match, and suggested it could be a one-hundred-percent match to Nikov's. He listed the governor's e-mail and telephone number and told people to call and write.

He sat back admiring his work, took a deep breath. He sat and waited for the comments to start posting. His mouth was as dry as dirt, his nerves jittery from caffeine and concern. Thirty minutes later, a text hit his phone. He was surprised to see it was Alexai Volkov.

"UR brave man."

Yeah, or foolish.

Within the hour, the blog had received more than fifty comments. In two hours, more than three hundred. Ethan drank two more cups of coffee before the threats started coming in, many written in Russian.

Then what he most dreaded—but thoroughly expected— an instant message like the one he'd received before appeared on his screen.

"Ethan Stantz—You are a dead man."

CHAPTER 33

The day was sunny but unusually blustery, a wind sheering off the foothills and swooping over the city like an eagle. Formerly fluffy white cumulous clouds stretched and thinned into round circles, what Ricky liked to call flying-saucer clouds. As she nudged the door open to his room, Jess was relieved to find him still sleeping soundly. He had a good thirty minutes to continue sleeping before he needed to wake up for school. For a moment, she stood there in the doorway and watched him sleep, wishing she could see his dreams. His room was decorated like the galaxy, all things planets and stars, and she couldn't help but see the parallel to a young Mikael Kriskan, with dreams of being an engineer for NASA. Now, he was languishing in a prison on the barren landscape of the Colorado plains, instead of blessing the world with his talents, while the real killer walked free.

That was not justice. It was her mission now to get him out.

She went downstairs to the kitchen, fixed a pot of coffee, opened her laptop. Clicked on Ethan's blog and began to read. As she scanned the contents, she could hear the wind howl and whistle outside, mirroring the whirlwind she felt inside. She wondered what Nikov and Dimitry would do once they saw their names on the page, questioned whether the angle they'd decided upon to fight for his freedom was the right one. She hoped Brett's presence and surveillance could keep Ethan safe while they worked to get Mikael's conviction overturned.

She shut the laptop, sipped on coffee. Now that word had gone out, there wasn't much she could do. Unless she wanted to run down to Nick Whelan's office and confess the rest of her sins, which she wasn't prepared to do yet. Only if it was necessary.

She cooked pancakes, scrambled eggs, bacon. Ricky soon came downstairs. He always woke up to the smell of bacon. As he scooted onto a chair at the table, he watched her every move, making sure she did everything correctly. She dished him three small plates, one with each item, laid out multiple forks. Put the syrup in a separate small bowl. Most evenings he would feed himself, but he always acted up if one of them didn't feed him breakfast. She cut the pancake, dipped it in syrup, watched his little mouth open like a baby bird. Next was a forkful of scrambled egg. Last was the bacon, which he picked up and chewed himself.

"Where's Daddy? Is he still sleeping?" Ricky asked.

"No, kiddo. He got up early to go to work. Big day today. He told me to give you an extra kiss for him." When he was finished, she rinsed the dishes and placed them in the dishwasher, cleaned off the table. She asked Ricky to go brush his teeth and get dressed, and to her amazement, he did so without argument. In ten minutes, he returned, handing her his shoes. As Jess kneeled to slide each shoe onto his tiny feet and tie his laces, she felt her eyes swell with tears. Feeling stupid, she brushed them away.

"What's wrong, Mommy?" Ricky asked, patting her head.

What could she say? That the simple act of being a mom and helping her son put his shoes on could bring such joy? And yet, that was exactly how she felt. Joyous. She wanted to believe that all that had happened in the past two weeks was soon going to be resolved by Ethan's blog and their research into the Kriskan case. The governor would issue a stay of execution, the DNA would be a match to Nikov Petrovsky and the police would find evidence of Dimitry's presence at the Bermans' murder. Nikov and Dimitry would be arrested and charged with their respective murders, and Mikael would go free. Jess would find Anya and reunite her with her brother. It would all be fine given time.

She wanted to believe it so badly.

"I'm just happy to be spending time with you," she said. Kissed the top of his forehead. "Maybe after school today we can go sledding. Would you like that?"

"Yay!" Ricky said. She helped him with his coat, pulled a hat over his ears as they headed out the door. She felt the wind cut through her jacket, the blowing snow sting her face. Although the day was clear and the sky blue, it was difficult to see with the old snow flying. She used to think about spending days like this with David. Now, she just wanted to spend all her time with Ricky, helping him succeed and be happy instead of run from his issues. She was done running away, from everything.

After dropping Ricky off at school, she spent the next five hours grocery shopping and cooking chili and corn bread. It would be the perfect meal after sledding. In between, she texted Tom that she loved him and hoped he was kicking ass at the trial. The prosecution had completed presenting their case the prior day, and now it was his turn. That morning, while she'd watched him strategically dress in his sharpest suit, ready to defend the innocent, she felt proud she'd married such a man—a defender of the innocent. She wished she could tell him of her efforts to do the same thing.

At two thirty, she drove the SUV up to Ricky's school, texted Ethan while she waited for the bell. When it rang, a flood of kids came streaming out, some nonchalant, others giddy. One car pulled away with kids in tow, then two, then ten, and still there was no sign of Ricky. Anxiety clawing at her stomach, Jess put the phone down and got out of the car. *Where is my son?* She started to walk, then run, toward the school when he suddenly came charging out.

Her knees buckled. She knelt and hugged him, waved at the teacher standing outside the door. Ricky showed her two new colorings he'd completed. "One for you and one for Daddy," he said, handing them over to Jess. She hugged him again, a bit too tightly. For just a moment, she'd thought...

"Mom, you're squeezing me." He wriggled free.

Jess took a deep breath. "You scared me, buddy. I'm sorry." She picked him up and strapped him in the booster seat. Used the wipers to clear a thin layer of blowing snow from her window.

"Are we going? Are we?" he asked.

"Yep, Ruby Hill it is. Toboggan is already loaded."

Firing up the heater, she drove north to Ruby Hill, a longtime Denver favorite for sledding. With the prior day's fresh snow, the place was busy for a weekday afternoon, several kids and parents scurrying like ants across and down the hill. Outside the car, Jess helped Ricky slide his snow pants over his jeans, zipped his matching blue coat. She held his hand as they climbed the hill to the top and selected a spot that wasn't overly crowded—Ricky often had difficulties when too many people were around.

Jess sat on the toboggan, put Ricky in her lap, and pushed off. They started slowly, then picked up speed, spinning and twirling, screaming all the way down. Jess stopped by digging her heels in before they reached the orange plastic netted fence at the bottom of the hill that prevented people from skidding across the nearby railroad tracks. At the bottom, they lay on the ground and made snow angels before beginning the long trek back up the hill. Ricky held her hand all the way, pulling her faster.

After a couple more runs, Ricky saw one of his classmates and asked if he could ride with him. Jess took a break with a few other parents watching from the top of the hill as Ricky and his friend zoomed down again. With the snow blowing sideways with every large gust, creating low visibility, she didn't notice the man at the bottom of the hill who helped Ricky up and returned with him to the top of the hill. But as soon as Jess saw him, her heart stopped.

Dimitry Romanov had Ricky in his grasp.

"Mom, look who I found. He's says he's your friend."

Panic washed over her like an ocean wave crashing ashore. Terrified, she called to him. "Ricky, come here. Now."

Ricky briefly looked at Dimitry, pulled from his grasp and ran to her. Jess hugged him, rubbed his arms. "Are you okay? Did he hurt you?" She examined his face for bruises, his coat and pants for any rips or tears.

"No, Mommy." He glanced back at the hill. "Can I go back down?"

Jess held on, uncertain. She didn't want him out of her arms, but she didn't want him anywhere near Dimitry either. She nodded. "Okay, but stay with your friend, nobody else, got me?" She waited until he joined his classmate and the boy's parents before she whipped back toward Dimitry. "Don't you ever touch my son again."

He took a step toward her, a deep crevice lining his forehead. "What is taking so long, Jess Dawson? I am not a patient man. My client is less so."

"I've spoken to the defense attorney. I've spoken to Mikael. He doesn't want out."

"Not your job to worry about what Mikael wants. We'll take care of Mikael."

"He doesn't want anything to do with you or his father. He knows what kind of people you are. Murderers. Thieves. Ruthless thugs. The man would rather die than be with the likes of you and his father. Frankly, I don't blame him."

Dimitry hardened his eyes, began to chuckle between breaths. "Such harsh words, Jess Dawson." He grabbed her arm and pulled her to him, so close she could smell his breath, a blend of whiskey and tobacco. His fingers clawed into her forearm.

"Listen to me, little girl, I have run out of patience with you. You think you're in charge here? You think you can talk to me like dog? Huh?" He shook her. "I can, and will, kill you if you don't give me what I want. I will do your son first—I will torture him right in front of you while you watch—then kill you too. Then I'll go to the next juror, and the next, until I get what I want."

She attempted to pull away, but the more she moved, the harder he clamped down. She gasped, trying to get air. A few feet away, parents and kids played and cheered, unaware of the unimaginable words he was saying to her.

"Listen," she said. "I've been trying, we..."

He snarled. "Yes, I know about your little stunt, you and your blogger friend. You think you can intimidate me? You think I'm afraid of your police? You try to play my game, you will fail."

"But Nikov, did you know? Did you know he..."

He twisted her arm. "Enough. This is the last warning. You go tell your story to the judge. You let me worry about Mr. Petrovsky."

Ricky came running back up the hill, bright, cheery red cheeks glowing. With a little shove, Dimitry released Jess and intercepted Ricky, picking him up and holding him high above his head. Ricky was usually averse to a stranger's touch, but he squealed as Dimitry swung him around, once, twice, then held him in his arms. Like he'd been with Jess, his face was just inches from Ricky's.

Jess stopped breathing. She could feel her lungs freeze, her eyes tear, every part of her go numb. "Give me my son."

Dimitry pushed the boy's bangs out of his face. "Such sweet Ricky. Such sweet boy. Do you love your mom, Ricky?" Dimitry glanced over his head at Jess, the hard lines around his eyes deepening with his penetrating gaze.

"Yes."

"Do you think your mom should do the right thing? Best deal for her family?"

Ricky shrugged. "I don't know. I guess so."

"Hear that, Mom?"

Jess choked for air, reached for Ricky. "Fine, I'll do it. Please, just give him back." And she would. She no longer cared about her reputation or what would happen to David Foster or anyone else. Right now, she'd do anything to get this man out of her life and away from her family.

What the hell am I doing antagonizing a man who would give no more thought to killing a child than deciding what he'd eat for dinner later tonight?

"Good. I like to hear. No more waiting."

CHAPTER 34

Jess sat in the darkened confines of the bedroom, waiting for Tom to get home. Ricky had passed out shortly after dinner, exhausted after sledding and filled with chili and corn bread. She was thankful for that, so very thankful, because the last thing she wanted was for him to see the fear that continued to be etched upon her face, sense the terror that encapsulated her heart. Still it raced like a runaway train, feeling as if it could derail at any moment. Her tea trembled as she raised the cup to her lips.

After her run-in with Dimitry, and the death threats issued to Ethan over his latest blog, there was no longer any choice about what she had to do. She had to go to Nick Whelan and confess her sins, all of them, the heroin, setting up Kevin Ryland, the affair with David Foster. Initially, she'd hoped it wouldn't be necessary, not because she cared to save her own reputation, or David's, for that matter, but because of the intense damage to others that would result. To Tom and their marriage, to Ricky for losing the only father he knew—and that which she feared most—for the possibility that her ex's mother could use it against her, to try and make her look unfit and get custody of her son. Losing Tom would crush her, but if she lost Ricky, she thought she might literally die.

Yet, although confessing would be difficult and exposing her past to the world would be embarrassing, nothing was going to be as hard or painful as what she had to do in the next hour. As soon as Tom got home, she had to sit him down and tell him everything.

Jess was about to break her husband's heart.

She saw the headlights of his car pull into the drive, heard the garage door raise. She didn't go to meet him, just sat quietly in front of the vanity in the bedroom awaiting his arrival. She heard his keys hit the kitchen island, his footfalls pad up the stairs. He opened the door a crack to Ricky's room, peeked in, then came into the bedroom. He stopped in the doorway, turned on a lamp. He seemed surprised to see her sitting there.

"Why are you sitting in the dark?"

Jess didn't answer.

Tom removed his tie and shoes, placed them in their proper places in the closet. He undid the top button on his shirt and loosened his cuffs, rolled them up. Walking over, he kissed her forehead, then selected a brush from the vanity and began to pass it through her long hair. He stood behind her, watching her expression in the mirror, a faint smile on his face. "Finished closing arguments today," he said. "I think I convinced them. Should get the jurors' decision tomorrow."

She gave a slight nod. "That's good. Real good."

With the dim light, her face was cast in shadows, a pallor of gray mixed with a streak of pale yellow. He continued to brush, to admire and stroke her hair, caring for her. She turned slightly, unable to accept the look of adoration on his face, all that love cradled in his hands and in his caress. "Tom, stop."

He smiled at her in the mirror, cocked his head. "What? Why? I enjoy it."

She gently reached up and wrapped her fingers around his wrist. "Please."

His face grew contemplative at her tone. The smile disappeared and a crease formed in his brow. He returned the brush to the vanity and knelt beside her. "Jess? What's wrong?" He reached out and wiped away a tear as it trailed down her cheek. "Why are you crying?"

She grabbed a tissue, squeezed it in her hands. "Because of the way you look at me." She sniffed and wiped her nose. Shook her head. "Because I don't deserve it. I don't deserve you."

"What?" he said, his expression incredulous. "Of course you do. Jess..." He started to caress the side of her face, but she quickly stood, walked to the French doors that opened from their bedroom to the back deck.

"Please, don't make this harder than it already is," she said. "I just need to get this out." She gazed out into the dark, could see a few lone windows of light in nearby homes. She imagined what other couples were doing at that moment, watching a movie with a bowl of popcorn between them, reading their kids a bedtime story. Certainly not breaking each other's hearts. "You might want to sit down."

He studied her, the folds of his eyes twitching. She could tell he didn't like what he was sensing. He put his hand on a knee and pushed up from the floor. "Okay."

He took a seat on the edge of the bed. Folded his hands. "What is it? You finally going to tell me what's been going on lately? Why you've been disappearing in the evening, even the middle of the night? Why you seem so at odds?"

She nodded. "Yes." And then she purged it, all of it. First, that she'd sat on the jury, followed by what had happened during deliberations, about the threats from the

Russians, then the final damning news. "I've been having an affair with David Foster," she blurted. "For nearly two years now."

Tom slowly rolled forward, like he'd taken several kicks to the gut. He had. He grabbed a fistful of the comforter on the bed and curled into himself with elbows on his knees, hung his head as if he was about to be sick. A sound came out of him that made the hairs on the back of her neck and arms stand straight, a voice that didn't belong to her husband.

Every muscle in Jess's body went rigid as a searing pain like she'd never known—worse than childbirth—swept across her limbs and torso. Nothing hurt worse than the pain you inflicted upon another human being when their only crime was loving you.

He glanced across the room through stained eyes, the veins on his neck exposed, his skin a deep purplish red. He couldn't seem to catch his breath and she wondered if he was about to pass out. He held his stomach and rocked back and forth.

She went to his side and dropped to her knees. "I've not been a good person, Tom. I know that now. For the past few years, I've sat here and felt sorry for myself. For my dad dying, for my luck in getting an autistic son, for the money running out. I thought, poor me, poor Jess. How did I get so unlucky? My whole life, I took things for granted, my dad's money and love. Until I went to rehab, I didn't understand how his coddling after my mother's death caused later issues, my behavior when any kind of pain or difficulty arose in my life."

She wanted to reach out and touch him but knew better. "Instead of facing my problems, I've run and hidden from them, and it's cost the people in my life dearly. I've caused my husband great pain, and an innocent man sits on death row because of me. I can't run anymore. I have to face what I've done."

She glanced up. "You deserve so much better than me. You are so rare. You genuinely care about other people more than yourself. I don't think you understand how unique that is. What you give to people is a gift."

Tom buried his face, shrinking away from her. He raised a hand, as if he just wanted to be rid of her. "Don't, I can't take your compliments right now."

Jess stood and backed away, giving him space. Every part of her being felt as if it were collapsing—head, shoulders, arms, legs—pieces of her crumbling and falling on top of one another like a rock slide.

"I can't tell you what to do now, Tom. For me, for Ricky, I'm begging for your forgiveness. But if you can't, I understand. I won't fight a divorce, and I won't take anything from you. I know I've already taken so much."

As she stood in the desperate, lonely silence, feeling her body shiver, she felt dirty and ashamed. How badly she wanted to cleanse herself of everything she'd done, baptize herself in healing waters. "Tell me what you need from me. Tell me what you want me to do to fix this, and I'll do it, I swear," she pleaded.

Tom regarded her, wiped a hand across his mouth, as if trying to rid himself of the bitter taste of her words. "I don't want anything from you. I can't even stand to look at you right now." He rose from the bed. "I'll sleep in the guest bedroom tonight. Tomorrow, after work, I'll take Ricky to a safe place until this matter is settled. He doesn't deserve to get hurt by this. Go do what you have to do. After that, you can talk to my attorney."

CHAPTER 35

Jess paced across Ethan's loft, sank into the sofa. She hadn't slept, and it felt like she was carrying an extra thirty pounds on her back. Shaking beneath her oversized sweater as if she was back in withdrawal, she told Ethan and Brett about her confrontation with Dimitry and her prior night with Tom. "I'm just so heartbroken," she said. "But also, I'm so damned pissed off. I mean, that bastard had my child in his arms. He threatened to kill him in front of me."

Brett ground his teeth. "I'm sorry I wasn't there for you."

"It's okay. You can't be everywhere at once, I know that."

She sat up, rubbed her head. It throbbed like a hangover after a two-day binge. Out of the blue, she let out a scream that made both Ethan and Brett flinch. She reached out and swept every newspaper and internet article Ethan had researched and printed from the coffee table to the floor. "I hate this man. I hate him!"

She punched a pillow once, twice. Jumped from the couch and began to pace the room.

Ethan raised from his workstation. "Okay, maybe we should settle down."

"Yeah," Brett said. He patted the back of a chair. "Come sit back down."

Jess cast him a glare. His pained, pinched face informed her he had no more experience or knowledge of what to do with a hysterical woman than Ethan did. "I can't. I have to walk this out. I have to think."

She stepped over the papers now spread across the floor, passed by Brett, who'd flattened himself against the wall. "I don't understand what Dimitry really expects to happen. So, what if I do go and tell Nick Whelan and a judge of the events that unfolded fourteen years ago? David will just deny it. What's going to make them believe me over him? Nothing. Why doesn't Dimitry understand that? Why doesn't he go threaten David some more? Make him confess."

"Because he has no leverage with David," Brett said.

"What? Of course he does, his wife, his reputation. He could be disbarred."

"Doubtful," Brett said. "David may confess to the affair, but he could deny all wrongdoing in the trial itself. But your son. Your son is leverage. A mother will do anything to protect a child."

She punched her fist into the palm of her other hand. "We have to do something," she said. "This can't be just about freeing Mikael and convicting Nikov anymore. We have to hang Dimitry. He killed John Berman and his wife, and Kevin Ryland. We have to find out what evidence the police have on those cases, see if there is something we can tie to Dimitry. I mean, he stabbed those people, and he's letting a seventeen-year-old kid take the fall. We can't let that happen. And Kevin, my God, poor Kevin. What he must've endured."

She stopped by the wall of floor-to-ceiling windows. Outside, the sky was a dull gray, additional impending snow barreling over the Rockies. People bundled in wool coats and parkas walked the street seven stories below, in a hurry to get home or back to the office. Others sat inside warm cafés, enjoying coffee and lunch with friends. Just another normal day for the rest of the world while hers fell apart.

"I can check with my sources, see what kind of evidence might link him," Ethan said. "But you've got to believe the guy is pretty disciplined when it comes to cleaning up after himself."

"What do you think he did with Berman's daughter?" Jess asked.

"I'm not sure I want to know," Ethan said. "He could've cast her into kiddie porn for all we know. Think of what Mikael said Nikov told him about Anya."

Jess put her hands on her hips, fought the bile rising in her throat. "I know, that's what worries me. And Anya, I promised Mikael I would find her. How do I find a girl who's been lost for fifteen years in Russia? I need to ask Alexai about her. See if he knows anything."

Brett sauntered over to join her by the view. "I think the best thing we might be able to do to get Dimitry is set him up. Catch him in the act of his next crime. He doesn't know I'm following him. Sooner or later, you have to believe he will go for another juror."

"Great," Jess said. "How will we entice someone to volunteer for that duty?"

"We won't. If I strictly track him, I can tip the police as soon as he acts to take someone out no matter who he goes for, intervene if necessary."

"So, the police could at least charge him with attempted murder," Ethan said.

"I don't want you getting hurt, Brett, and I don't want someone else nearly having to die in order to make an arrest, especially when that someone else is probably myself or Ethan, or God forbid, my son," Jess said. "And if you stick to point on Dimitry only, that leaves Nikov to, what? Wreak havoc elsewhere? You know he has to be majorly pissed off at Ethan about that blog, alleging he killed Kriskan's parents."

She walked the length of the wall, arms crossed, walked back the other way. "I can't ever let that man get ahold of my son ever again. I will do anything—and I mean anything—to stop him."

As the three stood in silence, thinking about their plight, a heavy knock erupted on Ethan's door. All three of them stopped breathing and turned toward the thud. "Expecting someone?" Brett asked.

Ethan shook his head. He walked over, glanced through the peephole. "Shit, it's the DPD again, Walker and Rouche, and they've got company with them."

"The police? What would they want?" Jess whispered.

"Well, I did practically invite them in when I released the latest blog," Ethan said. He stood back and opened the door. "Detectives, good to see you again. Come in."

After they entered, he glanced down the hall in each direction before he shut the door. Jess and Brett huddled in the corner, near a wall displaying paintings done by a local artist depicting various Denver landmarks. Jess could sense Brett's apprehension. She wondered if he'd had some previous run-ins with the police.

"Mr. Stantz, this here's Special Agent Barry with the FBI. He heads up major crimes for the Denver division. And this here's Agent Moore with the CIA. We'd like to talk to you about your latest postings." Walker glanced at Jess and Brett. "Is there someplace we can speak in private?"

Ethan glanced over his shoulder. "They should probably stay. They are interested parties to our...situation." He introduced Jess as his fellow juror. "She's the one I told you about, who was cornered by the Reaper in the café. We now know that man to be Dimitry Romanov."

"He also followed me to Ruby Hill two days ago," she told them. "He grabbed my son and threatened him. My son is in my husband's custody now. Until this whole thing is over."

Walker stepped forward. "Why haven't you come to the police?"

"He told me he'd kill me, any of us, if we asked for help. And you know, I believe him." She adjusted the scarf around her neck, felt it tighten against her jugular the way she imagined Dimitry's hands would do the next time she ran into him. "The man is a cold-blooded killer, of that I have no doubt. You need to do as Ethan suggested in his blog—you need to find evidence that he murdered John Berman and his wife, and Kevin Ryland as well."

Walker leaned his substantial self against a barstool near the kitchen island. Rouche followed suit. Agent Barry crossed his arms. "How did you identify Romanov?"

"Research," Ethan said, "Along with Jess's ID. And Nikov Petrovsky, because of his tattoo. Brett here saw the two of them speaking in a cigar bar. Probably plotting all our deaths."

"Okay, guys," Rouche said, raising his palms in surrender. "Let's try to calmly deal with this situation. You are clearly very fearful, and if what you state in that blog is true, I understand your concern. We're here to help. But I have to tell you, releasing those names and making those allegations has caused quite a stir with some of our local—say—more ethnic communities."

Ethan nodded. "Well, it was meant to in a way. We were afraid one of the Russians would take one of us out if we came directly to you, so we decided to put the warning out to the masses, let others know what Nikov implied in his talk with his brother, and to let Dimitry and Nikov know that we knew who they were. I admit it may not have been the smartest thing. I've already received several death threats, so to say I'm keeping a tight watch on my surroundings is not an exaggeration."

"Maybe one of their enemies will take out Nikov and Dimitry before they take us out," Jess said under her breath.

"I'm going to pretend I didn't hear you say that," Walker said.

She wheeled toward him and the others. "He threatened to torture and kill my son in front of me. So, apologies if I don't feel anything but relief at the thought of his death."

She paced, hands on hips. "Can't one of you guys, the FBI or CIA, arrest them on some violation? Ethan says both Nikov and Dimitry are on your watch lists, as known associates of the Saint Petersburg Twelve."

FBI Agent Barry picked up several of Ethan's articles near his workstation, examined them. "Yes, Mr. Stantz seems to know a great deal about some things he shouldn't," Barry said pointedly, taking a moment to steady his gaze on Ethan for an extra moment.

"But unfortunately, the answer to your question is no. Nikov Petrovsky is part of several ongoing investigations—art forgery, receipt and distribution of stolen goods, sex trafficking, all included—but any arrest now would prove futile. Unless the detectives here can obtain direct evidence of his involvement in these local homicides you refer to, we don't have enough to detain him."

"Ditto the CIA," Moore said. "Although I am quite concerned as to the reasons the Russians want to afford Mikael Kriskan his freedom. I don't need to tell you, we don't need that kind of inventor falling into enemy hands."

"You got that right," Brett said, speaking for the first time. He stood with his back to them, staring out the east windows toward the downtown skyscrapers. He turned to see Moore frowning at him. "Three tours in the middle east. Iraq and Afghanistan," he explained.

Moore nodded. "Thank you for your service."

Walker spoke again. "Look, at this point, I think it's best you all just lay low. No more blogs, no more talking with death-row inmates, no more spying on Russian mobsters."

He glanced at his partner, Rouche. "Criminy, just saying the words makes me want to lock the three of you up for your own safety. Don't you know who you're dealing with here?"

He thundered his towering self across the floor. "Let us do our jobs. If you see or hear anything suspicious, or you get contacted by this Dimitry or Nikov again, you call us right away."

Jess looked up at the man, about a foot taller than she, the other three men behind him, backing him up. "Well, no offense, gentlemen, but I can't just sit back and wait for justice," Jess said. "Fourteen years ago, I did my civic duty sitting on a jury and deciding a man's fate and I fear we made a terrible mistake. If Mikael Kriskan didn't kill his parents, I can't sit by and watch him die."

"You really believe Kriskan didn't kill his parents?" Walker asked. "I was there, at the scene, and let me tell you, I still have nightmares."

"Yes, and knowing what you do now—that a man like Nikov Petrovsky is his brother—who do you think was more likely to commit such a heinous crime?" Jess asked. "A nineteen-year-old college student from the Colorado School of Mines with no motive whatsoever to kill his parents? Or a Russian mobster intent on removing his competition for his father's affections and money?"

Walker smirked. "She may have a point," Rouche said.

"And what of Anya, who was never found?" Jess asked, her voice rising. "That Nikov took her makes sense, especially after what you just mentioned, that he's involved in sex trafficking. God only knows what that girl has been through."

She turned back to Ethan and Brett. "Speaking of which, we need to find her. That, too, would prove Mikael is innocent—if she came forward and testified."

Walker shook his head. "See, there you go again."

Rouche took a few steps toward her, concern on his face. "Jess?" he said. "May I call you Jess? Please don't get involved any further in this. Go be with your son. Let us do our job. You and Mr. Stantz don't need to work on this anymore."

Jess grabbed her coat, slid it on. "Well, you're wrong about that. I do have to work on this. So, while you do your job, I'll do mine. Let's just hope one or the other of us finds something that can make this end well—for all of us."

CHAPTER 36

E than Stantz couldn't remember the last time he'd stepped inside a strip club. Just walking toward the structure off Glenarm Street made him feel odd, like a kid about to get caught sneaking a peek at his father's girlie magazines. He didn't know why. He felt the same way every time his friends made him come to such a place, typically during someone's bachelor party. The guys thought it was such a turn-on throwing money at girls who swayed their hips and shook their boobs in their faces, but somehow, Ethan always left feeling anything but aroused. Instead, he felt like a lesser human, ashamed to be part of the gender that still needed women to parade around naked and treat men like royalty to feed their egos.

He reread Alexai's text, assuring him Nikov Petrovsky had not been at the club all evening and making sure that hadn't changed. Initially, Ethan had been reluctant to leave his loft, but Alexai insisted he had information that would be of utmost interest to their cause. Brett had left earlier in the day to track Dimitry's movements, and Jess had set out to learn whatever she could about Anya Kriskan before she disappeared, so Ethan was left to his own devices to travel solo to the club. He blended in with the partying masses of singles in LoDo, then hopped on a Sixteenth Street shuttle bus to Glenarm, before he risked walking the two blocks south.

Inside, the music was pulsing as a sultry woman with hooded eyes wearing nothing but a thong danced onstage. A line of men sat at the bar surrounding her, never dropping their eyes. In front of each was a drink and a wad of cash. Ethan quickly averted his gaze and nodded at the barrel-chested bouncer posted by the door before one of Alexai's associates intercepted him. Ethan followed him up the stairs where Alexai was stationed in one of the private rooms, surrounded by his entourage and a cast of women.

Ethan cringed as he realized a girl was straddling Alexai's lap. His associate noted Ethan's arrival, and Alexai motioned him over, unconcerned about the interruption.

Ethan hesitated, wondering how the hell he was supposed to hold a conversation with the man while a mostly naked woman gyrated over his groin.

He slunk over and stood at Alexai's side, unable to look anywhere but toward the front of the room. Several other scantily dressed women checked Ethan out, probably waiting to see who could be of service. He recognized a couple of the girls as those with Alexai from their previous encounter.

"Honey, give it a rest," Alexai said.

Ethan waited as the girl climbed off, feeling like he'd walked into a porn shoot in progress. He noticed a spot of moisture on Alexai's trousers, tried not to throw up. The woman popped a piece of gum in her mouth, adjusted her thong, went about her business.

Alexai pointed at a chair. Ethan obediently sat. "So, comrade, you are good?"

Ethan nodded. He really didn't want to be here right now.

Alexai studied him, a smirk on his face. He clearly sensed Ethan's discomfort. "You would like a girl?" He waved his arm at the women standing nearby. "Take your pick."

Ethan laughed under his breath, a nervous energy zapping his lungs. "No, I'm fine. I mean, yes. Girls, hell yes. But, no, I, uh, have a girlfriend. Waiting."

What an idiot. He sounded like a teenager on a first date.

Alexai laughed. "Me too. Many. Hard to keep them all happy." He sat up, shifted his trousers, mercifully moving that spot away from Ethan's vision. "Did you bring the money?"

"I did. You want it here?" Ethan asked.

He shook his head. "Give it to my associate."

He motioned for one of his men, who promptly came over and took the envelope from Ethan's hand. In exchange, he gave Ethan a flash drive. Ethan quickly slipped it into his pocket, wondering if the sweat pooling beneath his arms was beginning to show.

"What's on here?" Ethan asked.

Alexai leaned forward. "Proof of what you asked for— other times Mr. Petrovsky has been here in the States, corresponding to certain crimes."

"You mean like the Kriskan murders?" Ethan felt his eyes grow wide.

"Among others. Oh, and I have this as well..." Alexai reached for a brown paper bag beneath his chair. "Consider it a gift."

Ethan glanced in the bag. In it was a sealed plastic bag containing a cocktail glass, like one used for whiskey or bourbon.

"Don't touch it," Alexai said. "I swiped it from the table after Mr. Petrovsky departed the other night. In it, you should find remnants of his saliva, so you can test his DNA, yes?"

Ethan crumpled the bag closed. He wanted to get up and dance on the table himself. He looked at Alexai, broke out in a grin. Alexai matched it.

"You're welcome," Alexai said. "A toast to our business together?" The server brought two shots, and for once, Ethan downed it. One day hiding in his apartment receiving death threats, the next toasting with a shady Russian in a strip club. He was starting to feel like a real reporter.

Ethan stood to leave. "Thanks again."

"Good luck. I hope you get your man." Alexai motioned for the girl to return. "And Mr. Stantz? I know you are brave man, but I don't have to remind you the kind of man you are dealing with, no? Watch your back."

Ethan skipped down the stairs, wasting no time. He couldn't wait to get home and see what was on the flash drive. After he showered.

He started to exit the club when his phone rang. It was Jess. "I was at your apartment. You didn't answer the door. I got worried," she said.

In the background of the club, there were several whoops and whistles, some cowgirl song playing. "Wait. Where are you right now?" she asked.

He walked outside, breathed in the grimy industrial air. "Just leaving the Diamond Cabaret. On foot."

"Wait, you're at the strip club? Ethan, get out of there, now. I'm on Fourteenth approaching Glenarm, and I'm right behind him."

Ethan leaned his head toward the street to his left. "Who him? Dimitry?"

He didn't need to await her response, however. Beneath the streetlight on the opposite corner, he saw the man with shoulder-length blond hair, dressed in a fine wool coat and red scarf, and he knew immediately who he was—Nikov Petrovsky. As soon as their eyes met, Ethan jumped from the steps and broke in a dead run.

He darted in and around the valets, a couple walking arm and arm, another man coming out of the nearby Denver Press Club. A horn blared as he dashed across the street, a taxi as it barely missed hitting him. A second one sounded as he turned and ran straight up the street, between the parked and oncoming cars. Behind him he could hear shouts and similar gestures to the man chasing him.

Back on Sixteenth Street, most of the mall stores were closed, but several people continued to troll the streets, including the hyped-up twentysomethings waiting to enter the dance clubs and couples out on dates. Ethan hoped the sight of so many people would deter Nikov from chasing him, but a quick glance back indicated no such thing. He was on his feet and coming fast.

At the next block, a large group of street kids and musicians were gathered, huddled around the square sharing cigarettes and conversation. Ethan knew many of the regulars, teens and twentysomethings who lived on the streets for various reasons. Ethan had written many a story on them while working for *Westword*, and they knew him to be one of the good guys. He hated to put them in harm's way but knew it might be his only chance to escape.

As he ran into their pack, he shouted at one of their dreadlocked leaders about his pursuit, then bolted out the other side. To his satisfaction, the man quickly commanded the group to spread out and create a chain behind him. As Nikov approached, they confronted, then surrounded, him. Ethan cut into a restaurant he knew adjoined a hotel and bolted up the stairs to the skywalk that linked to their sister hotel across the street.

From the skywalk, he watched in horror as Nikov took out two of the street kids with a single blow, then bloodied another's nose and left the kid unmoving on the sidewalk. Down the mall, others ran to join them, to take up for their brothers being attacked, but there was a caution as they grew close. Maybe something in the tailored clothes Nikov wore, or the refined accent with which he spoke, gave them pause and finally made them stand back. Ethan hated that some got hurt but was thankful they'd given him a chance.

As soon as Nikov cleared the crowd, Ethan fled into the hotel. From a hallway, he stopped and looked out a window to the street below, watching where Nikov decided to go. Guests of the hotel passed and eyed him cautiously, he with his hands on his knees and gasping for breath. *Maybe I should start running those five miles per day again.*

In the confines of the hotel hallway, he waited while Nikov charged down one side street and then another, seeking any sign of him. Ethan smiled as Nikov kicked a trash can, frustrated at his loss. Once he was out of sight, Ethan headed into the lobby and asked the bellboy to call a taxi. As soon as the car pulled up under the awning, Ethan slid into the back seat. It wasn't far to his apartment, but he didn't wish to risk any more time on the streets. At the lofts, he told the driver to drop him off in a dark spot, so he wouldn't be seen exiting the vehicle. When Ethan was sure the coast was clear, he threw a ten at the driver and darted for the door.

As he raced into the elevator in his building and up to his loft, he glanced at his face in the mirror. Although it was early February, he was sweating profusely, with a dark stain down the front of his shirt and under his arms. He could feel the hysteria settling in, fearing that when the doors opened to the seventh floor that Nikov would be standing there with a knife, but it proved only his imagination. He burst down the hall to his door and quickly unlocked it, checked every window and door inside, especially those that led to his balcony. He lived in a secure building, but he wasn't foolish enough to believe Nikov was a man who would be stopped by such obstacles.

When he was satisfied that he was safe, he held up the brown bag in his hand, shook it like a fist after winning a prize. "Got you, you little Russian bastard."

CHAPTER 37

Nick Whelan wasn't expecting Jess and Ethan when they descended upon his office the next morning like a couple of uninvited bears to spring camp. Their entry caused a bit of a stir, as it broke up a group of staff members muddling about, all looking somber. Nick explained that the governor had set the date for Mikael Kriskan's execution that morning. In less than six weeks, Mikael would be dead.

Jess and Ethan stood in his office, their heads bowed. "I'm sorry," Jess said, her heart tumbling at the news. She pulled out a chair. "But that's why we're here. Maybe we can help."

She introduced Nick to Ethan, who stood next to her holding a large box. After shaking Nick's hand, he found a place to stash the box, cleared a stack of documents from a second chair and took a seat. In his hand, he clutched the paper bag as if it contained gold.

"I'm ready to tell my story," Jess said. "Are you ready to hear it?"

Nick Whelan, previously appearing forlorn, perked up. "Can I record you?" From a desk drawer, he removed a micro recorder, set it on the desk. "It's proved more reliable than my phone," he explained. He retrieved a fresh pad of paper and pen to take notes and informed the receptionist to hold all his calls—although he knew there would be many given the morning's events. "Okay, shoot."

Jess settled back in the chair, took a deep breath. She started with her friendship with Kevin Ryland, how they would go out for drinks after court had ended for the day, which eventually led to time at his residence, where she discovered how much research he'd conducted on the case.

"Ethan has all of that evidence now. He took it, after getting permission from Kevin's family, of course, to see if we could prove that Kevin had conducted research during the time of the trial, and you can see by the dates of many of the items printed, they are from that time."

Nick glanced at the box. "That's his research, there?"

"All of it, yes. Much was done afterward, during the appeals process, as he kept following the case. Mostly because I think he was hoping an appeal would come through to alleviate his guilt," Ethan said.

"His guilt?" Nick asked. "Over what?"

"He never believed Mikael was guilty of those crimes," Jess said. "The reason he voted guilty in the end—the only reason—was because of me."

She glanced at Ethan. He squeezed her shoulder, urged her to carry on. She explained to Nick her heroin use during the trial, how she'd taken some hits with her for deliberations, when they'd been sequestered, but had run out as a few days turned into many. "I was in withdrawal and sick, I mean, really sick."

Nick sat up, dropped his pen momentarily, stroked his tie. Jess could see the wheels spinning in his head. "I'm sorry to hear that. It couldn't have been easy."

"It was the most miserable time in my life," she said. "But that's not the story. One night, when I went outside to get some air, to try to stop shaking so badly, I was approached by a man. He spoke from behind a hedge so I couldn't see his face but said he could get me what I needed—if I voted guilty."

Nick Whelan reared back, moving like Jess had just thrown a punch at him. He clawed at his chest. She hoped he wasn't having a heart attack. "Who? Who was he?"

Jess shook her head. "I don't know. I figured, though, he was someone from the prosecution, because he wanted my vote, you know. But honestly, I didn't ask at the time. I was just desperate for the fix."

"And he gave it to you?"

"Yes, but only one hit. See, he asked me what was taking so long, and I made the mistake of telling him my vote wouldn't matter because two other jurors were holding out. He told me to change their mind or I would be facing weeks of withdrawal, that he wouldn't be able to risk helping me any further."

Nick studied her, his expression turning to one of incredulity. "What did you do?"

She tilted her head toward Ethan. "Ethan was easy as he was on the fence anyway, but the other...Kevin Ryland."

She took a deep breath. "I seduced him and planted heroin in his room and reported it to the court attendant. Later, they came to Kevin and threatened him with charges of juror misconduct, drug possession and distribution. He knew it would cost him his career, so he changed his vote."

And there it was. It was done. Jess folded her hands in her lap. Felt relieved.

But Nick said nothing, just sat there with his mouth agape for several minutes—likely trying to wrap his head around everything he'd heard. Jess felt uncomfortable in the silence and wrung her hands and tapped her feet.

Finally, Nick got up, stepped between boxes and briefs. "I think I need more coffee." He filled the pot with water from the cooler outside, fixed a fresh pot. While it brewed, he leaned against the wall, still thinking.

"Do you have any proof that the prosecuting attorney was part of the team that visited Kevin Ryland? Did you ever see him with the courier?"

Jess looked at the floor, thinking about David, how he would react learning Nick Whelan knew the truth. "No, I never saw him and Kevin said David Foster wasn't the man who approached him either. It was probably the same man who approached me, but unlike Kevin, I never saw him so I couldn't say for sure. But... David Foster knew what was going on, I can tell you that. He was the driving force. He confessed to me many years later that he was the one who sent the courier to help me."

Nick narrowed his eyes, stared daggers at her. "Are you messing with me right now? Why in the hell would David Foster tell you such a thing—admit he tampered with a jury? Why would he even be speaking with you? You understand, your credibility is on the line right now."

She glanced at Ethan again for support. She didn't think she could express to him how thankful she was that he was here helping her get through this, because she was pretty certain that, without him, she would bolt from the room right about now. She was on the hotseat and it was getting hotter.

Ethan nodded, urging her on once again. "Because for the past two years, David Foster and I have been having an affair."

Nick blinked. "What? Say again?"

Jess repeated herself. She explained how they'd met at a charitable event, one many lawyers attended. "He approached me, asked if I remembered him. Things went from there. But you have to know, if I include the affair and his confession in my testimony, he will fight like hell to make me out to look like a liar, and honestly, between my past drug use and what I did to Kevin Ryland, he's got a pretty good shot at shredding me into bits."

Nick Whelan laughed. "Damn straight he does. He's one of Denver County's top prosecutors, probably in line for getting elected attorney general someday. He's known to make mincemeat out of the strongest of witnesses."

With one hand on his hip, he rubbed his face, the back of his neck, his head. "So, Foster's a dirty prosecutor. This just gets better and better."

He poured a fresh cup of coffee. "Anyone else?"

"Please," Ethan begged.

"Ditto," Jess said.

Nick prepared two more cups, handed them over, returned to his desk. For the next few minutes, the three sat sipping, contemplating the situation, Jess and Ethan waiting for guidance. Jess felt as if she could throw up at any moment but was relieved to be free of the information she'd held within for fourteen years.

Finally, Nick started talking, more to himself than either she or Ethan. "Okay, so Foster would fight back, and not that I don't believe you that you've been having an affair and he confessed to you of his involvement, but if we include it in your testimony and it erupts into a *he said, she said*—from a judge's perspective, I think he would side with Foster. Without any direct proof of his involvement, I think getting him riled would be a mistake. So...as much as it pains me not to expose Foster for what he did, I recommend you write the affidavit and just include the parts about the courier and the actions you undertook to get Kevin Ryland to change his vote. I'll take a look through the materials you collected from his home and document his misconduct of researching the case on his own during the trial."

He made a little steeple with his hands, blew air through his fingers. "I have to tell you, though, although it's one hell of a story, it may not be enough. I've already thrown so much at the state and federal level, I don't know if one more special hearing will make a difference. But I'll try to get someone— anyone— to listen, and I thank you for coming forward."

"Maybe this will increase the odds." Ethan picked up the crumpled brown bag, set it on Nick's desk. "It nearly got me killed last night, but it was worth it."

Nick scooted it toward him, peeked inside. "What's in the plastic bag?"

"Nikov Petrovsky's glass. You should be able to get DNA tested from the saliva, right?" Ethan asked. "See if it matches the partial DNA strand or other DNA that was never identified during the trial?"

Nick pointed at the bag. "Where did you get this?"

"Does it matter? It was a gift. Along with..." Ethan opened the box, removed a flash drive. "This has information, airline and car rental receipts showing when Nikov traveled to the States, including a two-month period during the winter the Kriskans were murdered."

Nick raised an eyebrow. "Is that so?"

"Yes," Ethan said. "There's also some other damning evidence of Nikov, a video taken of him beating a man, a photograph of him holding a gun to the head of another, along with news accounts of similar cases with no suspects—I think alleging Nikov is involved in those cases as well. I realize that doesn't pertain directly to the Kriskan case, but..."

"But it demonstrates the type of man Nikov Petrovsky is, paints his character as a man who could commit such atrocities, when a young Mikael Kriskan could not."

Nick rapped his knuckles on the desk. "The unfortunate thing is, no judge I know will allow these items to be submitted as evidence. You know, probable cause, warrants, chain of custody and all that." He raised an eyebrow, as if they, and especially Jess, should know more about the law.

Jess sighed. "That's true, but if the DNA proves a match, then you could get a warrant and get the items yourself," she said. "Right?"

"Yes, but in the limited amount of time we have? I don't know." Nick sighed. "Look, I have a friend at the CBI who owes me a big favor. I'll get him to expedite the DNA analysis, and I'll file for a special hearing with the trial court to get your charges heard, but I need to ask you, because I know the judge will ask as well—why are you just coming forward now, after all these years? Simply due to the threats to you personally, or because you truly believe Mikael is innocent?"

"I admit it started with the threats," Jess said, "but now, like you, I do believe in Mikael's innocence. So does Ethan. Once upon a time, Kevin Ryland also believed in his innocence, and was planning to hold out for a hung jury rather than convict a man he believed had been set up. I'm responsible for him changing that decision, and as a result, I condemned Mikael to death. There are no words to express my level of regret, no way to give him back the fifteen years I took from him. But I have to do whatever I can not to take his life. Whatever it takes, I'll do it."

CHAPTER 38

Two days later, Jess intercepted David as he left his downtown office, walking along Seventeenth Street on his way to meet several other attorneys in a new high-profile case he was currently working on. She had to step quick to match his gait. "I wanted to let you know, I've written an affidavit and given it to Nick Whelan," she said.

David stopped dead in his tracks. His skin turned a violent red. "You did what?"

Jess raised her hand to stop the tirade before it began. "I didn't include anything about you or our affair. Just about Kevin's research during the trial, and that an unknown courier approached me and offered me heroin in exchange for my vote. I also made myself the sole scapegoat for Kevin's change of heart, stating that I willingly slept with him and planted heroin in his room, then informed the court attendant. Nothing implicates you as a player, although you should know, Nick Whelan knows the truth."

He grabbed her arm, pulled her around a corner where they'd be less visible. The wind whipped and dovetailed between buildings, sending loose plastic bags swirling in the air. "I don't understand. Why are you doing this? All because of that Dimitry character? He can't, he won't, do anything. If he was going to do something, he would've already done it."

"You're wrong. Just last week he got to Ricky. He had my son in his arms. In his grasp, David. Issued me an ultimatum—no more time." She issued him a look of dire concern. "Don't you understand who these guys are? They have names for them. The Butcher. Spider. The Reaper. And they're not going to stop until they get what they want."

"Mikael Kriskan is scheduled to die in less than six weeks, Jess. Unless the governor grants clemency at the last minute, nothing is going to change that, and this governor has no empathy for murderers."

"David, Mikael is innocent. I truly believe that, and you should too. No one knew about Nikov Petrovsky fifteen years ago, knew anything about Mikael's real family. But now, we have Nikov's DNA and proof that he was in the States at the time of the murders, and if that DNA comes back as a match to any of the DNA collected at the scene, you have to admit it's likely Nikov is the real killer."

His brow furrowed. "You have his DNA? Proof he was here? How?"

"It's a long story."

David shoved his hands into his pockets, grinded his teeth. "Okay, I'll give you that. If the DNA comes back a match, then that would warrant a stay of execution and a reexamination of the evidence. So why can't you just leave it at that? Why add in your affidavit?"

"We need as much ammunition as we can get. I'm also trying to find Mikael's sister, Anya. Nikov all but told Mikael that he has kept Anya as his girlfriend all these years. If we can find her, she can testify against Nikov. That would seal Nikov's fate and overturn Mikael's conviction."

David walked in a circle, a deep frown on his face. She could tell he didn't want to buy into the idea that he might've tried and convicted an innocent man, but she knew she was making inroads.

"Look, I know how much you wanted to convict Mikael for murdering his parents, your beloved professor, but you have the wrong guy. If you go before the judge and tell them you believe, as the original prosecutor, that the new information might warrant another look, I think that would add extra pressure upon the court to grant a stay of execution. They expect the defense to act on Mikael's behalf, but if you come forward, they have to listen."

David stopped circling. "Damn it, Jess, I just don't know."

She kept on. She couldn't quit now. "Mikael remembers moments from the night of the murders now. He said he remembers Nikov's tattoo, this spider he has on the back of his hand."

"See, that's just it, Jess. You're basing all of this on what a convicted killer is telling you. You don't know what he really remembers. He could be making this whole thing up."

"The conversation between Mikael and Nikov was recorded. Nick says he doesn't come right out and confess of course, but his words could easily be construed as a confession."

"Judges don't make decisions on what could be, only on what is."

She kicked a rock, feeling her frustration mount. "David, he's telling the truth. You should've seen him. How angry he was. The determination in his voice, the fire in his eyes. The words he used to describe his memories were very specific. That's not the kind of thing he could just make up."

"He's had all the time in the world to make stuff up and practice being very convincing. I'm just not that gullible to believe that a few weeks before his execution is to happen, he suddenly has visions of a man with a spider tattoo on his hand as the real murderer. I mean, what's next? The one-armed-man theory?"

Jess shook her head, balled her hands into fists. She growled. "You are so infuriating. You just can't stand the thought that you could be wrong, can you? Seriously, you would rather see an innocent man die before risking a bruise to your ego? Don't tell me that. Don't tell me you are that narcissistic."

He froze, his jaw clenching. She could tell he didn't like her choice of words. He glanced down at his shoes, polished, like the rest of him. "Look, I'll think about it. If a DNA match is made, then I'll think about it. Or if you find Anya Kriskan."

Jess sighed, worried that was the best she was going to get out of him. She tried a different tactic. "David, what you did, what I did, we owe it to Mikael Kriskan to give him a chance. You've got your career, and it isn't going to hurt you to let this one go. Plus, you can try and convict Nikov Petrovsky, a genuinely evil man. You can be a true hero. And Mikael, maybe he can go to the feds and get protection, or go into hiding on his own, but at least we'll be free of the guilt of putting an innocent man away for fifteen years. But if we let this execution go forward, his blood will be on our hands forever."

She issued him one last pleading look. "It's the only way, David. It's the only way Mikael—and the rest of us—are all going to live. Because these people are ruthless killers and they will stop at nothing to get to Mikael. And if he dies, I fear they will kill the rest of us as payback. The Russians will not take no for an answer. So, do as you say, you think about it, but don't take too long. You may not be afforded the time."

She walked away, leaving him with that thought.

CHAPTER 39

Dimitry drove up the winding mountain road, following a trail of glowing red taillights as they twisted around curve after curve climbing into the foothills of the Rockies. An equal gathering of headlights passed going in the opposite direction, swirling down and around the other side. The falling snow grew heavier with the increased elevation, and the slick roads were beginning to back up traffic.

After evaluating all the jurors, Dimitry had decided Gerald Fowler would be his next target. One, because the man thought himself invulnerable. Two, because he lived in a modified fortress, with security cameras and entry detection notification devices surrounding the place. Third, because he owned a number of guns. He was what Dimitry referred to as an American cowboy, a man who watched too many movies and thought himself the hero. Killing Gerald would send a message to the others. If Dimitry could get to Gerald Fowler, he could get to any of them. Anywhere. Anytime.

Near the town of Bailey, Dimitry pulled the truck off the highway and ventured higher into the hills on a narrow, gravel road. Here, the snow came down harder, flakes the size of quarters drifting in the headlights. During his prior visits to the property, he'd staked out a good area to park the truck about halfway up the road that led to Fowler's house, in a clearing under a pack of trees well away from prying eyes. The black pickup would also be more difficult to see in the dark, one of the reasons he'd requested it as a rental.

He pulled off the road into the space, turned off the headlights, and cut the engine. He slid on the ski mask that covered everything but his eyes and matched the rest of his clothing, all black—coat, jeans, and boots—all necessary to be no more than an unknown motion on any camera lens. He slid the hunting knife into the sheaf tucked into his waistband. His plan was to lure the man out of the house deep into the woods, then attack him. Fowler would come out armed, of course, but guns didn't matter when you couldn't see your enemy approach. And unless his fighting skills were military grade, he'd be no match for Dimitry.

Staying off-road, he hiked the remaining hill through the woods until he ran across a six-foot-high wire fence complete with a *No Trespassing* sign, one of the perimeters Fowler had set up. It was also here Fowler had set up various motion-detection devices, to alert him inside about predators outside. Dimitry took out the small explosive devices he'd created and tossed one over the fence, moved twenty feet around the perimeter, and threw in another, and continued on until he'd circled the entire property. He knew Fowler was likely inside now monitoring multiple cameras, having been alerted to motion inside the perimeter, but it would be nothing compared to the chaos that would ensue when Dimitry actually set the explosives off.

Knowing he'd be shot instantly if he was discovered climbing the fence or cutting through it, Dimitry climbed a nearby tree instead, a lodge-pole pine, which grew high enough so he could get over the fence without detection and was sturdy enough to hold his weight. From the top of that tree, he maneuvered from one pine to another until he could safely reach one inside the perimeter.

He climbed down the tree inside, but before dropping to his feet, he set off one of the explosive devices on the opposite side of the property. It created quite the commotion, splintering branches and brush, and as it did, he hit the ground running to the location he'd planned days before to station himself. From there, he set off two more of the devices, shattering snow and breaking the silence of the night. He knew Fowler had to be scrambling inside, monitoring his cameras and grabbing his gun.

Somewhere to his left, he heard a rustling behind the fence, but wasn't worried—it was most likely a deer fleeing his scent. Not wishing to detonate the last two devices yet, but wanting to keep Fowler confused and panicked, Dimitry picked up several rocks and hurled them at various spots around the property, which would send off all kinds of new alerts and signals.

Then he crouched low in the brush and waited.

Soon, the front door opened and Fowler stood on the porch, rifle aimed toward the darkness. He reached inside and killed the lights, so he would be on equal levels of visibility with whatever was outside. Dimitry could see him move slightly left, waiting, listening.

Dimitry threw a large rock to his right where it hit a tree with a *whunk*. Shifted lightly, launched another to the same spot. A scraping sound, like bark stripping from a trunk, broke the silence. Fowler stepped off the porch, rifle at eye level, ready to kill. "Whoever is on my property, you'd better know I will shoot."

Dimitry exploded one of the last remaining devices, near the same location that he'd thrown the rocks. That one caused the edge of an evergreen branch to explode, spraying bits of ice and snow everywhere. The rifle quickly scoped to Fowler's left and fired, reset and fired again. Just as Dimitry had expected, Fowler was a cowboy, caring little whether it was animal or human in the brush. A daring man who could brave his enemy. A reckless man who knew no bounds. A foolish man who would soon die.

"Come on and show yourself. Hell, I've been waiting for you."

Dimitry crouched lower, removed the hunting knife, stayed steady. When no other signs of disturbance came from the woods, Fowler began to make his way across the yard, no doubt curious to see if his bullets had made contact with anything. Dimitry stayed patient, waiting for him to get past the clearing before making his move. He knew the cameras stationed near Fowler's front porch would have good visibility of the yard and the road leading up to it, so Dimitry wanted to pounce only once Fowler was in the woods. That way, the video would be murky at best, with action tucked behind the trees.

Dimitry held his breath. He loved this time, the moments hunting the prey. He thought it amusing that of all the items Fowler had bought to protect his property, the one thing he'd forgotten was a dog. Sending a dog out first to scope the area would've given Dimitry's position away as soon as the dog scented him out. With no dog, Dimitry would have no trouble getting behind Fowler and attacking him before he knew he was present.

As soon as Fowler first stepped into the cover of densely packed trees, Dimitry sprinted across the lawn like a cougar. He leapt on Fowler's back and drew the knife deftly across the man's throat, then jumped away as the rifle swung wildly and a shot rang out. The minute the blood began to spurt, Fowler dropped the gun, fell to his knees, and desperately clawed at his throat.

Dimitry stood back and watched the man flail. He started to topple him onto his back and finish the job, when out of nowhere, he, too, was attacked. A man from the woods, sight unseen, tackled him from the left and, before he knew what had hit him, knocked him to the ground. Dimitry was surprised by the man's strength, the grip of his arms like the jaw of a pit bull as he tried to pull them apart. Dimitry rolled and dug the heels of his boots into the ground until he found leverage to separate himself from the man. On their feet, the two exchanged several punches, to the abdomen, the face. Dimitry was surprised to see the man duck and waver, as if he were a practiced fighter.

Stepping back, Dimitry realized the knife had fallen from his hands and lay on the ground. When a kick to his chest once again landed him on his back, he quickly rolled and grabbed it before jumping back to his feet. With his left hand guarding his face, he fisted the knife with the blade exposed beneath the pinky on his right, thrusting it forward. The man jumped back—once, twice—the blade missing him by inches. It was then Dimitry knew he'd seen him before—the man in the cigar bar with his many scars.

He thought for a moment whether he should continue to fight the man or run when multiple bright lights suddenly illuminated the house and made his decision for him. The police cars had come up the drive without so much as a sound, and now they were here. Dimitry made a break for the woods and circled back around the way he'd initially come, except this time simply climbed and hurled himself over the fence. His feet were quick racing down the hill on the other side, jumping over logs and snaking between trees as thick as stalks in a cornfield. He felt a sharp branch grab at his jacket and tear it. Felt others claw at his face and head. Voices from high above the hill screamed out for him to stop, but he wasn't about to be caught by the American police. Near him, the beams of their flashlights bounced and flickered as they approached from behind.

When he reached the midpoint where he'd started the journey up earlier, he could see the road was now blocked off by yet another police car—and worse, they had his truck surrounded. He stopped momentarily, his breaths pulsing hard and harsh, considered his options. He wondered how the police had known of the attack so quickly. Perhaps the motion detectors had automatically triggered an alarm, but his gut said something differently. He thought the answer rested with the man who'd attacked him

He quickly sensed motion to his right, suddenly saw a bright light illuminate his face. Through the eyeholes in the mask, he saw an officer, his gun drawn and pointed his direction, yelling at him to put the knife down. Dimitry quickly assessed the man— older, mid-forties, a paunch around his waist—and decided he would take him. He could see the man's hand shake, and Dimitry refused to die here, in a country not his home.

He quickly dropped and rolled toward the officer, hoping the shots that rang out didn't hit him, then jumped him from below. He deftly relieved him of his gun, then stabbed him in the abdomen. The officer fell. A shot rang out behind him, and Dimitry once again fled, this time with the officer's gun in hand in addition to the knife. He had to get down to the highway and carjack a vehicle. It was only a matter of time until the entire Jefferson County Sheriff's Department bore down on the scene and released the dogs. He had to get back to the city.

CHAPTER 40

Jess woke the next morning to a nightmare that turned out to be real. All over the television was breaking news about the overnight attempted murder of Gerald Fowler, another former juror in the Mikael Kriskan case, along with a deputy from the Jefferson County Sheriff's Department. Fowler was in critical condition, fighting for his life. The officer was stable, having undergone surgery overnight. But the manhunt for the alleged attacker was on, and that attacker had been identified as one Dimitry Romanov. They were now dissecting Romanov, of his ties in Russia and his alleged association with Mikael Kriskan's biological father. Denver police were promising to take a closer look at the murders of John Berman and his wife, as well as the supposed suicide of Kevin Ryland. News of the intimidation of other jurors was also part of the conversation as the anchors explained they'd received information that at least two others had received threats. With another juror fighting for his life, the media had to wonder what the remaining jurors were feeling at this time.

Jess could tell them—they were feeling it was simply a matter of time before they met the same fate. That Dimitry had acted on his threat to go after another juror left her bone cold.

They continued with an interview of the Denver police chief, asked him if anyone had approached him about the department providing protection for the remaining former jurors until Kriskan was executed. He said no one had yet discussed it with him, but he was open to the possibility.

Then the reporter turned back to the camera. "Still, one former juror doesn't think the intimidation will stop even after the execution. In fact, he believes if the governor permits the execution to move forward, the jurors could face a lifetime of looking over their shoulder. He spoke only on condition of anonymity."

They cut to him, a man hidden by shadow with a voice disguise. But Jess knew, the man had to be Ethan. "If Mikael Kriskan is executed," he said, "I believe these Russian gangsters will continue to hunt down the former jurors and kill them. If one of their men is captured, they will send another, and another, to come after us. I know it doesn't make sense. I mean, if Mikael Kriskan dies, what is there to gain? But these aren't the kind of people who see reason. Vengeance is reason enough."

The reporter shook her head. "Terrible. It's like a movie, except it's real."

The anchor asked about the governor's intention to grant a stay of execution given these extraordinary events. "No, in fact, these events have the governor pushing the opposite direction, stressing the need to go forth with Kriskan's execution and possibly even move up the date. He says he will not cave in to these intimidation tactics."

Jess groaned. Their actions to get Kriskan released was having the opposite effect. This was not good. She prayed they would hear from Nick Whelan soon.

She turned on the gas fireplace to warm the house, stood looking out the patio doors off the kitchen. New snow had fallen overnight and covered the deck and Ricky's play set in the back yard. A heavy weight fell on her heart. She missed him more than words could express. She missed his footsteps running across the hardwood floors, the smell of his hair when she kissed the top of his head, his little hands wrapped around the back of her neck when she picked him up. Mostly, she missed watching him fall asleep tucked soundly in his bed, knowing he was safe from harm, and away from the hands of that Russian bastard.

Since their last encounter, she couldn't believe the fury that had grown in her toward Dimitry Romanov. She not only wanted to see him captured and tried for Berman's and Ryland's murders, she wanted to set and carry out his sentence herself, wanted to flip that switch that would allow the lethal combination of drugs to enter his body and watch him die. She'd never felt such a hatred rise in her toward any human being before, and at times, it was frightening—what she felt she could do to him.

She could only imagine, then, how Mikael Kriskan felt about his brother, Nikov.

She wondered what Dimitry was up to now, whether last night's failed attempt and encounter with the police would have him fleeing the country. Part of her hoped so, to never see his face again, but the other part of her wanted desperately to see him pay for what he'd done.

She jumped at the sound of her cell phone, breathed a sigh of relief when she saw it was Tom. "Oh, thank God, it's you."

"Jess, I'm seeing the news. Are you okay?"

"Yes, for now." She told him about the events of the past few days, writing up the affidavit, getting proof of Nikov's travel to the States during the time of the Kriskans' murders, his DNA.

"That's good, Jess, really good. I have to believe that will be enough for the courts to listen and change the outcome, governor be damned. When will you know?"

"Soon, I hope. I can't take much more of this anxiety." She paced the kitchen, trailed her hands across Ricky's drawings on the refrigerator. Felt that weight again. "How's my bug doing?"

A sigh. "He's doing good, given the circumstances. You know how everything needs to be familiar with him, so the change in surroundings is causing some extra tantrums. But I just keep telling him it's temporary and he'll be home soon."

Jess took note of the *he'll*, instead of the preferred *we'll*, and her heart ached. Ached for Ricky and Tom, for Mikael and herself. She had to remind herself that if she managed to get through this nightmare, she'd still have to undergo another—a divorce. Disrupting her and Ricky's entire life. Things weren't going to be good again for a long, long time—if ever.

She asked to speak to Ricky, and Tom put him on the phone. Since their separation, he'd been certain to call Jess every night and let them talk. For the next ten minutes, she chatted with her son, assured him she was okay and everything would be back to normal soon, even though she knew she was lying to him.

Reluctantly, she hung up with a promise to call later.

Jess stood in the kitchen, stared at the cold, empty house. With the television muted and nothing but the stir of wind whistling through the pines outside, she didn't think the silence had ever been so numbing. What was she supposed to do with these empty days with no one to take care of? She didn't think she'd ever felt so alone.

She was happy when Ethan phoned a few minutes later. He told her of Brett's encounter with Dimitry the night before, that he'd been the one to tip the police off the moment Dimitry had arrived at the house. They'd wanted Brett's name, but he'd refused, and when they'd arrived, he'd fled on foot, just as Dimitry had. He didn't want to answer complicated questions as to why he was following the Russian or become a suspect himself in Fowler's attempted murder.

"Brett fought Dimitry. He's pretty banged up," Ethan said.

"Damn," Jess said. "But he's okay?"

"He probably saved Fowler's life, but he regrets not getting involved before Dimitry attacked him. He said Dimitry just went right for the guy's throat, didn't even give him a chance to fight back."

"Where do you think Dimitry is now?" she asked. "On his way back to Russia?"

"Could be. Hard to say. He's not at the condo he rented in Governor's Park and the police have his truck, I can tell you that," Ethan said. "I got a call from our DPD friends again this morning. They wanted to know what I knew."

"I saw you on the television. I assumed that was you too," Jess said.

"It's been a busy morning."

Jess laughed. It did sound like he was amped up on a gallon of coffee. She heard the call-waiting signal on her phone, told Ethan to hold a minute. Answered the other line. It was Nick Whelan. "We're a go for a special hearing this Friday. The trial court judge wants to speak with you in person, and Ethan Stantz as well. You'll be ready?"

"Yes." She shook a fist in the air. It was the best news she'd received all year.

CHAPTER 41

The special hearing was scheduled to be held in front of the Honorable Alfred F. Bailey, a trial court appellate judge with over twenty years of experience hearing appeals. He was an older man with white hair and age-spotted hands, slightly stooped at the shoulders beneath his black robe. Jess and Ethan sat at the defense table while Nick Whelan stood at the podium, offering oral arguments. David Foster, as the original prosecutor, had also been called in after the judge had read the claims of misconduct. He sat quietly at the prosecution table, as far away from Jess and Ethan as he could possibly sit, rubbing his face every so often. He did not look like a happy man.

Nick started with Mikael's statements about Nikov Petrovsky's visit, his claim of being Mikael's half-brother, the admission he'd not come to help free Mikael but to ensure the completion of a job he'd started many years ago and backed it up with the recorded conversation from the prison. Nick elaborated on Nikov's ulterior motive, that once Nikov learned of his father's rogue child, he plotted to locate and remove Mikael from the picture so he alone would be assured of gaining his father's inheritance. He further explained Mikael's remembrance of the tattoo on the back of Nikov's hand, that seeing it had renewed his memory. He reiterated the prior testimony of a blood spatter expert and his certainty that the knife had been held in Mikael's hands by a third party. He then provided the proof of travel documents, indicating Nikov's presence in Colorado during the time of the murders.

"Neither the defense counsel at the time, nor Mr. Foster here, were aware of Mikael's biological history at the time of the trial or had any knowledge that someone in his family might have had such a motive to set Mikael Kriskan up for the murder of his parents. I believe this issue alone—that we have a new suspect in the case—warrants a stay of execution be issued so all parties have time to look into these matters."

The judge looked over the documents, hands slightly shaking, and frowned behind thin-framed glasses. "I understand the DNA sample you had expedited came back inconclusive," the judge said. "Do you have any proof this man Nikov Petrovsky was actually present in Kriskan's home?"

Jess glanced at Ethan with a horrified expression. This was the first she'd heard that the test hadn't come back as a match. She wondered why Nick hadn't mentioned it before their appearance. Probably no time.

"True, Your Honor, but, as you stated, the test was expedited because of the urgency in this matter, and I believe with more thorough testing, a match will occur. But first, we need the time to make that happen."

"How did you obtain these travel documents?"

"They were provided to me, Your Honor, by an interested party," Nick said. "However, again, if time is granted, I can and will obtain a warrant to retrieve the same documents so they would be admissible."

The judge grunted. "So, these could've been forged."

"I don't believe so, Your Honor," Nick said.

Jess felt her nerves dance. So far, this wasn't going the way she'd imagined.

"Mr. Foster, do you have an opinion on this matter?" the judge asked.

David stood, straightened his suit. "Your Honor, I admit I was not aware of Mr. Petrovsky's relationship to Mikael Kriskan at the time of the trial, but without conclusive evidence that he was in or near the location of the Kriskan residence the night of the murders, I'm not at liberty to believe the original verdict should be overturned at this time or further investigation be ordered."

Jess shot him a damning look. She couldn't believe his denial to understand that they'd all made a terrible mistake. He refused to acknowledge her glance, as if she didn't exist.

Judge Bailey shifted gears. "I would like to speak to the juror about this alleged misconduct. Ms. Dawson, will you approach, please?"

She rose from the defense table and took Nick's place at the podium.

The judge gave her a stern head-to-toe examination. "Ms. Dawson, what you've alleged in your affidavit here is most disturbing. So, I would like to hear, in your own words, about this person who approached you during deliberations and your relationship with Mr. Ryland."

Jess gathered herself, took a deep breath. She started with her addiction, starting eighteen months prior to serving on the jury, an on-again, off-again habit lasting nearly a decade. "After my third stint in rehab, I quit for good and have been clean for six years. But while I served on the jury, I was an addict. I brought a couple of hits with me into deliberations, thinking that would be enough, but by day five things got very bad for me. One night, when I went outside to get some much-needed air, I was approached by a man who remained hidden in the brush and waited for the court attendant to not be present."

The judge eyed David to see if he displayed any reaction. He didn't. "Did you see this man? Know who he was?"

"No, Your Honor," Jess said. "He never showed himself to me."

"Did this man say he represented the prosecution?"

Jess watched David stroke his tie. He was playing it very cool, as if he had no stake in this at all. "No, not implicitly. I assumed he represented the prosecution because he offered me a fix in exchange for my vote—a guilty vote."

The judge's eyes thinned into slits. "And how did Mr. Ryland get caught up in this?"

Jess once again explained her sins. How she'd mentioned to the courier the outcome wouldn't change with just her vote. How he'd suggested convincing Ethan Stantz and Kevin Ryland to change their votes as he wouldn't be able to help her further. Saying it aloud to someone in charge, in front of Nick, Ethan, and David—all their judgment upon her—proved more difficult than she'd imagined. She might as well have cut open a vein and bled out upon the floor.

"And you didn't inform anyone else of this matter? Another juror, the defense, the court attendant?"

She cast her eyes down. "No, Your Honor."

"So, just so I'm clear, a man approached you and gave you heroin in exchange for a guilty vote? Then you convinced Mr. Stantz here, but found it necessary to set up Mr. Ryland with sex and drugs in order to change his vote? Is that your testimony?"

She now felt like she was the one on trial. She could feel the redness covering her cheeks and neck. "Yes, Your Honor."

He waved a hand over the bench. "No other interference. Just you and this unknown man who decided to take it upon himself to extort your and Mr. Ryland's votes? Were you present when this man approached Mr. Ryland about the drugs?"

"No, Your Honor. Mr. Ryland told me later what the courier had presented to him—either vote guilty or face drug and misconduct charges."

"Uh-hmmm," the judge said. "Well, I would ask him myself, but unfortunately, I can't, can I? Since Kevin Ryland is deceased, he can't be here to speak in his defense nor corroborate your story." He glanced at Jess over the top of his glasses.

What is he insinuating? That I'm making this whole thing up?

Anxiety gnawed at her belly. He had to believe her. If he didn't...

The judge shuffled papers, tapped the edges straight. "Just when you think you've heard it all... Tell me, Ms. Dawson, why did you wait so long to come forward with this information?"

She cast her gaze down at the podium. "I was ashamed, embarrassed. It's not easy to admit what I did. But as his execution neared and I began to believe he was innocent—when I learned about Nikov Petrovsky and his actions—I knew I had to come forward. I deeply apologize to the court for waiting so long."

The judge grunted. "You may sit, Ms. Dawson. Mr. Stantz, could you approach?"

Jess turned and traded places with Ethan, giving him a raised eyebrow as a wish of good luck. Judge Bailey was a harsh, no-nonsense kind of man. Jess was glad her time in front of him was over.

Ethan rocked on his heels. "Your Honor," he said.

"Mr. Stantz, like Mr. Ryland, you, too, have followed this case since you sat as a juror, know the history of the appellate attorney's numerous attempts at appeals."

"Yes, sir," Ethan said.

"Then why has it only been within the last month that you've begun to advocate so deeply for Mikael Kriskan's release or retrial?"

"Because, as Mr. Whelan stated, this evidence just came to light."

"Not because some Russian mobster was following you, maybe intimidated you?"

"No, not at all."

"So, you've received no threats? No unexpected encounters with these violent men?" The glare over the top of the judge's glasses was menacing, daring him to lie.

Ethan cleared his throat. "Well, yes, I have received threats, like many of the others. Over the computer and phone. And I was pursued one night by Nikov Petrovsky. Chased, actually. After I wrote of the conversation he had with Mikael Kriskan, the alleged confessions he made."

"Accused him of the murder of the Kriskans, didn't you?"

"I said it was a distinct possibility that should be looked into, yes. I mean, you heard the tape. It sounded like a confession to me."

More grunting. "Perhaps. Perhaps not."

Ethan's brow twitched. He looked at the judge quizzically. "Your Honor?"

Judge Bailey swayed on his seat, took off his glasses. "Mr. Stantz, you're a crime writer, yes? You examine crimes and seek out all the angles, explore various theories?"

Ethan nodded.

"So, isn't it possible," Judge Bailey said, "that perhaps Nikov Petrovsky visited his brother and issued these alleged confessions not *despite* the conversation being recorded but precisely *because* the conversation was being recorded? That in reality, these confessions are contrived confessions intended to do exactly what the Russians want—create another suspect and overturn Mikael's conviction? Set him free?"

Jess felt her heart stop beating. She and Nick glanced at Ethan, saw him wrestle with the judge's words. He rubbed his beard, appearing to give it thought. The next words that came out of his mouth fluttered, like butterfly wings.

"I uh, guess so, yes. I hadn't thought of that theory."

The judge motioned his shaky, bony hand across those that stood before him. "You see how all of this looks, right? We've got one Russian out there intimidating jurors and threatening to kill them if they don't do something to help set Mikael Kriskan free. We've got his brother making himself to appear as a possible suspect and new, sudden evidence is just handed to the defense to muster support. Now, two jurors sit before me doing exactly what the Russians have asked of them—to help free Mikael Kriskan by advocating for his innocence and claiming juror misconduct. To me, at least from my perspective, the Russians seem to be running the show."

Jess saw Ethan take a deep breath, glance her way. He appeared as worried as she was. "Your Honor, I see how you could believe that," he said, "But I truly believe..."

"Nevermind," Judge bailey interrupted. "Let's move on. Your fellow juror has alleged juror misconduct. During the trial or afterward, did you, Mr. Stantz, have any knowledge, awareness, or suspicion that Mr. Ryland or Ms. Dawson were engaged in such unethical behavior?"

Jess flinched at his choice of words.

"No, Your Honor, not at the time. I only learned of Mr. Ryland's research when I went to his residence after his death and received the research from his sister. I could tell by the dates and times that he'd conducted much of the research during the actual trial. I only learned of Jess's—Ms. Dawson's—other situation when she told me a few weeks ago."

"Did Mr. Ryland ever try to convince you to change your vote based on his research?"

"Not personally, but during deliberations, he argued against convicting Mikael Kriskan for the murder of his parents based on some of the things he'd discovered. He was the last holdout."

Judge Bailey shook his head. "Right, until Ms. Dawson allegedly slept with Mr. Ryland and planted heroin in his room and an unknown courier gave him an ultimatum," he said. "Got it. Okay, Mr. Stantz, you can sit back down."

"Mr. Foster, would you approach?"

David walked to the podium and buttoned his suit coat. Jess nervously watched, wondering if David would falter from his story in any manner.

"Were you at any time informed by the court attendant of Ms. Dawson's condition, or told of the man who'd approached her and offered her an illegal substance?"

"Your Honor, I was told a juror was sick, but I don't know anything about a man offering a juror drugs in exchange for a guilty vote. Obviously, that would warrant a very serious charge. And as to Mr. Ryland, I have no knowledge of him changing his vote either."

"So all of this is news to you? You didn't send a courier representing your office to this woman and the jurors to get a sense of how the deliberations were proceeding, make sure things were going your way?"

David frowned deeply. Stroked his tie again. "Absolutely not, Your Honor."

Jess leered. *Liar.* She wanted to throw up.

"Do you believe this young woman and man and the allegations they are making?"

David briefly glanced back at Jess. She clenched her jaw, felt the icy stare she directed at him. "I believe like me, they have been threatened by this Russian, this Dimitry Romanov, and I understand their fear of him. As for the claims of misconduct, I don't have a comment."

Judge Bailey abruptly stood from the bench. "I'm going to need a few moments to review this matter." He gathered the documents before him and returned to his chambers. The four of them were left to sit in the courtroom, listening to their own breaths.

"I'm so nervous," Ethan whispered.

"I know. Me too," Jess said. And she was. Her nerves sizzled like live electrical wires downed by a storm, writhing uncontrollably.

Nick joined them, raised an eyebrow. "You did your best. Let's cross our fingers."

"He didn't seem impressed," Jess said.

"He really caught me off guard with that twist on Nikov's confession," Ethan said. "But I can't imagine that he could ignore this much information, not in a death-penalty case. I mean, right, Nick?"

Nick shook his head. "You never know. I've seen it go both ways. I've seen the smallest crack in juror conduct cause a mistrial and I've seen an entire new suspect with corroborating evidence presented with little more than a shrug. It's all up to the judge and only the judge."

When the Honorable Alfred F. Bailey returned more than an hour later, he asked all of them to stand. "You should know I consulted with the governor, along with a few of my colleagues, regarding this matter," he said. "I was interested in their opinion and I value their input in my decision-making."

"And? What do you think?" Nick Whelan asked when he stayed silent for longer than expected.

He frowned. "What I, as well as the governor and my colleagues, think, Mr. Whelan, is that all of this is very convenient. A sudden brother, a flash of memory, a vague and suspect confession told to the convicted defendant. A juror coming forth with a misconduct allegation involving a party who cannot speak to, defend, or testify on their own behalf. Research done, yes, but not used to convince others to change their votes to not guilty but, in fact, may have influenced Mr. Ryland to alter his own vote to guilty. Unfortunately, we will never know. Therefore, I can only rule that this research had no material impact on the overall decision the jurors made to convict Mikael Kriskan for the death of his parents."

He shifted uncomfortably, gave each one of them a serious once-over. "So, I'm going to do you all a favor. First, let me say to each of you—especially you Ms. Dawson and Mr. Stantz—I understand the tremendous pressure you've all been under since these...mobsters arrived in our city. And I want to assure you, should evidence evolve of their participation in your fellow juror's deaths, Mr. Berman and Mr. Ryland, they will be prosecuted to the fullest effect of the law.

"But in no way, in my good conscience, am I going to allow such thugs to interfere with our legal system and our methods of justice. To do so would only serve to open the doors to future such acts of intimidation in other trials."

From the corner of her eyes, Jess could see Nick shift, uneasy, fearing the words the judge would next say. He was like a father who'd spent many a year living in a hospital by his ill son's bed, and now the doctor was in the room, preparing him for the most terrible of news. His eyes pleaded and begged with Judge Bailey, but Jess could already see the writing on the wall.

"I do not find any material culpability in this matter. The date for Mikael Kriskan's execution will stand."

CHAPTER 42

Jess stood in the corner of Ethan's loft, staring out the floor-to-ceiling windows that faced east, and watched the sunrise of a new day. She'd slept on the couch rather than return to the solitude and peril of her own house, fearing if Dimitry were still hiding out locally, he would come for her. The colors of the sky were like that of a lollipop, a faded pink and orange with a swirl of yellow. It pained her that Mikael Kriskan would never see one of these again.

She sipped her coffee, thought again about the special hearing before the judge. She replayed the pleas made by Nick Whelan, her confession of the courier and setup of Kevin Ryland. She still couldn't believe the judge had dismissed her story as full of utter untruths. The timing coupled with the Russian's intimidation tactics had actually worked against them, making it appear as if her testimony was a lie, that she'd made up the story simply to do what the Russians wanted—overturn Mikael Kriskan's conviction. If only the DNA had come back as a match, Jess thought that would've been the only thing to change the judge's mind.

She couldn't imagine how Mikael would react to the news. Her heart was heavy.

A door creaked open down the hall, and Ethan appeared in sweats and a T-shirt, his shoulder-length hair falling freely. His skin was pale and the lids of his eyes hung low. "Sleep much?" Jess asked.

He shook his head, opened the cabinet next to the stove, retrieved a coffee mug. He filled his cup with water, poured it into the coffee maker, popped in a pod of dark Columbian. "You?" he asked.

"Not much," Jess answered. "I heard Brett snoring earlier, so he wins the prize."

Ethan leaned against the counter, awaiting his fresh brew. "I just keep asking myself what more we could've done."

"Me too. I keep wondering if I should've fully exposed David for being involved, told the judge of our affair and David's later admission to me of his actions—if that would've made a difference."

"No, it wouldn't have. Like Nick said, it would've made your allegations even less credible, like a scorned lover trying to get revenge. Without proof, it's his word against yours."

"What if Dimitry sends his pictures of David and myself to the media?" Jess asked. "Or if we can find Anya and have her testify?"

"What good will it do now? Foster will claim the pictures are photoshopped, another tactic of the Russians. The judge will probably think we hired an actress to pretend to be Mikael's sister and tell a false story. He made it pretty clear he thought we were all acting out of sheer desperation to save our own asses. I don't think that Judge would believe anything now."

Brett sauntered in from the living room, wearing plaid boxers and a white tee. "I'd say good morning, but I know it's anything but," he said. He took milk from the refrigerator, poured a glass. He turned to Jess. "You sleep at all? I told you I would take the couch."

"Very little, but it wasn't the couch keeping me up, believe me."

They sat around the kitchen island, staring into their respective cups, unsure what to say. Ever since the judge had uttered those final words—that Mikael Kriskan's execution would stand—Jess had felt on the verge of a nervous breakdown, walking a hire-wire between collapsing into a mess of inconsolable tears and pushing aside a rising panic that made her heart feel as if it was about to leap from her chest.

There existed no place of comfort, no peaceful resting spot, and if Mikael Kriskan was executed, she doubted there ever would be again. There would only be endless days and nights of seeing his face and hearing his desperate pleas to set him free and find his sister, Anya.

Ultimately, she feared her failure to save him could be the one thing to crack the fragile barrier that prevented her from scuttling back into her own dark shell, the one familiar place she crawled inside when she needed all the bad to go away. It was the only place she knew that could quiet the voices in her head and erase the visions from her memory. And Jess knew—if she returned to that needle, she would never, ever be able to escape it again.

Her hands shook as she raised her cup. "I've never felt so unsettled in my entire life," Jess said. "It's like I'm going through withdrawals all over again, but without the drugs."

"My mind just keeps searching for new answers, but it's stuck in a maze. I keep rounding corners only to find the entryway blocked. I double back and go a new route to no end. I feel trapped in a virtual hell," Ethan said.

"I hate to ask," Brett said, "but do either of you feel there is any truth to what the judge said about Nikov purposefully confessing?"

"No," Ethan said.

"Me neither," Jess said. "I saw his reaction to Nikov's words, the anger and torment he exhibited. That wasn't an acting job."

Jess rubbed her face, brushed her hair back. "I just don't understand how they can do this, why nobody will listen when it seems so obvious to us now that Kriskan is not guilty of committing these crimes. And that bastard, Nikov, continues to be free, able to abuse Anya. It's so unfair I can't even put words to it."

She stood and began to pace the living room, as she had done so many other times in the past month. There didn't seem to be enough miles to walk to make her feel less restless. "I wish we could just execute him instead of Mikael. After all he's done, to Mikael's family, to Mikael and Anya—he's the one who deserves death."

"Maybe we can just switch them out," Ethan said, laughing.

Brett chuckled. "Good luck with that. Not as easy as switching dog tags."

Jess stopped pacing. Stared out the new day's sun, promises of new beginnings.

Switching. No, not easy. Impossible, in fact. Yet, as soon as she'd said it, her mind wouldn't stop thinking about it. A switch. Bad guy for the good guy.

Mikael and Nikov did have some resemblance, and Mikael had several friends on the inside of the Sterling Correctional Facility who might be willing to help.

She turned toward Ethan and Brett. "You know, the man does have friends."

Ethan laughed out loud. "Jess, seriously, you are losing your mind," he said. "It would be beyond impossible. Armed guards, security cameras everywhere. And even if you got past all that, although they do look alike, Nikov has that damn tattoo. That's a dead giveaway. I mean, besides the obvious problems of fingerprints and dental match they probably do before executing someone."

"It is a nice fantasy, though," Brett said. "I'll give you that."

"Well, I can't help it. It sure would solve all our problems. Set Mikael free, execute Nikov, arrest Dimitry for the other murders. We wouldn't have to spend the rest of our lives hiding."

Ethan huffed. "Well, you're right about that, because we'd spend the rest of our lives in prison—for trying to help a convicted felon escape prison and murder someone else."

Jess stood in the rays casting through the windows, soaking up the sun. Maybe she was crazy, but for some reason, she didn't want to let the idea go. "Well, just for the hell of it, set up a meeting with Alexai, would you? I'd like to hear his thoughts on the idea."

CHAPTER 43

E than and Jess met Alexai in his private home, a five-thousand-square-foot spread on several acres of land in Castle Pines south of Denver. The place was a fortress, armed with security cameras, two Dobermans, and an outside guard. Inside, the place was lavish, decorated like the lobby of a mountain resort, with expensive leather furniture, hardwood floors, and a bearskin rug highlighting the den. The fire gave off a warm glow to the otherwise dark room. "Thank you for coming," Alexai said. "I am glad we could arrange a meeting."

"Thank you for sending a car for us. We don't exactly feel comfortable going out these days," Ethan said. "I don't know if you're aware, but Nikov came for me the night after I left the club."

Alexai frowned. "I am sorry to hear that. I did not know. Is that why you are here? You want some of my men, for protection?" He waved at one of his men. "They are most useful. Maybe all your jurors need. I hear one is in hospital."

"It's true," Ethan said. "Dimitry got to him, but I hear he's going to be okay."

"Yes, Dimitry is now wanted by police. I haven't seen him, but I will tell you, he is still in the States, still in the area. You tell your people not to let their guard down. They need protection, I can provide until you can get Mikael free, yes?"

Jess and Ethan shared a glance. "Well, about that..." Jess said. "Mikael's attorney got the DNA tested and unfortunately, the results came back inconclusive. He was able to get a special hearing with a trial court judge, and he presented the information you gave us, proof of Nikov's travel here, along with some other testimony, but the judge, he denied it all. He believes Nikov's confession to the Kriskan murders is just another ruse to help get Mikael released. He ruled that Mikael's execution will stay as scheduled."

Alexai's dark eyes turned even darker, the lines in his face near his brow revealing themselves like dried river beds. "That is not news I wanted to hear."

Jess could see his chest rise and fall with his heavy breaths. He glanced over at one of his men. "Get us three glasses and bottle of scotch." The well-dressed man went over to the bar, filled three glasses with ice, brought them to the table, poured.

Jess picked up the glass, sipped. She never drank anything harder than wine, afraid of her addictive nature, but if there was any time to take up drinking, it was now. "I have a proposition for you," she said. "Nikov is a terrible man. You said so yourself. He murdered your father."

"Nikov is most evil man I know."

"And Mikael, a good man, is scheduled to die in two weeks."

"Most unfortunate," Alexai said.

"This is not justice," Jess said.

"No, it isn't," Alexai agreed.

Jess felt a storm rage in her heart, a thunder rumble deep in her core. She had to churn up her deep-seated hatred of Dimitry and Nikov in order to utter the words she was about to say, to make such a proposal. "It would be better, say, if Nikov Petrovsky was in that room. On that table, with an IV in his arm."

Alexai drank. "Yes, most definitely. I wish it were so."

Jess steadied her gaze, kicked back the scotch, wiped her mouth. Alexai shifted his eyes from a dark and distant place across the room back towards her. When Jess had regained his attention, and thought he understood what she was suggesting, she issued a single nod.

Ethan sat to her right, not breathing.

He raised his chin. "What are you suggesting Jess Dawson?"

"I know it sounds crazy. I'm just wondering, could it happen?"

Alexai studied her for the longest time, glanced back at his comrade, pointed at Jess. A huge smile crossed his face. "Do you hear this, my friend? This American woman wants to cook our Russian friend."

Their laughter exploded into the room. Alexai slapped his knee, his gold tooth flashing in the fire's reflection.

Jess felt herself flush but remained firm. "Look, I know it's a long shot," she said. "I just want justice. Mikael has friends inside the Sterling Correctional Facility who might be willing to help, and at some point, they will have to transport him to the federal penitentiary in Cañon City for the execution. I know there are cameras and guards and all that, and I don't know how to get around any of those things, but I figured if anyone could pull it off, it would be you. That's all. That's why I came."

Alexai gradually stopped laughing, drank his scotch, poured another for the three of them. He selected a toothpick from a nearby table and began to pick his teeth. He sat in the big leather chair for several minutes without speaking.

Just after the grandfather clock in the room chimed nine times, he spoke. "Let's say, just for—what do you say in America—for kick's sake, it could happen. You would seriously do it, yes?"

Jess glanced at Ethan. His eyes nearly exploded from their sockets. "Uh, sure," Ethan said, a nervous vibrato to his voice. "That would solve everyone's problems. But as I told Jess, it isn't possible. He will have multiple armed guards during transport. The vans are equipped with security cameras. And even if you got past all that somehow, there is a complicated identification process that occurs before a man is executed. All his identification features have to match what is listed on the death warrant. Unless you can clone Mikael, it's not going to happen. There's no way in hell."

Alexai slowly sat up until he sat on the edge of the oversized chair. He met Ethan's gaze. The deep scar beneath his left eye seemed to twinkle. "Mr. Stantz, hell is our specialty. Your friend, Ms. Dawson, appears to understand that. Do you?"

He snapped his fingers. "Go print a map of route from Sterling to Cañon City," he said to his associate. The man nodded and left the room.

The toothpick Alexai continued to chew splintered. "You are right that Mikael has many friends inside Sterling. Outside too. I know of two guards who will be on transport. Both of these men are good men. Very aware of Mikael's story. They do not wish to see Mikael die."

Jess's heart raced. They were actually talking about doing this.

His associate brought in the map. Alexai leaned over, studied it. "It is very fortunate for us that the death-row inmates are kept in separate facility here in this state. I don't know if that occurs anywhere else. Here, the guards at Cañon City will not know Mikael. They will have no reason to believe the man who is brought to them is not Mikael Kriskan. Still, it is as you say, the identification process will have to match."

He tapped the map. "Somewhere near here is where we would make the swap."

"The swap?" Ethan asked.

"Yes, Nikov for Mikael. Your job will be to find Nikov and bring him to us. In exchange, we give Mikael to you. You take him where he wants. Go to see his Anya. I don't want to know."

Ethan laughed, a slightly hysterical, you've-got-to-be-kidding kind of laugh. He glanced from Alexai, to his associate, back to Jess. None of them were smiling. Their eyes were fixed. Serious. "You're not kidding?"

"This is no joke," Alexai said.

"Nikov. How would we locate him and subdue him?" Jess asked. "Kidnap him?"

Ethan wheeled toward her, looked at her like she was insane. His mouth was agape. She could tell he couldn't believe they were actually discussing this either.

Alexai stood, paced the floor. "Nikov is planning to spend the week in Vail during the execution. Celebrating his brother's death for murders he committed. You figure out way to get him alone, drug his cocktail. You bind him, put him in rental van. Bring him to me."

Jess wrung her hands. Ethan was a mess of nerves beside her, his feet bouncing against the floor. She thought about what they were doing, what charges could result after committing such actions: kidnapping, assault, attempted murder. They'd spend their lives in jail. But if they pulled it off, they had a good chance of returning to a normal life, without fear of retribution. And they'd have the satisfaction of knowing the right man had been executed.

She didn't see that they had a choice in the matter.

"How will you get past the identification issue?" she asked. "The death warrant will be prepared at Sterling; the identification will be done at Cañon City. Just the tattoo on Nikov's hand will give him away instantly."

Alexai grinned. "Tattoo is no problem. We have methods for removing. It will burn, but I will take pleasure in removing it. Those in Cañon City have seen photographs of Mikael, sure, but not in person, and fifteen years in prison changes a man. He and his brother bear some resemblance. We rough Nikov up a little. Make swollen his face, bandage his hand. Say he was most uncooperative during transport. Why would they ever believe he is not the right man?"

"His attorney will know," Ethan said. "Won't he be present at the execution? So will Mikael's extended family. And then there's Nikov himself. He'll be able to tell the guards he isn't Mikael. There will be far too many people who know to keep their mouth shut."

He was borderline hysterical know, Jess could tell. She reached over and put a hand on his shoulder. Alexai walked over and did the same. "It is okay," he said. "Calm down. You let me take care of such matters. You focus on finding Nikov and getting him to me. Everyone will need to play their part perfectly. There can be no mistakes."

"What's in this for you? To take such a risk?" Ethan asked.

"Nikov killed my father. He cut him up like an animal and put his remains in a barrel of acid to dissolve what was left of him. Now, I will get payback. Make good on a long-ago promise."

CHAPTER 44

The next night, Brett confirmed that Nikov and his associates hadn't yet relocated to Vail but remained at the Hyatt downtown on the twenty-third floor. Included in his entourage were still the same two bodyguards and the same two women, one a dark and sultry woman of about thirty, the second a bit younger and fair-skinned, with strawberry-tinted hair. He said the women often went to the hotel pool but always had a bodyguard in tow. He was convinced now the women weren't hired locals but Russian nationals, probably permanent girlfriends of Nikov's he'd bought and paid for. The minute he said it, Jess grew still, wondering if it were possible one of them was Anya Kriskan.

"He wouldn't be that stupid," Ethan said. "Would he? To bring the girl back to Colorado where she lived as a child?"

"Who knows. The man doesn't fear anything," Jess said, "and he has them under constant guard. He's had control of her for fifteen years. She's probably completely brainwashed." She walked over to where Brett sat. "Let me see those photos again, the ones you took of the women earlier."

He pulled out his phone, scrolled. Jess compared the pictures to ones she'd collected of Anya as a child, the last one a middle-grade yearbook. "My God, I think that could be her. Look."

Brett and Ethan both came over, examined the photos. "Wow," Ethan said.

Jess grabbed her coat and purse. "I'm going to get a room there, see if I can get close to her. You said they go to the pool? She has to go in the restroom sometime, right? Surely, the bodyguard doesn't follow her in there."

"Are you sure that's safe?" Ethan asked.

"I think so," Jess said. "I don't think Nikov knows who I am, what I look like. It's just you he knows, because of the blog. My enemy is Dimitry, but I think Alexai is right, he still has to lay low."

"I haven't seen him in days," Brett said. "Good thing too, because I'm pretty sure he recognized me that night, put two and two together."

"But the police haven't contacted you? Your tip is still anonymous?" Jess asked.

"As far as I know," Brett said. "Which is preferable, especially given the situation we find ourselves in now. The last thing we need is the police sniffing around and watching any of us if we attempt to make this switch go down."

Ethan grunted. He fidgeted about the kitchen, looking like a dog in need of water. Jess told him once again it would be okay. He laughed. Who would've guessed she would be the one keeping a clear head in the midst of sheer chaos now instead of Ethan?

She left the men at the loft with a promise to check in later, drove to the Hyatt, valet parked. Walked through the lobby filled with contemporary art and furniture. At the front desk, she booked a room with the same level access as the suites, including a private bar and rooftop lounge, and of course, the pool and luxury spa. Upstairs in her room, she changed into a swimsuit overlaid with shorts and T-shirt and headed to the pool.

She arrived with a book and cell phone, selected a chair at the opposite end from the locker rooms and the entry door so she had a good view of the entire area. Currently, only one other couple and their two children were enjoying the water, otherwise she was alone. She sat and waited, one hour, then two. She wondered if this was what it was like to be a private investigator, hanging around hotels and businesses, waiting to take photographs and video of the unsuspecting.

Shortly after four p.m., two women meeting Brett's description entered the pool, wearing slinky bikinis with cover-ups, followed by a burly man dressed in black clothing better reserved for a bouncer at a bar. She slid the book up just enough to cover her face but still be able to see over the top of the page. Jess didn't want to approach them right away or do anything rash, preferring to sit back and observe how the two women interacted with each other and the man assigned to them.

For the next thirty minutes, the two women swam laps and stood in the pool and talked while the man sat nearby, reading a newspaper. Jess couldn't hear their conversation but often heard an occasional word or laughter, and the more she watched and listened to the young woman with strawberry hair and fair skin, the more Jess was certain she was Anya Kriskan. Tucked inside her book, she had two photographs of her as a child, and the resemblance was uncanny. Even as a girl of twelve, Anya had hair with a natural wave, and her limbs were long and wiry, just as the woman in the pool. But what most convinced Jess the woman was Anya was her fair skin, sheer, like a thin layer of fabric had been draped across her body.

She considered what a great risk it was that Nikov would bring her here, back to the state where he'd abducted her and murdered her family. Had he brainwashed her to such an extreme that she no longer had any memory of the events? Even if he had, Jess thought a return to the area could trigger some emotional relapse.

Jess watched as Anya pulled herself from the pool and wrapped a towel around her waist, got comfortable in a chaise lounge near the man behind the paper. She pulled at strands of her hair, examined the tips, as if she were bored or thinking. The smell of chlorine was overpowering in the room, but the odor always reminded Jess of summer days at the pool, long, happy days of splashing, popcorn, and candy bars. Right now, Anya did not look happy.

Anya lifted herself from the chaise, said a few words to the man. He gave her a nod. As soon as she slipped inside the women's locker room, Jess saw her opportunity. Wrapping her own towel around her waist, she walked around the side of the pool opposite from the burly man and sultry brunette and entered the locker room. Inside, Anya was sitting on a bench in front of a mirror, staring at herself and brushing her long hair. Jess could see the sadness in her features, something she held inside like a permanent secret or a wish she couldn't fulfill.

Jess opened one of the lockers, acted as if she were about to put her towel in, decided against it. "You have beautiful hair," she said to the woman, attempting to the break the ice. "I always wanted hair that color." Jess squeezed out a few pumps of body lotion the hotel provided and began to apply it to her arms.

"Thank you," the woman said. Her gaze darted up and quickly back down.

Jess applied lotion to her legs, eyed the woman in the mirror. "I'm sorry to keep staring. You look so familiar. Did we go to school together?"

"No, I don't think so."

"No? You didn't go to Meadowood in North Denver? Elementary school?"

Her eyes cast down. She stopped twirling her hair. A ridge of concern.

"No, I'm not from here. Live in Russia." Jess noted she'd adopted the accent.

"I remember now. Her name was Anya. Anya Kriskan. She had a brother too, Mikael."

The woman's head quickly snapped toward Jess, and a little gasp of air escaped her throat. Her eyes were wild and fearful, as if harm would come upon her at any moment. She looked at the door, as if she was expecting someone to burst in. She rose from the chair, made a start for it. "I must go."

Jess grabbed her wrist. "No, no, it's okay. Anya, it's okay. *Shhhh.*"

Anya stopped and froze. Jess could instantly see the results from years of threats and abuse in that look. "I am not supposed to talk to strangers."

"Then let me introduce myself. My name is Jess, and I'm a friend of your brother."

She trembled beneath Jess's grasp. "You know Mikael?"

Jess nodded. She put a finger to her lips, motioned for a hot tub near the back of the room, led Anya there. The smell of eucalyptus grew heavy near the steam room.

They sat on the edge of the tub, let their legs dangle in the bubbly water. "Mikael asked me to find you."

Anya said nothing. Jess could barely make out her face through the steam coming off the tub but thought she saw a tear roll down the woman's cheek. "If they see you, us..."

"I know," Jess said. "I know who they are. Mikael, do you remember him?"

"Yes, some. They say he killed my parents."

"Do you believe that?"

She shook her head.

"Do you remember anything about that night?"

"Only little. I go to sleep in my bed. I wake with a man's hand over my mouth. He tells me not to make a sound. To close my eyes. He carries me out of the house, but first cuts me, my hand, takes me downstairs. Tells me not to look. The next day he tells me terrible things. That my brother killed my parents and they came to take care of me. Back to my parents' home country."

She was speaking quickly now, as if she wanted to get her story out. Jess wondered how many times she'd longed to speak her truth but had no one who would listen.

"But I know it isn't true. I overhear Nikov one night, bragging about killing my parents, setting up my brother to die. I cried. I cried so hard. To know I have spent so many nights with the man who killed them. I am forced to pleasure him, this man. I am not allowed contact with anyone. And now they are going to kill my brother. I see it on the news. He tells me if I ever say anything, he will kill me instantly."

Jess's heart was breaking. She thought back to the time her father had spoken to her about meeting her mother, imagined he felt then what Jess was experiencing now, sensing the brokenness and fragility of the human form in front of her. No wonder he'd felt such an obligation to care for her mother. Jess wanted to do the same for Anya.

"We can get you away from Nikov. You're a citizen of this country. You can tell a judge what you know, testify against him. You can set Mikael free. They will put you in protection."

She violently shook her head, looked as if she was about to run. "No. There is no escape from Russian mafia. I know what they will do to me, to us, if I go to the police. Nikov's father is powerful man. Violent. He will find us whatever it takes."

"Plus, who will believe me. Girl like me, I'm not worth life, that's what he tells me. I am weak. Mikael would not have me. I am..." She looked down at her arms, quickly covered them.

Jess gently took Anya's hands. "Anya? I know what you're going through. I've been there. I was an addict too. If I was in your situation, I would use too. But you can escape Nikov, and you can get clean. You are not worthless as he tells you. That is simply what abusive men tell women to keep them in control. I can help you, if you'll let me."

Jess reached back to get her book, thumbed it open, removed the photo she had of Mikael and Anya as kids standing in the backyard by a plastic pool. She held it up to show Anya. "Do you remember this?" She placed it in her hands and then handed her a letter Mikael had written and sent to Jess. "He told me to give this to you if I found you," Jess said.

She stared longingly at the picture, tears swelling in her eyes. She flipped the folded piece of paper over in her hands, seeming uncertain, but soon unfolded it and began to read. As she read it, she began to cry, tears falling softly down her face. It was at once both comforting and heartbreaking. She put her fingers to her lips and laughed softly. "He was always so funny. Made me laugh. Corny jokes. Such a nerd."

Jess tried to imagine that, the man in shackles and leg irons once cracking jokes. Jess knew at once she had to make their reunion happen. "Listen. We're working on a plan to get Mikael out. You could go with him. He would never turn away from you, Anya. He loves you deeply. You have to know that now."

Doubt etched itself on her cheeks and lips, but Jess saw a spark in her eye, an underlying wish or a hope for possibility. A new life. A new chance. "How is that possible?"

Just then the door opened and the brunette called out for her. Jess quickly stood and whispered, "Don't worry about the details. Keep a bag packed. Just the essentials. When it's time, I'll come for you. Until then, not a word, okay?"

CHAPTER 45

Jess and Brett were once again gathered around Ethan's kitchen island, plotting their next course of action. She updated them on all things Anya, including Jess's promise to get her out and away from Nikov.

"So now we have to kidnap two people? This is crazy." Ethan said, continuing to display an underlying hysteria Jess didn't think would go away anytime soon. She'd started having nightmares of her own, of Nikov Petrovsky and gold-toothed Russians chasing and imprisoning her, so she understood. It would be a long journey back to normal if they survived the next two weeks.

"Certifiable," Brett agreed. "So crazy it just might work."

"So, the guards are in on it?" Jess asked.

"At both facilities. Three in Sterling, one in Cañon City, but all key players," Ethan said. "Alexai doesn't believe the actual swap will be a problem but says the identification is the main obstacle. They will have to forge a new death warrant, with Nikov's photograph, fingerprints, and dental records, and they can't do that until they have him in custody."

"I still don't know what they're going to do about that tattoo," Brett said. "Tats can take up to a year to remove with laser treatment. What if he has more than the one on his hand?"

Ethan took a long swill of beer. "Dude, I don't think you want to know. As soon as Alexai started talking about acid compounds, I just held up my hand and told him to stop talking."

Jess cringed. Alexai was taking the payback personally.

"We need to figure out our part of the plan. How do we kidnap Nikov Petrovsky and transport him to the meeting place?" Jess said.

"I suggest we head to Vail as soon as he does, follow him around, see what his routine is. He doesn't know either of us, so we should be okay," Brett said to Jess.

"And, Ethan, if you wear a hat pulled low and a scarf around most of your face, I don't think he'll be able to pick you out of a crowd of others wearing the same."

"We'll all need to be bundled up and unrecognizable," Ethan said. "Hotel and business cameras and all that. If Nikov is eventually reported as missing, we can't let anyone be able to identify us or associate us with his disappearance."

"The last thing you need is Nikolai Petrovsky hunting you down," Brett said.

"No shit," Ethan said.

"Do you think we need to create a reason that Nikov left?" Jess asked. "Like, maybe we leave a note that he decided to take off with Anya alone? Or, is it better just to let it remain a mystery? Given that he's suspected of being the Kriskans' real killer and the Russian community's anger over recent circumstances, I don't know if his associates would report his disappearance to local authorities. They'd wait until they got back home, take the matter up with his father."

"Agreed," Brett said. "I think they'll suspect foul play from the get-go, but these aren't the type of men who will go to the police to solve their problems. They solve their own problems."

"Yes, well, let's just be sure they don't know we're part of their problem," Ethan said.

Jess headed to the refrigerator, grabbed a beer. "Okay, so no note and well disguised. Now, how do we get to Nikov?" She popped the cap on the beer, took a drink. "I hate to suggest this given my past...history, but you said Nikov is a big-time womanizer, right? So, what if I seduce him? I figure out a time and place to get him alone, lure him back to his room, then drug him. It's the oldest trick in the book, but it works. I could text you when he's knocked out. You could come and get him, take him to the van while I get Anya and then meet you."

"You're forgetting two things," Ethan said. "Two very big things. Mutt and Jeff stationed nearby. They don't exactly look like the type of men who would just invite you in if you knocked on the door."

"We'll have to drug them too," Jess said. She snapped her fingers. "We can bring in some room service. On the house, courtesy of Mr. Petrovsky. I can order it to our room, then dress as staff and deliver it to their room. We wait until they pass out, then I can get Anya."

"What drugs can we use? Something undetectable would be best," Brett said.

"Rohypnol, the same drug Nick suspects was used on Mikael. Date-rape drugs can't be hard to get. Wouldn't be surprised if Alexai already has some."

"Easy enough to get on the streets too," Brett said. "I'll take care of it."

She turned to see Ethan glancing back and forth between the two of them, his shoulders rising and falling as he laughed. "You're both plotting crimes like it's the easiest thing in the world. You're starting to think like them."

"Excuse me?" Jess said, joining him. "Who was it that suggested going to the enemy of our enemy in the first place? Who thought it was a good idea to intimidate the Russian mob publicly in his blog?" Jess tapped her bottle to his. "You."

"She's got you there," Brett said. "Who knows crime better than you?"

Ethan tossed his head back, threw his hands in the air. "I write about murders, not participate in them. So many things have to be executed flawlessly for this to work. Everyone has to play their part perfectly. And we're relying on and trusting a group of shady Russians to get the job done. Again, this is crazy."

"Let's just say we get all this accomplished," Jess said. "We get Nikov, take him to Alexai, we make the switch, Alexai forges the death warrant. That seems to take care of most of it, except for the actual execution. Nikov will talk to anyone who will listen and tell them he is not Mikael. How will that be handled?"

Ethan groaned. "Exactly. How do you prevent a man from talking? Also, like I stated before to Alexai, Kriskan's extended family will be there—his aunt Miriam included. What will she do when she sees it isn't him on the table? What will Nick Whelan do if he attends? And there will be members of the press. The press is always allowed in."

"Well, as I understand it, Nick Whelan doesn't plan to attend. He said he's saying his good-bye at Sterling, and for us, that's a damn good thing. It will hurt him to believe Mikael is dead, but he's a man with a conscience and he wouldn't be on board with such a vigilante act.

"And as far as the family, Alexai will get them on board," Jess said. "You know, you spoke to his aunt. She'll be happy to hear Mikael is free and the real murderer of her brother will die. And the press, I don't think that's a concern. They don't know Mikael personally, and if the death warrant checks out, what is there to question?"

"What about David Foster?" Brett asked. "Does he attend?"

"I don't believe anyone from the prosecution is present," Jess said. "And even if he found out later, I don't think he would say anything. Regardless of how brave he acts, he knows as well as we do that, if Kriskan dies, Dimitry will come for all of us."

"Dimitry, what do we do about him?" Ethan asked.

"We have to make him surface, have him arrested for the attempted murder of Gerald Fowler and that deputy," Jess said. "That takes care of him and Nikov, and Mikael goes free. Nikolai Petrovsky will wonder what the hell happened, but I don't think he'll send anyone else. He'll think Mikael is dead, learn Dimitry is facing life in prison, and he'll probably assume Nikov is dead too. That the rivals got to him for what he did to Mikael. It will be done."

Ethan exhaled a long, pent-up breath. "If we make it through this, nobody can ever, ever say a word," he said.

Jess nodded. "I don't think anyone will. Once it's done, we all have too much to lose."

CHAPTER 46

The snow in Vail was coming down hard, a blur of full white flakes that made the winter-loving villagers most happy. Through the sounds of ski boots clomping on snow and the chatter and laughter of skiers and boarders heading to and from the runs, Jess and Ethan trudged through the village, past shops with winter wear, breweries where the beer was flowing. Ahead of them, Nikov was snug in a long wool coat, red scarf, and gloves, looking every bit of the wealthy European he was. He caught the eye of many a woman as he walked by, and he often returned their glance. Men studied him, seeming to either admire or rebuke his swagger. Jess thought he had that kind of aura—one that both lured and repulsed equally.

In the hotel where Nikov and his associates were staying, a soaring cedar lodge that offered ski-in, ski-out access and private suites, Nikov strode through the lobby, stopped and flirted with the desk clerk as she handed him his messages. Jess noticed Brett standing next to the fireplace beneath a huge rack of antlers, warming his hands and watching Nikov's every move. As soon as the man disappeared up the stairs to the second floor, where he'd booked rooms 2127 and 2128, two suites with multiple bedrooms and an adjoining door, Brett joined Ethan and Jess for a brief chat. "What's the verdict?" Brett asked.

"Alexai says they intend to move Mikael tonight," Ethan said. "Two guards and a driver. All three are in. He says the transport will leave Sterling around eleven p.m. That means we'll need to have Nikov in tow by midnight in order to meet them by two a.m."

"Where's the van?" Brett asked.

"In the public parking garage at the moment, but once Jess gives the signal that Nikov has passed out, we'll bring it to the side of the hotel," Ethan said. "We'll take him straight from the hot tubs to the van, or worse case, from the room through ski-out access and into the van. Either way we'll avoid the hallway cameras entirely."

Jess nodded. They knew from their surveillance the past three nights that Nikov enjoyed the outdoor hot tubs every night just before he settled in for the evening. It was there Jess planned to seduce him and slip the drug in his drink, then wait for him to pass out.

"Early this morning, I was able to snatch a white coat and bill ledger from the kitchen," she said. "Once I have the food ordered, that's all I should need to look like one of the hotel's servers. First, I'll deliver the food, notify Anya, then go for Nikov. You guys wait in the van until you get my message.

"We'll just look like a couple of guys helping their drunk friend get home for the night," Brett said. "No one should expect anything out of the ordinary that doesn't happen here every day."

"I say we're ready, then," Ethan said. "I think we should all get some rest this afternoon. We've got a long night ahead of us." They returned to the room and slept as best they could until nine p.m. rolled around.

Brett was the first to wake and get ready. Ethan and Jess shortly followed suit. Brett checked his watch. "Okay, if the past few nights dictates future behavior, Nikov should be heading toward the bar about now. I'll go monitor the rooms and lobby, let you know where everyone is, if everything looks to be on schedule." He gave them both a fist bump. "We can do this. Be safe. Be aware."

While Jess slipped into black pants and the white coat she'd snatched that morning, Ethan ordered four espressos and four slices of the house specialty—a dark chocolate cake with raspberry drizzle—asked for delivery near ten p.m. After they arrived, Ethan wrote a note on the hotel stationary: *You need to try. Best in house! N.*

Alexai had provided him a sample of Nikov's handwriting and signature, and Ethan tried to match it. The man apparently always signed his name with a gigantic *N*, the lines elongated like knives. Appropriate.

Jess wrote a note for Anya, tucked it in the bill ledger. *It's time. Be ready. Will knock three times.* Brett continued to update them with Nikov's movements: "In the bar having a cocktail." Then, "Now back in the room."

It was agonizing waiting for the message that said he'd gone to the hot tub.

At ten-thirty, it arrived. "Okay, go," Ethan said. "We've only got ninety minutes."

Jess warmed the espresso in the microwave, made sure it was steaming hot. Added the Rohypnol to two of the cups. After taking a deep breath, she rolled the cart down to the second floor, knocked on door 2127. A man the size of a linebacker, with a chest that resembled the Hulk, greeted her. She suddenly wished she could add an additional dose of the drugs, was worried she hadn't included enough in the cups.

The man read the note, chuckled. "You can bring it in," he said.

Jess took the drugged tray inside, said hello to the other man in the room. He was equally large and smelled of vodka. She wondered what the hell they were going to do if the men didn't drink the espresso, started to question whether they should've sent up shots of a special whiskey instead. But she couldn't worry about such matters now.

"Are your friends next door?" Jess asked. "These pieces are for them."

The man followed her back into the hall, rapped on the door of 2128. Anya opened the door, froze. Her glance ping-ponged from Jess to the Hulk, back to Jess. "Can I set this down for you?" Jess asked Anya.

"Yes. On the desk is fine." Her voice quivered slightly.

Jess pushed her way past Anya, said hello to the brunette, set the tray down. She grabbed the bill ledger with the note, opened it up so only Anya could see it. "If you could just sign for it," Jess said, "I'll be on my way."

Jess watched Anya's eyes quickly read it and glance up at her. She took the pen and signed. "Tell the staff thank you. I am most appreciative."

Jess smiled. "Will do." She snapped the bill ledger shut and departed, shutting the door behind her and wishing the Hulk a good night. Back in the room, she leaned against the door and caught her breath, her nerves firing like ricocheted gunshots.

Now for round two.

Brett had texted that Nikov Petrovsky was outside in the hot tub and was alone. Jess quickly changed from that of server into snow bunny, overlaying a red bikini with an off-white hooded parka and snow boots. She tucked the drops of Rohypnol in her coat pocket and grabbed a recently opened bottle of red wine and a glass. On the way to the hot tub, she thought about Tom and Ricky and prayed for the first time in years—she could not screw this up.

Outside, she practiced a slightly off-center walk, placed a wry smile on her face. Nikov was in the tub up to his chest, a drink in one hand, cigar in the other. "Mind if I join you stranger?" she asked.

She let the coat fall from her shoulders.

His head turned and looked her up and down. He licked his lips, raised an eyebrow. She could tell he liked what he saw. "Yes, please. I love company of American women."

She removed her snow boots, lowered herself in the water. She could sense him staring at her nipples, which had hardened in the frosty mountain air. She snuggled under and purred, letting the water warm her, although inside, she was anything but. Her muscles tremored, knowing what she was about to ask them to do. Around them, light snow fell, highlighted by the hotel's twinkling white lights. "I love to be out here when it is snowing," Jess said. "So cozy, so romantic."

Nikov puffed on the cigar, blew smoke in the air. "I am surprised girl like you is alone here. You don't have boyfriend?"

"He's back home in Denver. I came up for the weekend with my girlfriends. But they didn't want to come out. I think they're asleep." She gave him her best smile.

Suddenly, his foot graced her leg, ran up the inside of her calf. He was testing the waters. Jess let out a little squeal. "Oh, someone wants to play footsie with me, I think."

That was all he needed. He put out his cigar, drank a shot of whiskey, poured himself another glass. Like her, he'd brought his own stash. He moved deftly through the water, closing in on her. She braced herself for his touch, hoped she didn't pass out. She let out a little gasp as she watched his hands—that tattoo with the snake heads—latch on to her waist and slither around the small of her back.

As she felt his fingers kneed into her skin, she thought of the damage those hands had done—to Mikael and Anya, to their parents, to friends and relatives. That Nikov had thought no more about killing the Kriskans than stepping on a couple of bugs on the sidewalk. That he would think nothing of killing her if he caught her drugging his drink. Thinking about what he'd done made it easier to handle knowing what they were about to do. Killing a man wasn't something she would've chosen if other methods were available, but it was a situation she had no choice in now.

Now one hand was on her ass, squeezing her closer. Acquiescing, she leaned in and wrapped her arms around him. As he began to nuzzle her neck, she reached behind him for the vial in her coat pocket. Quickly squeezed several drops in his drink and watched them dissolve. Tucked it back in her coat. She waited a minute until she pulled back. He kissed the top of her breasts, dipped his tongue inside her cleavage.

She tried to hold the bile that rose in her throat at bay.

She grabbed her wineglass, took a long drink. Pushed him back a little. "Whoa, cowboy, slow down a little. Let's enjoy the moment, shall we?" She held up her glass as if to toast. He reached back for his whiskey and clinked glasses. "To our new friendship," she said. She downed the remaining wine. He followed suit with the whiskey.

He set the empty glass on the edge of the tub, returned to her breasts "So, where were we?" She cringed as his hands massaged the whole of her, held her breath as his lips met hers. Soon his tongue was inside her mouth. She wondered how long the drugs would take, begged them to hurry the hell up.

A few moments later, he stopped. "Maybe we should take this somewhere more private? Like my room?" He looked her over, eyes roaming, like a fine whiskey he was ready to take part in. "I have some specialties there. Drugs to make you feel good. Some special toys." He ran a single finger down her arm.

Though her body trembled, and she'd hoped like hell he would pass out here in the tub, she couldn't cause him any suspicion. They were just minutes away from making this happen, making it real. And maybe it would be good to get inside, make sure the big guys had finished their dessert. "I'm getting cold. A fire sounds good. Let's go in," she said.

As she slid from the tub and back into her coat and boots, she noticed him waver slightly as he walked back through the water, then stumble as he swung his leg over the railing of the tub.

Jess giggled, pretending to be amused.

"I'm not so coordinated, no?" he said. He turned, laughing, slapped her ass cheek. "But other things, I am much more coordinated. No worries."

In the elevator, he leaned and kissed her again, so deep she thought she might puke. She hated what she was doing, but focused on the why, thought of Tom and Ricky, Ethan and Mikael. All the jurors' families, the safety of so many. Down the hall, he stumbled again. The drugs were definitely starting to take effect.

At the door to his room, he slid the key card in once, twice, to no use.

"Here, let me," she offered. She slid it in, turned the light green. She feared opening the door and coming face-to-face with Nikov's associates, still very much awake, but thankfully one was passed out on the couch and the Hulk snored from a nearby room. She took note of the empty cups and plates.

Nikov stepped sideways across the room, shoved the tray aside. "Hmm, my comrades have eaten all the dessert. Such pigs. Now they sleep it off."

Jess raised an eyebrow. *He didn't know how right he was.*

"But that just means we have time alone, right," Jess said, running a finger down his abdomen. "Time just for us."

Nikov pulled her close, kissed her once again. He fumbled about at the bar, poured a shot of whiskey, one for her as well. Jess downed it. She didn't like it, but right then, she needed it to calm her nerves and get the taste of him out of her mouth. After he drank his, Nikov sat on the edge of the couch, his head bobbing. "I am sorry, miss...I did not get your name."

And then it happened. *Whunk.* Nikov Petrovsky rolled forward and passed out.

Jess slipped inside the bathroom, spit, and rinsed, spit again. Texted Ethan and Brett. "He's out. In the room. Hurry."

"On our way."

She tiptoed to the sliding doors at the back of the room, stuck her head out in the cold. Brett and Ethan soon rounded the corner, fully bundled in parkas, hats, and gloves. They climbed up the snowbank, entered the room. They quickly propped Nikov back up on the couch, slung one of his arms over each of their shoulders.

Brett counted before they lifted. "One, two, three..." They stood. Gripping his hands and supporting his waist, one on each side, they began to haul ass. Brett nodded at the adjoining door. "Get the girl."

Nerves burning like torches, Jess went over, lightly knocked three times. Anya appeared, eyes as wide as saucers, bag in hand. The other girl, the brunette, appeared, her face flush. "This is Olga," Anya said. "Please. She can go too? I can't leave her with them."

Jess looked at the woman, her brown eyes pleading. "Of course, let's go."

She didn't have to ask twice. The woman grabbed an already-packed suitcase and threw on her coat. In tandem, the three shuffled out the door. Jess closed it as she left, the last to leave, and slid down the snowbank to the comfort of the heated van below. Inside, she turned to Anya, gave her a nod. Now, it would be up to Alexai and his associates to do the rest of what was needed.

CHAPTER 47

Mikael waited anxiously for the guards to arrive. He'd spent the day saying a string of goodbyes—guards, other prisoners, even the local chaplain. Nick Whelan had taken it the hardest of all, and after thirty minutes of agonizing tears and apologies, Mikael had called for the guards to take him back to his cell. Otherwise, he would have blown the plan. Mikael couldn't bear the thought of Nick fighting his grief and guilt for the rest of his life, believing he hadn't succeeded in freeing Mikael, but he couldn't risk the man knowing something that could make him appear involved if anything went awry. Maybe someday Mikael would send him a letter and tell him the truth. Maybe someday he'd mail him a photo of himself high upon a fourteener, looking down over the expanse below with a caption that read, "Heaven is Freedom." He certainly hoped so. He closed his eyes and said a silent prayer to his father and his father's God for it to be.

The double knock finally came. *Bang. Bang.* Mikael stuck his hands through the slot, awaiting the cuffs, for what he hoped would be the last time. Waited for the door to open. Took one last long look around his cell, at the made-up stars scratched upon the ceiling. Earlier in the day, he'd used a pen to write today's date along with his name in the far corner of the cell along with a single word. *Adios.*

The guard attached the leg irons, shut the cell door. Mikael could feel the man's hand tremble as he took hold of Mikael's elbow and began to lead him down the walkway. Looking down into the commons where the non-death-row prisoners gathered during the day, he could still see the sign they left him. *Rest in peace, brother. Someday, justice.*

But Mikael hoped that someday was today, when he finally got the chance to confront his parents' real killer—his brother, Nikov Petrovsky. He couldn't wait to see the look on his brother's face when he realized what was happening, when they removed Mikael's chains and prison attire and slapped them upon Nikov and shoved him in the prison van.

It would be a moment frozen upon his memory for all time.

And he would relish in its glory.

He followed the guards down a hall he'd never been through before, an area going past the kitchen to the delivery area out back. There, two armed guards met them and conducted checks of credentials before bringing up the van. Mikael simply stood and let the frosty night air fill his lungs, hoping this was the first of many breaths he'd take outside in the great outdoors. He thought he might want to go live in the woods for a year and stare at the evening stars for nights on end, when the sky was clear and moon was full, nights just like tonight.

After the guards had made their routine checks both inside and outside the vehicle and were satisfied with the results, Mikael was placed inside the van with two armed guards. The driver got in the front, radioed some instructions, and soon they were off.

Mikael sat quietly, listening to the rumbling of the tires upon I-76, wishing he could see the landscape passing by outside. It had been so long since he had seen anything other than concrete walls, even the sight of dark sprinkled with distant lights would fascinate him. The icy air of the night whipped through unseen cracks in the back of the van, creating a steady whistle and chilling him with a thin blast of cool air. The cameras inside the van stayed steady upon the cargo, showing Mikael and the two guards huddled in the back from multiple views. In the front of the van, there was a number of other monitoring and security devices as well, including more guns.

The guards made small talk as they drove. One spoke of his daughter's upcoming dance recital, the other about the Broncos' off-season trades. Three-plus hours into the drive, Mikael began to panic that what he'd been told was a lie, until one of the guards tapped the face of his watch. "Just about halfway," he said, glancing at Mikael.

That was his cue. *It is really happening.*

Mikael cleared his throat, said he needed to go to the bathroom. The two guards regarded each other, as if seeking each other's permission, until the one with the watch shrugged. "It's a long trip. I need to go too."

He looked into the front seat, tapped on the window with the barrel of his assault rifle. Made a motion with his hand. The driver nodded, held up five fingers. "Five minutes," he said to Mikael, giving him an extra-long stare down. Mikael nodded and sucked in a deep breath. He thought of all the ways this could go wrong.

Just as the driver had indicated, the van began to slow in a few short miles, then exited the highway. Two minutes later, they were climbing steadily into the mountains over pavement. After another five, the van began to bump and grind over what could only be a dirt road.

And then it stopped.

Mikael's heart raced like that of a running greyhound, nearly exploding from his chest. He couldn't believe this was really happening. These people, these guards were risking their lives, helping him to freedom. He wondered if Jess and her friends had been able to locate and abduct his brother.

The driver spoke to someone on the radio, notifying them of their stop. After securing the front cabin, he walked around to the passenger side and slid the van door open. As was protocol, both guards exited first, weapons at the ready. They scoped the area to make sure the coast was clear, making a show of it for those watching through the body cams back in Sterling. "Don't think anyone wants to see me take a piss," the one with the watch said. "Signing off for ten."

The minute the cameras were off, everyone moved into action. Mikael was helped from the van and his cuffs and leg irons quickly removed. The driver threw him a bag containing a pair of jeans, a sweatshirt, and a ball cap and told him to change his clothes. The headlights of another van suddenly approached and stopped about twenty feet away. From the other direction, a second vehicle, a single person behind the wheel. As soon as the headlights all went dark, the occupants descended. First, a well-built man of maybe thirty with green eyes and a military buzz cut. Second, a lanky man with longer hair and a beard. And finally, Jess Dawson, hidden beneath an off-white parka and fuzzy hat.

Mikael stood to the side, rubbing his wrists.

From the second vehicle, a man slid from behind the wheel, handed a package to Jess. He approached one of the guards, laid a hand on his shoulder, spoke to him in Russian. The guard nodded. Clearly, this was the man in charge, the one Jess had worked with to set Mikael free. But it wasn't until the man got closer and Mikael saw the two-inch scar beneath his left eye that Mikael realized who he was—Alexai Volkov.

Mikael's knees buckled. He couldn't believe it.

Alexai reached out and embraced him. "Good to see you, my friend. It's been a long time. Not since we were kids. Many years. Too many."

Mikael couldn't speak, his emotions overwhelming him. "Why?" he choked out.

"You know why," Alexai said. "Ms. Dawson has your papers. New name, passport. For Anya too. When you leave here, you go. I do not want to know where."

Mikael felt his heart palpitate. "Anya? She is here?"

Jess joined them. She smiled. "In the van."

From the back of the other van, he could hear the muffled sounds of rage, several kicks against the inside door. "Your brother's not too happy," Jess said. "He started waking up about twenty minutes ago. We have a hood over his face so he doesn't see any of us or know the girls are with us. They've done well to keep very quiet. We'd prefer to keep him in the dark until we leave."

Alexai motioned to the guards. "Get him. We don't have much time."

When the side door opened, Nikov could be heard yelling into the rag that filled his mouth. "I will kill you, whoever you are. I will kill you."

The guards dragged him from the van and dumped him at Alexai's feet. In addition to the hood and gag, his hands and feet were bound. Mikael watched his brother writhe on the snow-covered ground. "Take off his hood," he said. "I want him to see my face."

Jess and the two men stepped back into the shadows, evidently preferring to keep their anonymity, but Alexai proudly stood with him, caring little if Nikov saw who had made this happen. "It's my honor," Alexai said. He tugged at the fabric around Nikov's neck until it loosened, then lifted it over his head.

Nikov blinked several times in the headlight's glare, then squinted, as if he couldn't believe who he saw standing before him. With great satisfaction, Mikael delivered two blows to his sternum, several others to his face. He reached and grabbed Nikov's throat and ripped off the gag, thrust his head up so he'd have to look at him.

"How's that feel now, my brother? To be on your knees like a dog while I am free of restraints?" He punched him two more times and Nikov spit at him. Alexai laughed.

"You. I will kill you, my brother!" Nikov screamed.

"You already had your chance. Now, it's my turn," Mikael said.

Mikael glanced up at the night sky, stars sparkling like the icy crystals covering the ground. He took a deep breath, released the air with force. "Ah, fresh mountain air fills my lungs. I did not think it would ever be so again."

He leaned down to whisper in Nikov's ear. "You should breathe in, while you can."

Nikov whipped his head around—to Alexai, to the guards who stood idly by with their weapons, then back at Mikael. "You'll never get away with this," he yelled at all of them. "The moment they find him missing from prison, you'll be the most hunted men in the world. All of you will go to prison or die for helping him escape."

Mikael turned around to look at the guards, raised his hands. "This is true?"

Together, they began to laugh.

Mikael could tell Nikov wanted to reach out and rip out their very hearts.

He reached down and placed a hand on Nikov's shoulder. "I don't think you understand, brother. I won't be missing, so there will be no need for the police to look for me. See..." he said, waving toward the van. "You are going to take my place. Lie on that special bed that has been prepared for the killer of my parents. The guards at the chamber, they don't know me from you. I look different now than my arrest photo. Much older, yes?"

"Yes," Alexai said. "And considering how uncooperative you're being right now—how you tried to escape when these gentlemen were nice enough to pull over and let you take a piss—they had no choice but to rough you up a bit, get you back in the van, sedate you."

He nodded at the guards. "I'm sure they will recommend you remain highly sedated until your execution. For your safety."

Alexai smiled, his gold tooth flashing an extra shine.

"The authorities will know something is wrong when I arrive. I will tell them every detail, and when they test my blood, I will be set free. You will be wanted men. I will hunt and find, torture and kill every last one of you in the slowest way possible."

He snarled at Alexai. "Just like I did your father."

Alexai hurled his fist into the side of his face, knocking him on his side.

Mikael picked him up by the hair, yanked his head back. "What do you think it will feel like when the drugs enter your veins? Huh? Others, they tell me—the first injection is hot, like liquid metal running through your blood. Then, the second—ice, stopping all flow to your heart, oxygen to your lungs. Finally, your eyes will close, brother, for the last time."

Nikov gritted his teeth, screamed, resisted Mikael's grip on his hair. "I hate you, always hate you," he said. "You are bastard child."

Mikael looked him dead in the face, his gray eyes not flinching. "The feeling is most mutual." He released his grip and let Nikov drop to the ground. "You are a dead man."

One of the guards took Mikael's arm. "It's time for you to go now," he said. "All of you." He pushed Mikael toward the group near the other van. He turned toward the others. "Five minutes people."

Mikael joined Jess and the two men he didn't know, watched as the guards dressed Nikov in the prison attire he formerly wore before clamping on the cuffs and strapping on the leg irons. The driver of the van forced Nikov's mouth open and swabbed some thick unknown substance across his teeth and gums, forced his jaw to clamp down.

Nikov fought the entire time.

As soon as they were done with the dental imprint and the driver indicated he had what he needed, Alexai came back from his car with a canister of a mixture that looked like some kind of witch's brew. Mikael wondered what the hell Alexai was about to do when his old friend rolled up the sleeve of Nikov's jumpsuit to expose the bulk of his right arm, displaying the tattoo.

Alexai strapped on gloves and started to apply the mixture when, standing next to Mikael, Jess Dawson gasped.

Alexai glanced over his shoulder and met Mikael's gaze—he hadn't realized the foursome of guests was still there. "You best go now. Take the girls and get lost. You will not wish to be present for what is next."

CHAPTER 48

The day of the execution, the death-penalty advocates descended upon Cañon City like a human plague. With the first execution to be conducted in the state in more than forty years, the media, too, had lined up, local and national, their news vans parked for a mile stretch around the prison. In the skies above, news helicopters flew in circles and filmed the crowds. Jess, Ethan, and Brett watched the events unfold on the television from the safety of Ethan's loft, wanting nothing to do with the crowds or the expected fighting and pepper spray that were sure to come. One group in Denver was holding a candlelight vigil at the state capitol building and nearby Civic Center Park, chanting prayers for the soon-to-be deceased Mikael Kriskan. At 12:05 a.m., the time he was scheduled to be put to death, they planned to release lighted lanterns into the air.

For the past two days, since Jess, Ethan, and Brett had abducted and handed over Nikov Petrovsky into the hands of the authorities, the three had barely eaten, slept, or spoken. Every time one of their phones rang, they collectively gasped, expecting news that the switch had been discovered. Every time there was a knock on the door, they were certain it was the police, arriving to slap them in handcuffs and seal their fate. So far, it hadn't happened. So far, all had been quiet on the western front.

The short drive to Denver after they'd left Alexai and his friends had been a joyous reunion between Mikael and Anya, and the two had spent the entire night up in Ethan's loft—crying, talking, and hugging it out. Jess had learned of Olga's own family tragedy at the age of fourteen and subsequent sale to Nikov, who'd kept her captive for even longer than Anya. The following day, Jess helped her arrange a flight to New York, where she planned to reunite with relatives. After that, Jess purchased a used car with the remaining money from her trust fund and titled it in Mikael's new name.

Then, just earlier that morning, Mikael and Anya had hit the road for a destination unknown. Jess often imagined them driving down the highway and chattering like baby birds—maybe heading east through the Kansas prairie, or north through the

Wyoming tundra. Jess had given Mikael the names of several rehab centers in nearby states and made him promise he would get Anya in rehab as soon as possible.

"Where do you think they are?" she asked Ethan and Brett.

"Somewhere Mikael can look at the stars," Brett said. "That guy is a dreamer."

"I don't care as long as they're safe," Ethan said. "I just hope they're not watching this."

Jess glanced back at the television, the talking news heads continuing to analyze, dissect, and discuss all things Mikael Kriskan. Jess wondered what was happening inside the prison at Cañon City at that exact moment. It made her nervous to think of those in charge taking Nikov's fingerprints and comparing them to the death warrant, searching for any distinguishing scars, marks, or tattoos on his body. She wondered what kind of stories Nikov had told the guards since his arrival, and what lies the guards had told the authorities in Cañon City concerning Nikov's injuries.

She didn't want to think about his hand.

What had Alexai done to remove that tattoo?

She shuddered.

"You finished the new blog and published it?" Jess asked.

"Yes, it went public as of ten minutes ago," Ethan said. He sat at his workstation with his chin cupped in his hands, staring at the screen absently.

"Do you think Dimitry will respond?" Jess asked.

"Definitely," Ethan said. "Maybe in person."

Jess laid her head upon the table. She was tired, so tired, but sleep wasn't an option. "You told him? Made it clear that we tried?" she asked again.

"Yes." She could tell he was tired of her asking. Ethan had told the audience that both he and another juror believed Mikael to be innocent now. He spoke of their time pleading with a judge to issue a stay of execution and grant time to investigate a case of alleged juror misconduct and new evidence against Mikael's brother, but the judge believed they were only coming forward because of the intimidation by the Russians.

He said the blood was on the judge's hands now and asked for understanding from the public, that the new information about Nikov Petrovsky hadn't come forward until the very end, an end that proved too late. He asked for the family's forgiveness and for that of the public-at-large, all of those who supported Mikael Kriskan.

The haters, of course, came out in force, the anti-immigrant, pro-death trolls who cared little of the truth. #InjectHim and #Eye4Eye started to trend.

To the Reaper, Ethan included a direct message: "We did our best."

"I bet Dimitry is nearby," Jess said. "Just waiting to come for us."

"If he is, he'll run into a bit of a surprise. I asked our DPD friends to keep watch. They're on surveillance right now, waiting for him," Ethan said.

Jess turned her head. "Comforting. Why didn't you tell me?"

"I'm telling you now."

She glanced out into the darkness, eyed the clock—11:33 p.m. She closed her eyes, hung her head, took a deep breath. She wondered what Tom was doing right now, hoped Ricky was sound asleep. She wanted badly to talk with him. She knew he would sit in bed until the time came then click off the television a minute before it happened, say a silent prayer in the darkness.

At midnight, Ethan brought out three individual candles, handed one to Jess and Brett, lit them with a match. They dimmed the lights in the loft and waited for it to happen. All across LoDo, they noticed the lights go out one by one—the individual lamps in apartments and lofts, the strands of white lights that constantly hung across Larimer Street, even the signs on the restaurants and bars.

People stood on the street and halted whatever they were doing, lit a candle for Mikael Kriskan. It was a historic moment in Denver history, and not a good one.

The news anchors became more somber. One of them announced the governor had officially denied clemency. At 12:05, the station went dark.

Jess, Ethan, and Brett sat in the silence, listening to the irony of their own heartbeats. Before them, the television screen displayed only a candle with a flame. When it was over, they added Mikael's name below the photograph, along with his date of birth, and now, his death.

Jess started to cry. The mixed emotions she felt, joy at Mikael's freedom conflicting with the guilt of another man's death—no matter how evil that man may be—overwhelmed her.

She could see Ethan and Brett struggling too.

A few minutes later, her cell phone rang. Hoping to hear from Tom, she was disappointed to see it was David. Maybe—finally—he was experiencing remorse. She accepted the call, said hello through sniffs. Her voice shook.

On the other end, David sounded despondent, as if he were stumbling across a distant, dark planet. She could tell he was outdoors, the wind whistling in the background. "Jess, what did you do?"

She felt a sharp pain invade her chest. "What do you mean?" She had never heard him like this—his voice like chalk, an angry, choking quality to his words.

"What...did...you...do?"

A coldness swept over her. Tears replaced with fear. *He knows. How?*

"I was there," he said. "I cleared it with the state to watch the execution."

She gasped. Brett and Ethan shot a look at her, concerned.

"Mikael's aunt Miriam was there and identified the man on the table as her nephew, as did cousins and an uncle. The warden was concerned because the man kept rambling about not being Mikael. The guard explained he'd hit his head in the accident and may have a slight concussion."

Jess frowned. "The accident?"

"The van carrying him from Sterling rolled on transport."

Her mind raced. So, that's how Alexai had done it—planned to explain the bruises and bandaged hand, blame any statements Nikov made mumbling about not being Mikael Kriskan on a concussion, head trauma.

"His bandaged hand. I stood there looking at it, wondering if it was possible, when the warden turned and asked me if this was the man I had tried and convicted. And the relatives and the guard, they all glared at me—daring me to say otherwise. I could see it etched on every feature of their face. I was stunned, out of my mind."

She heard his breaths, quivering, could envision him standing in the biting cold outside the prison, shuddering more from the shock of what had occurred than the weather.

"So, I ask again, what did you do?" he said.

Jess steadied herself. "The only thing that could be done," she said.

The other end of the phone was silent for several minutes. They exchanged the sounds of breaths and the wail of a distant siren. "I don't know if I can live with this."

"Yes, you can, and you will," Jess said. "And you won't mention it ever again. Understand? Not ever."

CHAPTER 49

D imitry Romanov sat in the darkness of his hotel room reading Ethan's words. Since his run-in with Gerald Fowler and the unknown man who'd intervened in his death, Dimitry had been forced to keep a low profile. But now, with Mikael's execution, he would have no choice but to carry out his promise to his client. Jess and Ethan had tried, he would give them that, but the remaining jurors—as well as David Foster and this judge who had denied to listen to Jess's claims—would have to die. He would make a statement loud and clear.

Nikolai Petrovsky would be most angry upon learning Dimitry had failed to save his son, but his fury would not compare to the outrage he would have when he learned it was his other son, Nikov, who'd put Mikael in prison in the first place.

"Nikov Petrovsky," he said aloud to the dark. "You play your father for a fool, tell no one of your own deeds? Now, you will die, along with the others." He downed a pour of whiskey, slammed the empty glass on the table. "I will take joy in killing you."

He felt the footsteps behind him more than he heard them. "No, I don't think you will, my friend," a voice said into the dark.

Dimitry started to wheel around when he felt the end of a gun nudge the back of his head. "Don't move. Let me see your hands."

The voice was familiar, of Russian roots, but removed. Still, he couldn't match the voice to a face, not immediately. Though his anger smoldered, Dimitry did as commanded, raised them to his side. "You are going to shoot me?"

An envelope landed in his lap.

He looked at it, kept his hands in place. "What is that?"

The gun again nudged his head. "Read it."

Slowly, Dimitry opened it, removed a photograph and a note. The picture was of Mikael Kriskan standing next to a mountainside, along with a thin woman with strawberry hair. The photograph was dated two days ago.

The note said simply: *Mission Accomplished. JD.*

Dimitry stared at it, an odd sensation crawling up his spine. He turned the photograph over, studied it closer. "This is not possible. This is lie."

"No, my friend. I'm afraid it's the truth."

"Just a half hour ago, they say Mikael was executed."

"He was."

A new envelope landed in his lap. He opened it. Out fell Nikov Petrovsky's signature ring and gold chain. Dimitry picked them up and examined them, felt his eyes narrow.

"What are you saying friend? Where is Mikael? Where is Nikov?"

"I just told you."

No, it couldn't be.

Dimitry felt the laugh start deep in his belly and grow in intensity until he was nearly howling. The man standing behind him with the gun to his head didn't interfere.

Minutes later, Dimitry set the photograph and items on the table next to him. "Well done, Jess Dawson," he whispered. "Well done."

He glanced at the picture of his daughter and his late wife that sat on a nearby table, the one he took with him everywhere he traveled. Such beauties they had been— he'd always thought his Viktoria could win the pageants. If only he could've saved her.

If only she could've saved herself, like Jess Dawson.

He picked up what remained of a cigar from an ashtray, lit it and puffed. Selected his empty glass from the table. "Would you mind?" Dimitry said, holding it up.

The man took the glass from his hand, filled it with ice and whiskey. Handed it back to Dimitry. For the next ten minutes, the man with the gun let him smoke and drink in peace.

Finally, when he had finished both, he felt the gun return to the back of his head.

"Yes. I know what you are here for, stranger," he said to the man standing behind him, making no attempt to turn around. He didn't need to be a witness to his own murder.

Dimitry Romanov set both feet squarely on the floor and rested his hands on the arms of the chair. He stared longingly at the picture of his daughter and his wife, then slowly closed his eyes. They were the last thing he wanted to see.

"Well, my friend, what are you waiting for?"

CHAPTER 50

They promised to have no contact until the third month after the execution. Today, on the anniversary, Jess and Ethan met at the same back-corner table of the café next to the brick wall where they'd met again for the first time. It was a bit of a shrine now to all they'd been through. Unlike the time of their initial meeting, the weather outside was comfortable now, mid-seventies with a bright-blue sky, a spring filled with hope, optimism, and new beginnings.

Ethan sauntered in wearing a plaid shirt over a T-shirt and jeans, his hair wrapped in a little bun. Jess arrived in yoga pants and a matching pullover, having gone for a run earlier in the morning. They stared at each other across the table, their customary latte and mocha between them, both not knowing what to say or where to start.

Jess finally broke. "Well, Ethan. I think...I think we did it," she said.

He nodded, his eyes wide and wild. "I still can't believe it. But things have really quieted down. I've not heard from a soul in at least eight weeks, not the media, not even Walker and Rouche of the DPD. They came to talk with me after they discovered Dimitry Romanov to see what I knew—if there was anyone in particular I suspected. They actually think it could've been Nikov Petrovsky who shot Dimitry before he fled back to Russia. I of course, didn't say anything differently. You?"

"No. Not a word."

"David Foster?"

She shook her head. "He knows better." She stirred absently. "Everyone has kept their mouth shut. I haven't heard even a trace of speculation that the execution didn't go exactly as planned. All the photos they published of Mikael in the papers and online afterward, they're all pictures of him at the time of his arrest and later at Sterling. None of his last days."

Ethan released a huge breath of air. "This never would've been possible without the two facilities," he said. "We got so lucky. Sometimes, I still break out in hives thinking about taking Nikov out of that hotel room, carrying him out to the van. I was running on pure adrenaline and fear."

"I know, me too."

"And he was never reported as missing?" she asked.

"Not that I know about," Ethan said. "You saw they dropped the charges against John Berman's son? Once they had Dimitry's DNA, they found evidence of him being there. They believe it was Dimitry who killed them, attempting to imply that Mikael's parents had been killed the same way."

"Which we know is true," Jess said. "I still can't believe the appeals courts ignored Nick's findings with the new blood-spatter evidence. Nick had it right."

"The post-conviction appeals process and state courts have taken a hit with this execution. The majority of the public feels the justice system buckled under political pressure and failed Mikael Kriskan."

"They did," Jess said. "I really would've liked to have seen Dimitry go down for what he did to the Bermans and Kevin and Gerald Fowler, but I can't say I'm not glad he's dead. I feel safer knowing he's gone and he can't talk. But I worry for Bryn Berman. We may never know what he did with her."

"Bryn, yeah, that's the saddest part of this," Ethan said. "Where is she? I'm thinking of opening an investigation on the blog. Somebody out there has to know what happened to her."

"That would be great Ethan. If anyone could find her, it would be you."

He smiled at the compliment.

"I can't believe we conspired with a local Russian crime boss to pull this off," Jess said. "Sometimes, I look at myself in the mirror and ask what the hell I was thinking, that I must've been out of my mind. But the truth is, I was out of my mind. I was desperate to save him and us, my family."

Ethan stirred his latte. "You did surprise me, I'll give you that."

Jess stared out the window into the cut-away of the building next door, where Brett used to sit with his sign. Now in his place sat a large pot of blooming flowers, geraniums and azaleas. "How's Brett?"

"He's good. Real good. He got a job with a security firm, working events and concerts mostly, and he's volunteering down at the veteran's center, helping vets get reacclimated into society. Help with PTSD, Suicide prevention, that sort thing."

Jess felt relieved. "He sure helped us out. He's still staying with you?"

"For now. But eventually, he wants to get his own place. We're friends for life, though. That guy has some stories. He's a beast."

"Yeah, well, we gave him a pretty good story of our own," Jess said.

"No doubt." Ethan laughed.

"He's not the only one doing good." Jess rummaged in her purse, removed her cell phone. Broke into a big smile. "I got these last week." She pulled up the messages, handed the phone to Ethan.

Jess delighted as his expression turned from one of concern into outright joy. She saw tears swell in his eyes. He began to laugh. Showed her the photo he was looking at—Mikael in a selfie at the top of a mountain, overlooking a deep valley below.

"My first fourteener," the text said.

Then another, with Anya by his side at the entrance to a lush, mountainous park, arms wrapped around each other. In it, Anya was at least ten pounds healthier, with clear eyes and a bright smile. She'd dyed her hair a dark chestnut, looked like a completely different woman. "Three months sober. Wants to go to culinary school!"

Ethan wiped his eyes. "Man, that's so awesome. Makes it all seem worth it."

Jess nodded, put the phone away. Sniffled away a few approaching tears of her own. She'd spent more nights crying the past three months than in the past thirty years, but it had brought a cleansing, a purging of everything past. Her mother's suicide, her father's passing, her former drug addiction, her bad choices. In the last few weeks, she'd begun to sense a renewal, a strength and determination to live anew that she never thought she'd possessed.

It was a good feeling.

"They took their new names and moved to Washington," she said. "He invited us to come visit, but not too soon. For now, they're just trying to find their footing in their new reality, get to know each other again. He says Anya is the most resilient person he knows but appreciates her big, overprotective brother. She's been through a special kind of hell."

Ethan grunted. "I don't think hell would even begin to describe it. Held captive as a mobster's sex slave for fifteen years? I'm not sure there's enough therapy in the world to undo that."

Jess wrapped both hands around her cup, took a long sip. She offered a smile. "I don't know, seeing life through a clear reality, experiencing real love, and having new dreams? You'd be surprised what second chances can do for a person. Speaking of which..."

She reached across the table, took his hand. "I wanted to say thank you, Ethan. For granting me a second chance. For believing in me. For trusting me. After everything I told you, you didn't have to come along for the ride. You, Ethan Stantz, are a good man. I'm happy to call you my friend."

He fidgeted, unsure how to handle so many compliments. "It was a crazy ride."

She let go and laughed. "Certifiably insane."

They enjoyed the moment, let the sunshine fall through the window on their faces. It was warm and inviting. Ethan broke the silence. "I don't know if I should ask, but how is Tom?"

Jess took a deep breath. "Well, it's taken some time, but believe it or not, he wants to give us a second chance too. I don't deserve him. I know I don't, but I'm going to do everything in my power to give him the wife and life that he deserves, and Ricky, the mother he needs. Tom and I have started counseling, both together and separately. I think you'd agree I could use some outside perspective?"

He chuckled. "Maybe. But inner perspective too. That's important. Get to know the real you. Just, who is Jess Dawson?"

"This journey has certainly given me much to consider."

He nodded. "Me too."

She took another long sip. "So, what about you? What's next for Ethan Stantz?"

"Me? You won't believe it, but I've been fielding publishing offers. I'm giving serious consideration to writing true crime."

"Ah, Ethan, that's fantastic. You're the perfect man for the job."

"And..." His face lit up as he dug for something in his pants pocket. "I meant to give you this. My buddy at *Westword*, he mentioned they had an opening. I told him about you, and he said, if you want the job, it's yours."

He slid the paper with the guy's name and phone number across the table. "You'll have to start with selling ads, but you can present pieces on the side, and eventually, hopefully, get a cover story."

Jess took it and stared at it as if it were a winning lotto ticket. "You mean it? Really?" She jumped from her seat and hugged Ethan awkwardly. When she sat back down, his face was red. "Thank you so much. I can't express..."

He held up a hand. "I'm happy to do it. I believe in you, and besides, you may have given me one hell of a book idea." He winked.

"Fiction, though, right? Not true crime."

"For now. But maybe, someday? Who knows." He picked up her hand, kissed the back of it. They said their goodbyes with a promise to connect often.

As he departed, he gave her one more glance over his shoulder. "See you soon, Jess Dawson. Thanks for the adventure."

She held up her cup. "To new beginnings."

Thank you for reading The Fifth Juror. I hope you enjoyed it!
Please leave a review of this book on http://bit.ly/TheFifthJuror

ACKNOWLEDGEMENTS

No book is written without the assistance and input of several people and this book is no exception. Many thanks go to the following people: The team at North Denver Investigations; Michelle Hope, Editor; Melissa Yahr, Proofreading; Rose Boscia and my entire Advanced Reading Team for feedback; All mistakes herein are my own.

Note: Two years after this book was written, the state of Colorado abolished the death penalty in Colorado. At this time, none of the four prisoners formerly on death row will be put to death.

ABOUT THE AUTHOR

Lori is a writer of thriller and suspense novels. *The Advocate* is the first novel in her Women of Redemption Series. *The Fifth Juror* is the second. *The Tattoo Artist*, the third in the series, will be forthcoming in July 2020. The Women of Redemption Series: Women who may not be perfect, but who perfectly kick-ass when given a second chance.

Lori is also working on an FBI series featuring FBI special agent and local profiler Frankie Johnson. You can expect the first two books in that series, *99 Truths* and *The Art of Obsession* in 2020. Want a preview of Frankie Johnson? Check out Lori's short story, *The Fire Keeper*, in *BURNING: an Anthology of 14 Thriller Shorts* here https://amzn.to/2lbW1Fh

Like **FREE** books? Download a copy of Lori's novella, *The Rumor*—a psychological suspense short here: https://www.lorilacefield.com/novellas.html and enter to win her latest giveaways here: https://www.lorilacefield.com/news-and-giveaways.html

Lori is a lover of coffee, books, music, yoga, pilates, wine, travel and most of all, dogs. She lives in Colorado with three adorable Pomeranians. You can follow her on Facebook and Goodreads at Lori Lacefield-Author and on Twitter at #lorilacefield.

Manufactured by Amazon.ca
Bolton, ON